Foreword

At what point does life force you to go through that dark and intriguing tunnel that you have always refused to go through? Akim Brenda thought and thought lying on the warm sand trying to decipher with logic what only the heart can accept. She, who was all judgment and decision, found herself trying to deny a passion that, still dormant, was sobbing to escape. The bars of a learned prejudice buffeted her in a storm of decisions that drilled her rational brain. She stretched out on the towel and her eyes closed, keeping the warmth of a shy sun that was disappearing, accepting her defeat. She took a deep breath and a small indiscreet drop escaped under her soft eyelids. Unique and shy, the solitary tear, tried to atone with its delicate taste of the sea, a guilt too heavy to carry. Present and future, reality and desires, feelings and obligations collided like a high-speed train in a tragedy impossible to avoid. Ten days, only ten days were needed to collapse the foundations that she thought were indestructible. Ten mornings and a penetrating look were enough for her chocolate eyes to close in search of a passion eager to be born. Who decides about truth or lies? Who defines what is real or imaginary when the heart is the crazy motorist of your desires? Brenda clenched her fists tightly on the sand moistened by the night breeze, and stretched her refined body trying to relax the muscles exhausted from so much thinking. She must feel infamous, a traitor, a liar and hundreds of other adjectives that people give especially to women of dubious conduct, but not even all the insults and lamentations of the villainous society could erase the smile engraved on the body of a beloved woman. A soft, warm breath approached his ear and his body bristled, recognizing him by its warmth alone. That was not right, she thought saddened, she would be thrown into hell and the keys melted in the fiery cauldron of sinners, she would be slapped by society, but how can a woman refuse that oxygen that gives meaning to her life?

-Come with me... -He whispered like Adam to his Eve, and she accepted without arguing.

She could not think, only react. Her sinful and treacherous body responded to his command like a slave before her master. Love, lust, passion, tenderness, truth, lie, all empty words in front of a passionate body that does not allow her to recognize the will of duty.

A rough hand caressed her breast, now bare, cooled by the sea breeze as full lips caressed her neck. She stretched backward seeking further contact and a deliciously masculine smile pierced her to her depths. Closed eyelids never needed to open. She recognized his scent, his hands and that delicate warmth that emanated from his breath before brushing against her rosy skin. Next to him passions were a sinful secret that we dare not tell but he knew exactly how to make them come true.

The muscular arms grabbed her waist and knees and lifted her up like a sleepy little girl. A sinful mouth drove her wild as the sound of the sea grew ever more distant. Her feminine hands trailed down his torso until they crossed behind his neck as his mouth accepted every caress. Brenda felt transported to that place that poets write about but very few know about. That for which many sigh, others search desperately and some accept that they will never find.

Nothing felt better. Embraced, loved and desired, it was like being in heaven. Paradise existed and it was there in her arms. Brenda responded to every kiss and every caress by feeling like a complete woman. A main protagonist in her own fairy tale, one who could live her passion without feeling guilty or responsible for anyone but herself.

With the gentlest of care she was laid on a soft bed and for the first time opened her eyes to recognize her refuge. A gaze as blue and as deep as the darkest of skies flamed with desire for her. Her skin

Wild
Dr. Klein
Book II

Diana Scott
Published by Diana Scott
Copyright 2017 Diana Scott

Tabla de contenido
Wild
Dr. Klein
Book II
Foreword
First
A leap into the void
Hidden truths
With you
Not like this
Every man for himself
In the evening light
Today or never
I accept you
Kisses that kill
A matter of time
Last day
Forgetting yesterday
Forever and ever
The last night
Everything ends
Reality
Return to the truth
Walking among clouds
Do not leave me
Wait for me
Weather
Lies
Late and early
Days go by
Failures
Truths and lies
Prisoner of your decisions
Stones in paradise
An end, a beginning
A picture, a thousand words
Ultimatum
I don't see you

bristled anxiously and her breasts heaved eagerly to be loved. A man with a fierce and penetrating gaze was about to devour her as her heart pounded with the hope of being consumed.

"I'm sorry..." She thought before losing consciousness amidst the waves of a sea of kisses and caresses that danced to the rhythm of her moans.

First

...Coward for not trying, coward for not recognizing what you feel,
coward for not accepting that it is my heartbeat that wakes you up every morning,
coward for leaving without hearing me say I love you...
Akim

Ten days ago...
Brenda disembarked at the Ibiza airport, walked to the exit, handed in her documentation, picked up her suitcase and all without uttering a single word. Rachel walked just as silently, something quite unusual for her, but what do you say to your best friend when you see her "totally broken" and you have no idea what's going on in her crazy mind?

The former showbiz star elegantly raised the five fingers of her right hand, making them dance mischievously, and stopped a smiling cab driver who approached and helped them put away their two small handbags. Not small, very small! she thought annoyed. That's the price you have to pay when you run away in terror from husbands interested in finding out the truth, she thought grumpily.

The worst of misfortunes befell her that afternoon. Packing in fifteen minutes. My God! What woman in her right mind is forced to pack not one, but two suitcases in only fifteen minutes, she thought, scrunching her forehead. You pack a few outfits without being able to choose the new season's fashion brands and run away like a cat in front of a delicious bubble bath. Two bikinis, a few sets of underwear, two pairs of jeans, a little night dress just in case and run. All of them horribly folded, along with a bag with the indispensable seven pairs of shoes, in a beautiful Louis Vuitton bag. This is as far as we would have gone! She said to herself angrily, thinking that she wouldn't be caught dead using one of those neighborhood flea market suitcases that some greasy beings called poor people usually use as a travel bag. Rachel sat down next to her very friends as she pointed the helpful cab driver in the right direction. She looked for the fifteenth time at her friend who was still staring blankly without taking a bite.

"What happened? Why isn't Brenda answering my calls? Why did you change your destination?" Rachel still had Max's screams ringing in her ears. "What's going on! Why aren't you coming to Paris? Where's my wife!" he shouted angrily.

"And how the hell am I supposed to know!". One minute they were arranging a sweet trip to Paris and the next minute they were changing tickets to the first place she could think of to hide a friend who wouldn't stop weeping and wailing in Connor's arms. Good thing she was such a good actress that she came up with a Holiwood-worthy script and managed to appease some very inquisitive husbands. Sick Her Aunt from Spain turned out to be her epic play. Worthy of best director and lead actress. Yes, maybe not having a sick aunt in Spain was not a very solid lie, but when the water gets to your neck, creativity shows up in some rather curious facets, she said smiling to herself.

Rachel sighed nervously and decided like Brenda to lose herself in the scenery behind the window. She was plagued by many doubts, but now was not the time to burden Brenda with demanding gossip. When she was ready, she would talk. That was Brenda, always looking for the best moment and she understood and respected her above all else. They were both very, very different, and it is there, in the contrast, that true friendships are forged. Like Versace and Armani, she thought amused, that no matter how different they are, if you combine one with the other sometimes it looks divine, yes, that's how they were, divine each in their own styles. Her Brenda, sensitive, affectionate, responsible, educated and with a character as restrained as she was chubby in a Triumph girdle. One day you will explode, Connor told her, and apparently that day had come. Why and by whom? That was another matter entirely.

A small, trembling hand rested on hers and Rachel stopped thinking to caress it and instill courage in her. She didn't need to ask, the explanations would come, if Rachel was looking for her, she would be there, after all how many times was Brenda the one who had stuck her neck out for her? Countless, she thought, smiling as she remembered her antics as a little girl in a private boarding school. Now she was a grown woman. She was Rachel Zalazar, star of a couple of national movies, two commercials for depilatory creams and a starring role in four episodes of the great soap opera "Memorias de un macho", she thought, craning her neck and looking haughty. The great Rachel ready to burn her mascara for her only friend.

-Which way? -Brenda spoke with barely any energy and Rachel wanted to die of grief.

-That way." She pointed in a straight line with a certainty she didn't have. After all, she had never been there either.

Both tried to make room for themselves among a crowd of women of all ages and countries who gathered loudly in a hotel lobby that was even more crowded than the entrance. Young and not-so-young women wore smiling faces. They were all wearing the same T-shirt and Rachel noticed the logo printed in the center. A clenched fist and two fingers raised in victory. She smiled instantly, recognizing the group of London Amazons.

She was not sure if booking at the same hotel as her beloved Amazons had been a good idea, but the speed of events did not allow her to think of a less disastrous alternative. Sick her aunt in Ibiza in the middle of the season seemed like a good alternative, although now she was beginning to doubt it a little.

-Dear Pink. For equal pay, not one less! -shouted a woman barely five feet tall and with her fist in the air.

-Not one less! -the others exclaimed, stabbing at the sky.

Rachel, unable to contain herself, raised her hand to shout in time to the rhythm of the claimants who were squeezing more and more into the crowded reception area. Brenda watched her with her eyes popping out of their sockets trying to scream "Why?" and Rachel cursed at her uncontrolled temper.

"Typical trait of us big girls," she thought as she remembered Marilyn. She'd better explain herself before Brenda had a stroke.

-You see, it turns out that...

-Rachel! You bitch. You don't know how glad I am to see you.

-Well, I'm not exactly for.... -She said trying to explain herself when a lady as big as a beached whale approached her and squeezed her in her soft arms.

Rachel opened her mouth like a fish out of water while Brenda was looking for something to hit her in the head to free her friend who was starting to turn a greenish blue. The doctor was already holding her cell phone up and cursing for not having extended the warranty on her expensive Iphone when the actress managed to free herself.

-You see... -He said, coughing and trying to recover his oxygen. My friend and I...

The corpulent woman observed Brenda and, without warning, threw herself on the doctor, who was absorbed by an "immensity" of corpulent affection, astonished and with her cell phone raised.

-Buffy, this is Rachel, and if you let her go, I'm sure she'll tell you how pleased she is to meet you. He commented with an amused tone as he saw the perfect Dr. Klein being sucked in by a woman with a huge heart.

Brenda was released and craned her neck trying to get some oxygen into her lungs as the same rosy-cheeked, wide-hipped little girl screamed again with effusiveness.

-Pinks, we are beautiful, we are smart, we are unique, what are we!

-We are Amazons! We are Amazons! They all shouted in chorus and raised their fists in the air.

The doctor was trying to understand some of what was going on but didn't have a chance to ask. Buffy, who was still holding her back, joined in the enthusiasm of the fans. She raised her arm with such power that one moment Brenda was on her feet and the next she was thrown by the momentum like a soccer shot by a drunk. If it hadn't been for Rachel being in front of her and cushioning the blow, she was sure she would have swept the floor with her teeth. Both friends were trying to regain their balance when a young lady with a sign held high pointed the way for the Amazons who followed her like heated devotees before their messiah.

-Rachel! See you tonight. You'll see how happy Carol will be when I tell her you're here.

The group departed, leaving a desolate reception and a confused Brenda.

-Sweet, don't look at me like that. I haven't killed anyone. She said in the voice of a woman offender.

-But who are they, since when, why...? -Brenda spat out the questions in an incoherent torrent of doubts as she tried to rescue her handbag, which who knows why it was at the other end of the reception desk.

-Miss Salazar, Miss Klein. -Miss Salazar, Miss Klein. Room 271 and 274. These are your keys. Breakfast is served from nine to eleven o'clock and is included in your reservations. Dinners are from eight o'clock onwards. For further information please do not hesitate to contact me. Said a very friendly employee with a beautiful updo as she held out her hand with the keys to their double room.

-Esperanza, please accompany our guests.

-If you would be so kind as to follow me. Said a young girl with a wide smile and speaking perfect English.

Brenda reluctantly assumed that explanations would be delayed. The women accepted the bellhop's cooperation and stepped into the elevator without a word, although Rachel could feel her friend's accusing gaze. It was clear that there was more than one friend there with dark secrets and she was one.

The bellhop opened the door to the room, showed them the air conditioning instructions, and Rachel begged for time to stop so she could run away and not have to come clean.

-What, what? What!" he shouted as the employee closed the door.

-It's all right. I'll tell you everything but don't look at me like that. Sweet, you look awful when you furrow your brow, I told you about that cream.....

-Rachel! I don't look at you in any way. She said as she stroked her small wrinkle.

-Ok, Ok, Keep to calm. Let's see how I say it...

-The beginning is usually the best.

-Ha ha," she said wryly. It's all right," she said wryly. I've been an Amazon for six years, I've already said that. Well not one of those Amazons... I mean yes one of these Amazons but not one of those Greek movie ones although the truth is that if they proposed it to me I think that....

-Six? -Six years? -Did he say six years?

Rachel sat down in grief. She understood Brenda's hesitation.

-Yes. Sorry. She said with her shoulders slumped as she sat on the wide bed and traced the embroidered sheet of the bedspread with her finger.

"Yes, among so many others," he thought but kept silent so as not to interrupt.

-Sweet, I've never been as special or as smart as you or Connor....

-Don't say that... -. She replied indignantly but Rachel asked for silence with her hand to continue with her saddened statement.

-When I discovered that my forties had caught up with me before my big starring role, I knew my career was lost. Dreams of innocent years were erased in a big cream and caramel cake.

-Rachel, that's not so.... -Brenda lay down next to him.

Both rested on the mattress with their heads stuck together as when they were little and waiting in a cold boarding school to be picked up by parents too absent to miss.

-Yes, Sweet, that's the truth. I'm a star but unpainted. My role hasn't come to me yet, but don't worry, I've moved on.... There was a time when I felt useless and worthless, old and useless, but that's all behind me now. Now I see myself as I really am. I am a star in my own right, with or without a role, the great Rachel Zalazar, whoever likes her.

Brenda smiled half-heartedly.

-Why didn't you trust me? -The question conveyed a sorrow that made Rachel feel even worse.

-Sweet," she replied with special tenderness, "we are best friends and I know I count on you just as you count on me but there are certain tests of life that we must take on alone. And this was mine. You know, like when you have to change your hair color but you don't know which brand to buy. You try it and that's it. No one can give you their hair or their face, well the same thing happened to me. I faced my doubts and I assumed my.... years?

Brenda shook her head trying to divert her from a subject that was clearly so painful for her.

-Why Las Amazonas?

-Coincidence, accident, I don't know, the truth is I don't remember it well. Let's say that when I realized I was already at the first meeting. You know something Sweet, it's funny but when I'm with them I feel special. There we all have something that makes us feel important. We feel... - Rachel took a deep breath and continued - women without sin. Worthy of deserving the best.

-I could have helped you..... -Brenda spoke with a hint of jealousy in her words. How good a psychologist was she if she was unable to help her best friend when she needed her most?

-Of course you could," he said looking at her smiling, "You always could, but I needed to be the one to start walking. Sometimes secrets need time to mature and show themselves.... -He commented with a double meaning in his words.

Brenda could not answer. Both remained silent, analyzing the worn paint on the ceiling. They were both thinking but analyzing different worlds. Rachel was happy to come clean. She didn't like to admit that the weight of years frightened her and that she suffered for hundreds of lost opportunities but with the Amazons she had discovered that there were still a few thousand left to discover, Brenda however felt worse than before, now she was not only a bad wife, but a bad friend, a bad psychologist... a bad... woman.

The two of them, lying on the bed, analyzed their worlds while the minutes were lost under the dingy sound of an air conditioner eager to retire. Rachel waited and waited. She was sure Brenda would open up. What was wrong with her that she didn't offer half of what she demanded? The actress smiled half-heartedly looking at the white paint on the wall. Her friend was not much better off than she herself had been six years earlier. The wonderful Dr. Klein, the one everyone went to for a solution to their problems, was at a loss and had no strength to trust?

"Poor thing." She thought saddened, Brenda was a heartbeat away from realizing that the perfect, molded Dr. Klein deserved to have moments of imperfection. Rachel thought and thought of the thousand and one ways to get Brenda to open up. She would counter-attack with all her artillery. Brenda would come out of that deep sorrow in spite of herself. She was going to help her friend no matter what. She was ready to begin her verbal assault when a soft sound of deep breathing made her smile. It was Brenda and she was absolutely asleep. After a huge handful of painkillers that she and Connor managed to get her to take, she was finally getting some rest.

-Rest my Sweet. He said as he maternally covered her with a delicate blanket. I'll be here when you wake up....

A leap into the void

> I am afraid of not knowing if you will ever come back, to recognize that without you there are no more stars to dream about...
>
> Akim

It was Lola's fifteenth WhatsApp and Akim would have thrown the cell phone down the stairwell if it weren't for the fact that he couldn't afford to splurge on a new one. That woman had the power to drive him out of his mind. He growled angrily. His head hurt as much as a thousand devils put together but he still angrily threw the cement sacks that bounced as they landed on the ground sprinkling a dark cloud of material around them. He had been on twenty such trips but he wasn't tired. Fury and rancor coursed through his blood. She was gone. By now husband and wife would enjoy each other's caresses. They might be having breakfast holding hands gazing at the Paris sky in an expensive hotel bed, then they would love each other shamelessly and promise each other eternal love while he bled to death inside. He cursed again and again those destructive thoughts that had always dominated him and desperately searched in his pocket for the demonic gadget to answer Lola's last message, "see you tonight". He threw it on his backpack and set about loading another sack of cement.

If he got tired enough and slept with Lola a thousand times, he might stop feeling his chest split in two when he imagined his doctor in someone else's arms. Maybe if he closed his eyes tightly trying to forget her, time would pass, his lungs would stop breathing, he would be buried under the ground and then he would stop thinking about that cruel chocolate-colored gaze that haunted him even in his darkest nightmares. He had to hate her, he had to, then why wouldn't he stop pining for her! A night with Lola had turned out to be a pleasant but all too momentary experience. He remembered the night before and invincible memories piled up in his head haunting him with a sense of guilt he didn't want to feel. The night before he walked naked to the restroom feeling the cold under his feet. His insides churned inside him. He felt dirty and disgusted. How many times had he called her name? How many times had he pronounced her name, ramming hard against the one who had no claim on him? He could no longer remember...

He leaned against the sink and ducked his head so as not to see himself in front of the mirror. He was disgusted. Lola didn't deserve treatment like that.

"Damn it! Even I don't deserve it."

-Come to bed. A honeyed voice whispered with his lips pressed against her back.

The young beauty hugged him around the waist trying to pull her man back to where she wanted him.

-Lola... -She murmured trying to apologize. Trying to say with a word what her soul could not.

-I don't care. He replied without regret.

Akim closed his eyes, knowing that he should not accept it. A good man would understand that this was wrong and that he should leave. Lola wanted him and he had already taken too much advantage of her.

-Lola..." He whispered again asking for some understanding and a hint of forgiveness.

-You can call me whatever you want, I don't care, but don't leave. He said, gluing their naked bodies together. You need me....

God, he hated to admit it but yes, he needed her. Lola was offering him what another was denying him and he...he was not a good man.

With strength and broken by the pain he drowned his sorrows in a hard and unromantic kiss. He needed to unload and she was his escape valve.

-I'm sorry...'' he said, hoarse with desire and holding her too tightly in his arms, showing that it was not love he was looking for.

Lola smiled accepting the challenge. No matter what she was looking for, Akim would always find it in her....

Brenda had sunk him further into his wretched life and Lola meant no cure however tonight he would return to his bed. He needed to feel alive before the madness of jealousy finally broke what little sanity he had left. The pain of feeling that he had caressed her with his fingertips and it had slipped from his hands was so deep that he doubted if he had ever felt alive before he met her. Maybe, maybe just in fits and starts, but with her life was transformed into eternal minutes of a song that he never wanted to end. Damn you Dr. Klein! I need to spring back to life and Lola is the only lifeboat at hand, he thought furiously. He knew he was using her and tried to hate himself for it but he could not. His heart was pouring out too much pain to think of a third victim. His grief was increasing a selfishness that he did not remember possessing and that consumed him from the bottom of his gut. It was not Lola's arms he sought. It was not her lips he dreamed of, she was not the owner of that beautiful voice that resounded in his ears and it was not to her that he dedicated his love writings, those that would never be read...

Nikola appeared smiling and Akim turned to throw the last bag of material he was carrying on his shoulders to the ground. She tried not to look at him so as not to punch him in the middle of his smile. She hated to see him happy, didn't she know he was tearing himself apart inside? Even his best friend couldn't watch his heart break into unrecoverable pieces! She decided to leave before awakening his understanding with her own fists. Fate had played one of its many dirty tricks on him and it wasn't fair that the world continued to spin and smile when he was suffering the insufferable.

-Will you know if you want to leave before I tell you the latest news? - Nikola said, trying to get her attention so she wouldn't leave.

Akim turned half his body to face him and Nikola swallowed saliva. When Akim gave you that cold, piercing stare and his broad shoulders tensed up further highlighting those arm tattoos, the sensible thing to do was to run while you could. Akim saw the fear etched in his friend's gaze and regretted his insistent bad mood. He closed his eyes and took a deep breath, trying to control his angry outbursts as he asked in what he thought was a friendly tone.

-Nikola smiled again, feeling a little more confident as he noticed the control returning to his friend's muscles. Akim's fist was a weapon only an idiot wouldn't fear.

-I happen to be coming from the headquarters building. Akim growled angrily as he remembered that this was Max Brown's workplace and Nikola, fearing for her life, left the suspense for another time.

-They are not together! -He dropped a bombshell in front of Akim who was looking at him expectantly waiting for explanations.

-You see, it turns out that Samir asked me this morning to go and get some plans from headquarters. I've been out most of the morning, I guess you haven't missed me because of course I look like a zero to the left in your life, but you know that...

-Nikola... -Akim stretched out the last vowel, trying to keep a calm that was on the borderline between madness and despair.

-Well, as I was saying, I went to get those plans when the brunette at the front desk told me she hadn't seen me in a while. You can't imagine my surprise.

Akim cocked his head to the side trying to follow that nonsensical argument but his friend was making it really difficult for him.

-I would never have imagined that this beauty would remember my face. Of course, I guess it's not just my face that attracted her to me. You know... - He said pointing to her body shaped by hard work.

Akim shook his head and reached for the wheelbarrow to continue his work. Nikola was undoubtedly losing his mind. Perhaps he had lost it many years ago, when at the age of sixteen he had to rescue him from the hands of Don Dmytro, the neighborhood hairdresser, who, catching him with his hands on his daughter's breasts, wanted to check the edge of his knife on his friend's neck. If it had not been for his strong hands, which were already showing their manners in those years, his friend would not have kept all his parts in the right places. He picked up the wheelbarrow trying to forget the infinite number of problems in which he had been involved thanks to the permanent collaboration of his friend's busybody, no, this time he was going to forget about it, his problems were enough to fall into another of his madness. Nikola held the wheelbarrow with both hands to stop him.

-What the hell is wrong with you? Aren't you interested in knowing that they are not together?

-No.

Nikola was shocked by the answer and Akim leaned against the wall crossing his legs and trying to explain himself. After all it was Nikola, his friend, his brother.

-She left me. They will meet in Paris. She may not have traveled yesterday but she will travel today. Brenda is history past and forgotten. He said with a sorrow most evident to even the blindest of the blind.

-I don't think so? - he replied with a smile.

-What do you know? -He asked, sitting up and stretching out his elongated body, interested in the answer.

Nikola feeling the center of his attention again continued to talk about the brunette at the entrance and her spectacular curves but

Akim's rough growl and his hands on his shirt lapel made him start a most accelerated summary.

-... she was furious, apparently she had to make last minute cancellations, book a hotel in Ibiza and twenty thousand other arrangements, and all in less than an hour...

Akim listened attentively to every detail. Nikola had not only managed to discover that both Brenda and Rachel were in Ibiza, but also that they were alone. She had cancelled her flight to Paris. The air of hope was beginning to fill her body. Their cursed honeymoon and those hours of passion he thought he imagined were gone. Nikola continued talking but Akim was barely able to follow. God, he felt devilishly happy. He shouldn't be, after all she had rejected him but he couldn't help it. A small glimmer of illusion lit up his face. "What if it had been for me?" he thought excitedly. "Fuck, of course it's because of me!" Akim remembered the warmth of her kisses on the sofa at home and smiled with a positivity unknown to him. She was running away, and if she was running away it was because she was scared and if she was scared it was because....

-What do you say, do you want it or not? -Nikola asked enthusiastically.

-I don't understand." Akim came back to earth and apparently his friend was looking for an answer to who knows what.

-The ticket, asshole, are you keeping it or not?

-Passage? Imbecile? -Akim fixed his deep blue eyes on his friend trying to understand something.

-Oh my God, if it wasn't for me," she said with an air of superiority. I see you're lost, I go back to the beginning, it turns out that the little brunette was crazy about my bones and I didn't know it but you know, it happens to a lot of people and...

-Nikola!

-All right, all right," she replied, shaking her head as if it was your loss. With the points from the ladies' card they were giving away a free ticket and since my pretty brunette was so upset I thought that if she gave me the points and I got you a free ticket....

-I can't believe it... I mean her, I mean you... And she gave them to you? -Her eyes glittered with distrust.

-And you still don't know, it turns out she's got a crush on my bones and we're meeting tonight, but I'm going out on time because lately....

Nikola could not finish speaking. Akim held him in a tight embrace and gave him two pats on the back with an effusiveness that almost ripped his lungs out of their sockets. He was elated. He would travel to Ibiza. He would look for her all over the island if necessary. He had to plan it well. How much time did he have?

-When is the ticket due?

-You leave in three hours.

-Three. Did you say three? But how the hell am I going to leave in three hours? He said with his soul on his feet.

He couldn't just disappear from work, it was impossible. His shoulders slumped and his eyes were troubled with the usual pessimism. For a moment he had felt like he was touching the sky with his hands, but now, as always, happiness was slipping through his fingers.

-Thank you, my friend," he said with embarrassed sincerity, "but I cannot.

-What can't you? Why can't you?

Akim just stared at the concrete mountain and Nikola realized that he had not told his story in full. He smiled to himself in amusement.

-And that's what you get for making me summarize. You know how bad I always was at literature," he said cheerfully. I called Samir to tell him that the doctor found you have an egg herpes," Akim arched an eyebrow and Nikola replied amused. It was the first thing that came to my mind. I remembered that my cousin had it and had a fever for almost a week and couldn't go to work," he said, lifting his shoulders in apology. No matter the reasons, the truth is that Samir understood perfectly. Moreover, he said something like these irresponsible young people and who knows what else, but the important thing is that he ordered you to take care of yourself and not to return until you are one hundred percent recovered.

-So I'm on vacation?

-It's more like medical leave, but it's the same thing. When I was coming I talked to your father and asked him to prepare a bag for you with some belongings. I figured you would say yes. He said lifting up a travel backpack.

Akim grinned from ear to ear and Nikola looked at his watch. If we leave right now on your bike, then I'll take it to your house so you don't have to leave it at the airport. The parking lots are expensive.

"Money, cruel and vile metal," he said to himself furious at feeling like the poorest of the wage earners.

-I don't have a pound in my pocket.... -Nikola smiled smugly and Akim's eyes widened expectantly, "The brunette too? -He asked as he watched Nikola type on her cell phone.

-No, asshole. Philips is an acquaintance who can help you," he replied, stretching out his cell phone, "but ask only for the money you'll need. The interest rates are not low. Akim smiled happily as he talked to this Philips the happiest thing in life. When he cut the call he hugged him tightly and Nikola sighed pretending to be angry.

-Little guy on the loose. Just the right amount of faggots.

Akim let go, picked up his backpack and went running in search of his helmet. He was in too much of a hurry. Someone was waiting for him in Ibiza.

Hidden truths

I close my eyes and I imagine you, I breathe and I feel you, you crossed my path and I discovered you.
Love by your side means much more what sweet songs sung to destiny.
Akim

The sun was beginning to fade into the orange sunset horizon and Brenda still had her legs wrapped in her own embrace. With her chin resting on her knees she watched the waves crash as she wondered over and over again how she had come to feel this way. She closed her eyes and sighed deeply. Even without wanting to, she remembered each of his caresses. That deep blue of his gaze followed her wherever she went. It didn't matter if she was awake or asleep, her body burned for him, for the sweet touch of his lips caressing the silky skin that yearned for him in supplication. She couldn't remember ever feeling like this, or even anything remotely like it. Yes, it was true that she was married and that Max had become her whole world but what she felt for Akim was something more raw, more primal. With him, security and duties became unnecessary feelings. The once vanished passion would present itself hungrily just knowing he was around. Just remembering him made her body tremble from her head to the smallest and farthest toe. With him the smile was present and passions were born without the need for obligations. Being by his side her feminine body reacted in a way that could not be possible, the lips rejuvenated expectantly and the soft breasts dawned from a deep sleep wishing to be sheltered in his hands. Why not meet you before? Why is life so cruel as to teach me what I can never live? I imagine that's the punishment I'll have to bear for living what I shouldn't with the one I can't. Loves and passions that will die in my mouth bruised by teeth that will hold it back preventing me from shouting what my heart desperately screams.

He thought, trying to make sense of everything that was happening to him, but none of his sage advice was any good. The scenario was changing. Now she was the protagonist of an unwanted tragedy. At this moment it was her own advice that she wanted to find but unfortunately it was not coming. Love, desire, passion, what the hell was inside her?

"Why me, why!" she questioned herself as she remembered how different her life had been just a few months before. Everything may not have been in perfect order but it mattered to her. It all fit. A little time and every loose end would have been restored, every lost sheep would have found its fold and every fissure in her marriage would have been patched but now.... Now everything was upside down. He ducked his head and looked down at the sand between his knees and began to draw with his finger in the sand. He shouldn't find himself like this. This couldn't be real. Yes, it had to be some of that, some kind of momentary mental derangement, why else would he still remember her perfume, her husky voice speaking in his ear or that little nibble on his lip that she always gave him before their first kiss?

-Sweet we have one problem.

Rachel approached from behind with her cell phone raised and Brenda immediately erased with the palm of her hand the name she had just absent-mindedly written in the wet sand.

-With this one there are about fifteen messages and I am no longer able to count the number of missed calls.

Brenda watched the screen even though she didn't have to. Max was desperately looking for her.

-Despite my lies, he still insists on talking to you.

Brenda closed her eyes and sighed, overwhelmed with guilt. She wasn't like that. Lies were not part of her life. She had never felt the need to lie, much less to Max, but how could she explain to him what even she wasn't able to understand? What was she supposed to tell him? I'm sorry, honey, but I've been dreaming of other arms for weeks, or better yet, I'm sorry, honey, but even though I love you very much, it's his kisses that I need in the morning and his body that I desire at night.

-God... -He said with his shoulders slumped and hiding his head between his knees again.

Rachel sat down next to him and looking at the horizon spoke confidently.

-Beautiful sunset. Brenda timidly raised her head and watched as the sun finished setting. Remember when we used to look out the window at boarding school hoping to wish upon a shooting star?

And how to forget it. Her only hope resided in that halo of light that always passed so fast that it never listened to her. Again and again she begged him to turn her into a boy and thus conquer her father's heart, but the stupid star did not grant it to her.

"Girl you had to be. You never know anything. Her father used to tell her, snorting with annoyance for not having a son. "I hope you find a man to carry you through because you're such a softy." He told her when she first fell off her bike. Yes, yes she remembered those old dull old stars perfectly.

-How old were we? Ten?

-Seven. He replied bitterly as he remembered his stern father.

-Yes, of course, there were seven of them.... -Rachel looked into her eyes for the first time and Brenda quickly hid the crystalline glow of sadness. Sweet, you know you can always count on me.

-I know, and I swear it's not that I don't want to... it's just that Rachel I...

-Sh, I don't demand anything from you. I know you too well and I've learned to respect your silences. I know when you're ready you'll talk to me," Brenda nodded with a deep lump in her throat, "but I think you should calm him down. Max may have his quirks but he loves you and he's worried. He won't calm down until he hears you. They both think we are in Spain because of Aunt Evangelina's passing.

Aunt Evangelina was the only family member Rachel still had alive and everyone knew how much she loved her.

-Did you say she was sick?

-With one foot in the holy sepulcher to be exact.

-God... God... -I'm so sorry," she said, "I'm so sorry. I didn't want to get you into this trouble. I'd better go and face my problems. She commented, remembering her father's constant complaints about her lack of courage. I'll leave. She said trying to get up but she couldn't. Rachel stopped her by resting her hand on her knee.

-You're not leaving and I'm not leaving. Max just wants to talk to you. I told him your phone was dead. Talk to him, reassure him and forget about him.

Brenda opened her eyes in wonder, not knowing if she had heard her friend's words correctly.

-Forget me?

-Yes. I don't have to be much of a priestess to understand that you need to think and you won't do that if you put others first. You need time for yourself and I'm going to help you get it.

-It seems easy. He replied with irony.

-It is. You always put the welfare of others before your own. In your practice your patients come first, in your marriage Max is the important one, in your life the right thing is always the way.

-It's not true," she said, somewhat offended.

-Sweet, whatever happened was important enough to break down your most solid walls and that worries me. You never show weaknesses, you are always perfect, consistent and right. Making this trip is the first plan I have not seen you plan and that scares me.

-According to you and Connor, that's exactly what I should do. She said annoyed.

Brenda was getting more and more upset, it seemed that her friend was demanding what she had been asking for for years. What was the point, she thought offended.

-Maybe, but not in this way....

-And what shape is supposed to be the right one!

Brenda screamed and got up in a huff. She had been lost for two days. She was trying to find her limits again but she couldn't find them. The perfect outline she had made of her life was beginning to fade and she felt disoriented. Profession, friends, home, everything followed a structured order necessary to be a successful woman. If one of the pillars moved, the meaning of her life was lost.

-We'll talk later. You're in no condition. Rachel said, trying to end the conversation.

-No! Now you say it.

-Suffering! -. He replied as usual, unable to hold his tongue.

Brenda looked at her blankly and Rachel again sentenced.

-You suffer and it's not just because of what you've been through. You suffer because of fear. I see it in your eyes. I recognize it because it is the same fear that dominated you every time you talked to your father.

Brenda tried to hide the tears that began to flow without permission. She was exhausted. She couldn't take it anymore. She felt like a liar, a traitor, unfaithful, selfish, weak and terribly scared.

Rachel hugged her, trying to calm her down but only succeeded in making her tears multiply. If the solution was so simple, why was it so hard for her to accept it? What had he given her that she couldn't forget him? The doctor cried on her friend's shoulder who wrapped her in a firm embrace. Once the tears and hiccups had stopped, Rachel wiped a tear from her face and coughed to put on that funny, flippant tone she used to use with those who didn't know her.

-It's super late. Talk to Max, tell him everything is fine and cover those dark circles under your eyes urgently or you'll get wrinkles and they won't let us in.

Brenda smiled as she wiped her face with the back of her hand.

-Enter where?

-Wait and see...

The room exploded with women. Hundreds, no thousands of them were pacing back and forth waiting expectantly for the big moment. Today was the big night. The annual convention of the Amazons was opening its doors in the city of Ibiza. Brenda walked somewhat unsure and dragged by Rachel's firm hand. Her friend moved like a fish in water. She greeted each other as if they had known each other all their lives and a small pang of jealousy shook her from deep in the pit of her stomach. She had always believed that the two were inseparable, acquainted with each other's most painful ashes, but it seemed that this was not the case. Rachel had a hidden side and it was called The Amazons.

-What do you think? -said Rachel, stopping in the middle of the crowd as she looked around for an open seat.

-Nothing.

What was she supposed to say or claim? She was the least likely to claim sincerity. He was still not confessing and that made her feel even worse.

-Turn, turn... Rachel ordered between her teeth, but Brenda did not know how to react in time before a beautiful, tall, dark-haired woman with the demeanor of a queen approached to greet them with that smile typical of hyenas about to attack.

-Rachel! I was told you weren't coming. What happened? Your hubby got tired of showing you off and gave you permission to attend?

Brenda crinkled her eyes ready to counterattack. Rachel may not have been the most enlightened of women or the most fluent in words but there she was to enjoy a good dialectical fight.

Truth be told, after recent events, it wouldn't hurt to let off a little adrenaline in something other than tears. He was about to respond when Rachel straightened the entire length of her back and smiled victoriously as she raised her hands in indifference.

-You know, honey, when you're like me," she said, emphasizing her lush contours, "it's hard to resist them. They all fall...

The woman shot fire out of her eyes and Rachel was in position to continue her attack when a young girl with ample curves and short height approached at full speed running directly into the back of the brunette who turned around in a fury.

-Sorry, sorry, I just had to find you before....

-You idiot! You can't do anything right. You're the worst of the assistants.

The poor girl adjusted her glasses with trembling hands as she clutched with the other one a myriad of messy papers.

-I'm very sorry Amazona leader but it's time and the sound operators still need to perform the tests. It's important because otherwise the pinks sisters won't be able to....

-Oh, shut up for once. You bore me. He said raising his hand in boredom.

-Rachel, I hope to see you later. He commented with an excessive dose of false politeness.

-We will be here.

The woman shook her head and left, followed at a fast pace by the assistant who ran after her like a faithful puppy waiting for an old and licked bone.

-And why is she looking at you with a face like she wants to kill you? -Rachel laughed heartily and answered just as amused.

-Her name is Carol and she is the lead Amazon. She commands more of the Amazons and yes, she wants to kill me.

-Why?

-I slept with his former darling. Brenda's eyes widened in horror.

-You mean before George? -She asked fearful of the answer but Rachel didn't answer.

-Sweet, you may know a lot of social theory, but you're missing a few practical classes. He replied as they sat down in two vacant seats.

-Rachel! You can't... -Brenda was about to continue but the angry look from the woman sitting next to her made it clear that if she didn't let her listen to the speech she would make her eat her purse.

-Sh, it's about to start. I'll explain later.

-Not at all. I want answers now and...

A loud squeak from the ladies in the back row and the half-hearted handbag of her seatmate made it clear to her that it was wise for any explanation to wait at least until the end of the speech.

Carol made her appearance on the dais wearing jeans and a T-shirt with the Amazon logo on the front. Hundreds of women cheered loudly as she solemnly raised her fist in the air and spoke with the energy of a confident leader.

-Dear Pinks! We are here one more year to make ourselves heard. We are here why?

The women jumped out of their seats and with raised fists and loud shouts responded at the top of their lungs.

-We are beautiful!

-And what else? -asked the leader.

-We are smart! -they shouted.

-And what else! -he asked again.

-We are unique!

-Why?

-Because we are women! We are Amazons!

-Yes Amazonas, we are women and we are here to defend what has been kept from us for years.

-Because we are! -he shouted, waiting for an answer.

-We are Amazons, ahoo, ahoo!

Rachel raised her hand and shouted in chorus along with her new companions while Brenda let herself be absorbed by the intense aura that surrounded the room. Hundreds of women united by the same feeling of equality. The warmth of an invisible sisterhood bound them all together and the doctor understood the reason why Rachel had joined their ranks. At that moment they were all sisters in the same cause. None were out of place. The environment accommodated tall or short, thin or not so thin, all were claiming a place that had been taken from them and to which they were entitled by birth. Brenda settled back in her seat thinking of the association of abused women with which she collaborated and thought how good it was to see how others who felt strong and brave raised the flag of equality for all, including in their requests those whose tired arms were no longer able to fight.

The speech was getting more heated by the minute and Brenda felt a pang of remorse in her veins. Upon first seeing Carol, she had gotten the wrong picture of the woman. Someone leading a group to such good ends could not be what she had first imagined.

She cocked her head to one side, as she always did when she was focused, as the leader's words touched every little portion of her being.

"...this is our world, our home. Let us work together to recompose the positions that were usurped from us. Let us be courageous and not allow indifference and fear to take their toll on our rights. Let us share our personal stories and experiences with those who have not yet discovered their own power. Let us raise our voices for all the marginalized women who wander without a destination because they feel alone. Let us raise our hands for those who suffer the blows and mistreatment of a cruel abuser who imposes his physical strength to belittle them. Let us smile in the face of the arrogance of those who consider us inferior and let us demonstrate to those hollow brains that they are the only ones who are useless. Each one of us here present has a story to tell and a hand to offer, let's not look away, if we are here today it is because others like us raised their hands and shouted loudly that not one more woman died because of male violence, not one more woman with lower wages than a man, not one more woman called a whore for wearing a miniskirt or pants, not one more woman insulted for daring to drive, not one more woman called a slut for not accepting sex from someone she has not chosen. Today we are here to pick up the legacy of our grandmothers and become writers of our own history. We have come this far so that politicians, scientists, lawyers, businessmen, artists and any man worthy of calling himself a macho man, will know that we are standing up and we do not intend to remain silent. We are women with dreams to fulfill, but our dreams are just that, our dreams, and we are no longer willing to be ordered how we should dress, what we should clean, how many children we should take care of or who we should love. Thousands of housewives broke imposed molds and became pilots, scientists, cattle ranchers, transporters, doctors, soldiers and hundreds of professions reserved only for men. They showed us the way, now is the time for us to stand up and walk the path without fear. We owe it to them and to all women who suffer today without knowing that there is a way out. We are the chosen ones to raise the flags on their behalf and tell them that all is not lost, that we are at their side to fight together. The time of oppression is over and our voices are the chimes of freedom. Let no one ever tell you that we are different or inferior because we are not, we are simply women looking for a better world, one in which we do not have to fight for the rights that were once usurped from us. Amazon sisters let us raise our hands to show the world that we are great, we are human, we are intelligent, we are dreamers, we are unique Why!"

-We are women! We are Amazons! -They all stood up and shouted loudly

and Brenda, unable to hold back her tears, hugged her friend while whispering a hateful thank you.

For several days he had lost his bearings. It may have been years, but that no longer mattered, now he had discovered the reason for his studies, the purpose of his work. She loved helping people and was happy to do so. The rest were simply pitfalls to face and she had the tools to do it, not for nothing was she the famous Dr. Klein.

Rachel accepted the embrace but with a slightly quizzical look on her face and Rachel, though understanding, simply held her arm and walked together back to the hotel. The two enjoyed each other's company under the warm light of stars that shone unabashedly on a delightful summer night.

Hope, you can't do this." A red-haired, freckle-faced young man pleaded in anguish with the young girl in his arms.

-You know I do." She released her grip and replied indignantly.

-She doesn't deserve you. Let's get out of here.

-Peter, please, you have to support me on this. You know how important this is to me. When she accepts who I am she will be proud.

-No, he won't. Stop lying to yourself! -The young man was beginning to lose his temper and the girl closed her eyes before answering coldly.

-You'd better go. I don't want to see you again.

-Are you breaking up with me?

-I'm just saying that if you're not going to support me in the most important thing in my life, you'd better leave.

The young man cursed before putting on his helmet and speeding off on his Vespa. The young girl hugged her folders and took off in the opposite direction from the women.

-Wasn't that Carol's assistant? -Brenda asked curiously.

-Yes, and I think she's the same one who greeted us at the hotel. Now I understand why I knew her face.

-Poor thing, what happened? Did she seem upset?

-Boyfriend fight, you know. I'm sure in an hour they'll be texting and apologizing to each other. Love is like that, I hate you, I love you, I need you? -Said Rachel without giving more importance to the subject.

-Brenda said, imagining who she was really thinking of when she said those words.

Walking without speaking he watched the cobalt light of the stars and the bluish reflection falling on the dark sea. Blue, everything in her world lately seemed to be blue. Damn color and damn eyes that haunted her no matter how many planes she had boarded.

-Rachel, why didn't you ever tell me about the Amazons?

Both stopped their walk and sat on the beach in front of their hotel watching the moon reflected in the swaying of the water. Waves of sea like a serene song danced slowly with the company of a couple of seagulls that silently and oblivious to the curious caressed each other under the deep melody of the sea.

-Shame, fear, pride, who knows? Maybe a little bit of everything.

-I would never have judged you, on the contrary, I would have understood and supported you," she said, convinced and somewhat disappointed.

-And I know that now, but when the situation gets to you and you don't see the way out, it's very difficult to understand that your friends are there to support you and not to judge you," Rachel spoke slowly, emphasizing each of her words as accurate stabs thrown straight at the target.

Brenda felt a huge jolt of reality hit her and she took a deep breath, realizing the meaning of her words. Rachel was her best friend and she had to trust her heart to her. She would never hurt him. But how hard it is to open up when for years you've only learned to shut yourself away in your own thoughts. Years of hiding who she was and encouraging what she wasn't had led her to this, a perfect professional, educated woman and responsible wife, but what was she like inside when no one claimed her? Did anyone know who Dr. Klein really was? Did anyone know what Brenda Klein thought, felt, dreamed or longed for? Maybe not but she hadn't made it easy either.

-Rachel, I... -Her saliva caught in her throat and her hands began to sweat. She had to acknowledge out loud something she wasn't sure she was capable of hearing from herself. I'm confused.

Rachel watched her quietly and Brenda knew it was time to take courage and acknowledge her mistakes. Better or worse, they were hers and she had to face them.

-There is a man... one I cannot forget. No matter what I do or what I think about, his gaze never leaves me. I have him here," she said, tapping her forehead with a finger. I want to forget him, I swear I want to but I can't. He's here like a disease that won't leave me. It's here like a disease that doesn't let me breathe. If I move, walk or sleep, no matter what I do, he's there disturbing my reasoning. I try to control myself but I can't.

-And it's clearly not Max.

-No, it is not. He replied with his eyes downcast in the sand.

-And have you thought about what you are going to do?

-No, I didn't even know this was happening to me until yesterday.

-Brenda felt like she was dying of embarrassment.

-Well, I don't. I'm dizzy, confused, angry. I'm dizzy, confused, angry. Why did this have to happen to me!

-And why not? Sweet, you are not the iron wonder. You are a woman with blood, body and heart, you have no reason to be angry with you. She said calmly.

-I had it all...

-My beauty friend, you know as well as I do that one man does not take the place of another if the place is not free.

-I love Max. He said quickly.

-And I don't doubt it, but Max is not your problem.

-No? I thought I was the only one." She replied annoyed.

-And therein lies your problem. Stop thinking about that new man or Max and start thinking about you. What do you feel when you are with him? What do you want in your life? Who do you want to be?

Brenda looked at her as if she had grown horns and Rachel smiled at her in amusement. For the first time in years she had managed to unsettle the perfect Dr. Klein.

-Mi sweet, do you remember when you cut your hair short like a boy?

-Yes. It was at fourteen.

-You never recognized him, but I'm sure it was because of that conversation that you overheard your father.

-You can... -He replied when he remembered telling his father the benefits of a son and the disadvantages of having a weak and incompetent daughter.

-He was an idiot for not recognizing the beautiful daughter in front of him. Follow your own steps and live your life honey.

-My father has nothing to do with all this.

-Maybe not directly, but true is true. Because of him you became perfect, educated and socially correct.

-I don't...

-You do. You hide your feelings as weaknesses that no one should discover. That asshole taught you that you were a weak and incapable little girl and you believed him. From those you sow these harvests. Sweet, think of yourself, live life for yourself and then we'll talk about what to do with everything else.

-Are you telling me to abandon Max over some silly thing?

-No sweet, I tell you to act as you please and think of no one else but yourself. Do what you feel and not what you must. Live according to your heart and you will see that the stumbles will hurt less.

Rachel got up from the floor shaking the sand out of her jeans leaving her alone with her thoughts. She was confused. Her friend's words had been neither gentle nor loving.

Thinking about her and her feelings? Wasn't she already doing that? What life was she living?

If you knew how much you provoke me doctor...-A thick voice that she thought was a dream made her open her eyes to discover that her bluest secrets were becoming a robust and muscular reality right under her nose.

With you

Discover in the beats of my heart your only way of living.
Akim

He couldn't believe it. He had just left the last hotel, it was late and he was tired. He had been asking from hotel to hotel all day but nothing. No Mediterranean Sun or Mediterranean Hot or anything like it. He unfolded again the paper he kept in his pocket that Nikola had stolen from the secretary. Would that be an a or an o? He wondered for the twentieth time trying to decipher the letter. God, he was desperate. He was hundreds of miles from home chasing a woman who wouldn't stop running. "I must be out of my mind," he thought despondently and knowing he should give up the search. A rather shrill and haughty voice he heard in the distance distracted him from his thoughts.

"That voice... I know her," he said hiding behind a pillar so as not to be discovered because he was sure that if the owner turned out to be who he thought she was, she would not be very happy to see him.

-No, 271 is my sweet friend's, mine is the other one. The receptionist looked at her like a weirdo and Akim couldn't hold back a smile. If uptight Rachel was there, her lovely doctor was not far behind.

He waited to see her enter the room, come out of hiding and knock on the blissful 271. If he had heard correctly Brenda would be there.

His heart was pounding like a runaway horse. What would he say to her? How would she react? Would she be happy to see him? Because he was. God, he was trembling at the mere thought of having her in front of him again. He leaned his forehead against the door. He felt both exhausted and hopeful. Brenda wasn't in Paris, she was in Ibiza and alone, that had to mean something. It had to mean something. His hands were sweating nervously as he knocked again but no one answered. Fear began to grip him, what if it wasn't Brenda the friend that uptight Rachel was meeting?

"No, no, don't be an idiot. It's her. It has to be her or Nikola I swear I'll castrate you this time," he thought grumpily.

Nothing, she did not answer. He walked towards the exit determined to return early in the morning when on the sidewalk in front of him, next to the sea, a solitary figure lying on the sand caught his attention. Same height, same figure, same hair. He walked slowly, begging the sky to hear him. As if he were a serial killer, he approached stealthily, with delicate steps and a crazy trotting heartbeat.

"It's her... damn it, it is..." He thought as he observed her stylish figure lying on the sand. It's her, he said to himself as he observed her long dark thick eyelashes resting on the beautiful cheeks rosy from the burning Mediterranean sun.

"How have I lived this long without you? How will I survive if I don't have you?" he thought somewhat uneasily. Gently he knelt behind her head and had to clench his fists tightly so as not to fall under the temptation represented by her long auburn hair. God, how he longed to caress her. No matter how many women he had drowned his desperation the scent of her body was still present under every pore of his skin. He remembered every single kiss he had ever given her, every single one. He took a breath trying to calm himself before speaking behind her ear in a soft voice trying not to frighten her.

- If you knew how much you provoke me doctor... Do you think of me? Because I don't stop dreaming about you not even one of my unhappy nights.

Brenda's eyes widened in fright. She jumped on the spot and tried to get up. She looked at him terrified and Akim hurriedly searched for some explanation, surely he thinks I'm a sexual depraved, a woman ripper or a serial killer, why else would he react like that?

-No Brin, no honey, don't be scared, it's me," he said, trying to calm her fears, but she was still looking even more out of sorts.

Akim held her by the arm as she stood up in agitation. Shit, that was not the expected reaction. Brenda moved trying to get out of his grip but he wouldn't let her. He didn't want to scare her but he wasn't going to lose her so soon either.

-You, you? What are you doing here? How did you know? -She asked between nervous and frightened.

Akim released his grip fearing to hurt her with his strength and tried to appear as serene as possible although his blood was bubbling with nerves on all four sides. He dragged his hand through his black hair to calm himself and speak with what little calm he possessed.

-They told me where you were.

-You followed me? What do you want? What are you looking for? -she asked nervously.

Akim smiled mischievously as he focused his fiery gaze on hers. Now that he could answer without looking like a fucking depraved man.

-You. I look for you, I want you, I desire you. He answered self-confident.

Brenda stirred on the spot. She was nervous, maybe a little agitated but not scared. She wasn't anymore, thank goodness, she told herself cheerfully. The fears left her delightful gaze and Akim breathed a satisfied sigh. At least tonight he wouldn't be spending it in a police station for stalking helpless female doctors.

-How did you know? -he asked, narrowing his eyes.

-Secretaries, you know, they talk too much. She replied, trying to make her smile look less nervous.

Brenda walked closer to the shore and Akim followed close behind. She looked beautiful. Her hair shone in the moonlight and her long shadow was reflected on the calm sea. The sea breeze sent a shiver down his spine and he wanted to embrace her and give her the warmth of his body but again he clenched his fists to restrain himself. He had to go slowly. She was surprised and frightened. The tension in her arms and the blank stare into the horizon showed a hundred fears that he would gladly quell but could not.

-You must go," Akim swallowed dryly when he heard her so determined.

No, he had not come all that way to give up like a well-mannered young man. No, he was not that kind of man. He would not go down without a fight. His mother may not have fought for his father's love but he was not his mother. He remembered the hundreds of sad looks in his home and vowed to himself that he would fight a thousand times if he had to. He wanted her too much to give up.

Sure of himself he came up behind her and without touching her but knowing that his warmth reached her he spoke in soft words.

-I can't. You're here because you can't forget me," she didn't deny it, that was good, "I can't forget you either. You are present in my every move. When I sleep, when I wake up, when I eat, when I walk, you're pinned to my chest like a pin that can't come off. Clinging like the sweetest of hopes, like the most painful of memories -. He said as he rested his rough hand gently and almost without touching her behind her delicate and feminine back.

-This can't be... You have to understand. I'm married, this is crazy.

Gently and trying not to frighten her he moved his other hand to the small hollow of her waist. With one hand on her waist and the other on the small of her back he continued to speak tenderly behind her ear.

-The only laws I respect are those of the heart. And my heart tells me that you are in each of its arteries. You keep me and hide me like a sin that must not be discovered but I know I'm there, deep inside you. Crying out for you to let me out to make you happy.

-Akim please... What are you trying to do? -He said as he turned to face each other.

"Everything, I want it all." He thought for sure but didn't want to scare her off. She needed time and he would give it to her. If she asked for it he would give her his life and leave this world happy in the knowledge that she had loved him. Brenda may not have known it yet but he was completely sure of his feelings. One recognizes the love of one's life when their lips are caressed with the first kiss. And Brenda was the love that many seek, others hide and a very few enjoy.

-I won't force you to do anything, I promise. Let's be friends. Get to know me. He said thinking that his lies would keep him out of heaven.

Brenda looked at him in confusion and he wanted to smile at her naivety. She might be older in age but in foul play he beat her by a wide margin. Friends? Of course not. He wanted all of her and all of her. He would fight with all his weapons, dirty or clean, it mattered little to him. In love and war the only thing that matters are the results. She represented an unattainable dream, too tempting to pose moral dilemmas. Another man had come into her life before him, he may even have had full legal rights to her, but the rules were not written for him. Since leaving his country he had learned that triumph was on the side of the strongest and these were not necessarily the most sincere. Truth, honesty, loyalty, what do they mean if at the end of the day she is cuddled in the arms of another man? No Dr. Klein, I will not let you escape. I have your doubts, I will soon have your decision.

-Are you offering me your friendship, no strings attached? -she asked curiously.

She sounded somewhat disappointed, or at least that's what he wanted to think, and it made him feel exhilarated.

-Of course," he lied cheekily. I don't think I behaved well with you the last time we met. He said mischievously, looking around her body with fire in his eyes, trying to remind her of those caresses on her couch. I won't deny that I like you, that's something more than evident, but I want you to know me as a person much more. He lied shamelessly again.

Brenda was no fool. She was suspicious so she decided to play the role of a good and understanding guy. He wanted her completely, he wanted to lay her down on the sand and leave all that empty bullshit but Brenda was not the type to be conquered with a good fuck, too bad for me, he said to himself amused.

-Are you trying to convince me that you came all this way out of friendship?

Akim grinned cheekily and moved in close almost gluing his chest to hers as he locked his burning gaze on her.

-I came because I want it all, you will decide which part is mine.

Her chest was rising and falling uncontrollably and Akim bit his mouth not to hug her and calm that little fire he knew was awakening in her. Thoughtfully she licked her lips and could see the wet glow in the moonlight and couldn't resist. She moved even closer and with her thumb she wiped the coolness from her mouth. Her heartbeat was as evident as her desire and Akim celebrated his victory. She was arousing his feelings but he managed to ignite his desire and that made him want to scream with happiness. He had to start somewhere and this was not a bad beginning. Nervous and trying to control his impatience he separated a few centimeters from her body and spoke with his voice a little thicker than usual.

-Are you afraid?

She saw it in his eyes. His question had upset her. Okay, first objective achieved.

-Why should I? I am not a child.

-Then you are not afraid to meet me," she hesitated and he decided to act.

He turned to leave. He walked with heaviness in his legs praying that his trick would work or he would have to crawl back begging for forgiveness.

-Where are you going? - "Yes! Yes!" He thought before turning to look at her with a disappointment as fake as his words.

-If you are not able to decide for yourself, you may not be who I thought you were.

-I don't need anyone's permission. She replied annoyed.

-So tomorrow at nine o'clock?

-What happens tomorrow at nine o'clock?

-Let's have breakfast together. There's a café nearby. It's called Tapeando con Manolo. I don't see a better way to start a good... friendship.

Brenda shuffled her feet on the sand and Akim became nervous. This was no time for her to hesitate. Not now.

-But if you want to back out or are not even allowed to have breakfast with me, then.... -he said, deepening his pride.

Akim -Akim, you have to understand that I...

-Sh, we talked about that," he said reaching over and stroking her hand. It was an ordeal to have her so close and not be able to touch her.

-No, we haven't really talked.

Damn, there she was again, the rational doctor. God, why couldn't she fixate on an airhead, he thought amused. Because then she wouldn't be as smart, or as bold, or as sweet, or as fabulous, or as perfect, he answered himself.

-Brin, I am here in peace.

-And how many days will you stay? -she asked interested.

-The same as you.

-Don't tease. She said with a broad smile that he wanted to savor in bites.

-Then stop forecasting, we are here today. That's all you need to know.

Brenda accepted his reply and left without a word. Without saying goodbye but also without refusing. Akim watched her walk away but did not follow her. She must have been stunned, her visit came as a bucket of cold water and he understood her perfectly. Somewhat calmer, he lit a cigarette and sat on the sand watching her walk away. His nerves were about to kill him. The situation was most unstable but hell if he was going to let it win. His mother lost his father's love because of her lack of courage and he would not be the same. Guilt at the memory of her instantly seized him. He thought of his poor mother waiting for an affection he never got back and felt somewhat regretful of his behavior. He was acting like that mistress he had always offended with a thousand insults and he regretted his childish attitude of those times. Now he saw it much more clearly. Love does not stop in front of gold rings or obligation books. Papers do not dignify true love, nor do they legitimize lovers of occasion.

His father fell in love with a woman out of wedlock and lost her. Today, history was repeating itself but with small nuances, today he was the third in discord and would not stop fighting fist to fist for the woman he adored. He would tear down any wall that stood in his way, whether or not it had graffiti painted on it by a justice of the peace...

Without stopping watching her as she entered the hotel, he took a second deep puff and silently asked for forgiveness. Forgiveness to heaven for not accepting a marked destiny, to his mother for not accepting the bonds of marriage and to her because even without deserving it he desired her beyond any reason and far from any forgiveness.

Brenda stopped in the doorway and he narrowed his eyes trying to see what was going on. He saw her reading a message on her cell phone and with her head down she put the device back in the pocket of her jeans. Fuck, it had to be him, he thought in annoyance. Without a second thought he rummaged through his leather jacket and typed to her with fingers still tense from nerves.

-Dream of me... please.... -He wrote pleadingly as he took another huge puff on his cigarette.

"In front of every message of yours you'll have two of mine, every two looks of yours you'll have four of mine and in front of every caress of yours..." He thought furiously, as he crumpled the cigarette in the sand. "No, his caresses won't be for you anymore. Not if I can help it."

He looked up at the sky and shook his head.

-I'm sorry mom, I know how you feel about lovers but if it's any consolation I'm not very proud of myself either. I'm sorry but I can't promise. I won't walk away. I've been pining for more than a year for what I don't have and dreaming of what I don't deserve, and I can't stand it anymore, either I die trying or I die for not having her -he said with a bitter smile-. As you can see, dear mother, my future is not very promising," he commented, looking at the sky for the last time before leaving the way he had come.

Not like this

Tell me you'll be mine forever, promise you won't leave.
Akim

Brenda was dragged by Rachel's hand without knowing the reason for such urgency.

-It's just that I... had an engagement... -She tried to say as she was wobbled through the streets towards the center of the island.

-Oh my god... my god. Run or we won't make it." He shouted over his arm to a Brenda who was running like a kite on a stormy day.

-Late for what! -she shouted, hoping to be heard.

The crowd was beginning to gather at a dead end and Brenda stopped dead in her tracks. She was starting to feel short of breath.

-Rachel, don't wait... -She said, trying to make it clear that they would be crushed to death by the crowd. -she shouted loudly as she broke free from his grip.

The woman not only did not pay him the slightest attention, but on the contrary, she went into the middle of the bustle. All the Amazons were in that alley. Hundreds of women were smiling and jumping nervously as if waiting for a big moment. The tension was palpable in the atmosphere and Brenda did not like what her instinct warned her. Rachel was lost like a needle in a haystack and Brenda cursing a thousand times did the only thing she could do. She threw herself on top of the group and elbowed her way through the group, trying to reach her friend's crazy friend. For heaven's sake, what was going on there? The crowd was so large and thick that she could hardly move.

-It's late! It's late! Rachel was screaming uncontrollably, but late for what?" she thought intrigued.

He finally caught sight of her. She was standing in front of Carol, the Amazon arguing like a madwoman.

-You can't do that! They're waiting for you." She shouted nervously trying to make herself understood.

-That's not true. You do it to earn points. The Amazon replied angrily.

-Carol, don't be stubborn. You're leading them right into a trap.

-No way. We will be all over the press. Today all the newspapers and TV news will be talking about us. We will be news. We will be heard.

Rachel snorted obfuscatingly as she grabbed the big Amazon by the shoulders and Brenda was fascinated by her friend's decision. Not since she was a girl at boarding school, when the creepy Mary the steamroller tried to steal her snack, had she seen Rachel so out of her mind.

-They will arrest all of you. You'll have a list of charges so long you won't get out for a year. Please Carol...

The woman narrowed her eyes watching Rachel intently but didn't seem to be thinking about anything other than achieving her own goals.

-We are unbeatable, we are unique, we are women fighting for our rights.

-But not like that! -Rachel shouted loudly, trying to convince her and attracting the attention of the group that began to surround them, interested in the discussion.

Carol, feeling that she was being watched, raised her voice to be heard by the group.

-Dear pinks, Rachel is trying to stop us," she shouted with an evil grin.

-No!" replied the female mass.

-He says we should stop. He says we should be afraid of the consequences but I say let's move on.

-You're crazy. I didn't say that. I said it's a trap!

-And how do you know that? -He replied with a wicked smile, "You gave us away?

Rachel shifted nervously and the others shouted loudly.

-Rachel traitor! -Machist!

-No! That's not true. They gave me the tip, it wasn't me... Damn it, Carol! You know I have a cop friend.

Not only did the leading Amazon not answer him, but she turned her back to him and addressed the increasingly angry mass.

-Pink Sisters! Amazons of freedom, the world must learn, we must show them how much we are worth. This is our moment." He said in a heated speech that had just begun.

-What's going on? -Brenda approached Rachel and asked in her ear as the audience cheered for their sovereign leader.

-Attempting to sabotage the mass of the centenary of the army. Today great personalities from the world of politics are gathered on the island. They try to enter and sabotage the event but someone has sold them out and they are waiting for them. If they are caught, they are waiting for years of prison.

-God... -. Brenda understood the seriousness of the subject. Who could have sold them?

-I have no idea, but I can't allow it. They were my sisters when I thought I was trash. He replied, clenching his fist in his mouth.

-Be calm... Maybe... -He didn't get to finish the sentence when Carol's increasingly loud voice caught his full attention.

-The world is ours. Men will surrender to our power. We are a superior race and we are ready to prove it. They are nothing in front of us.

-Yes, we are Amazons.

Brenda frowned. This was not at all the message she expected from a feminist leader. She worked daily to find her place in a male-dominated world but that didn't mean she hated the entire opposite sex. In her long years as a professional she had guided hundreds of women in their struggle to be themselves but that didn't mean turning their demands into a life and death war between the sexes.

-Are you ready?

-Yes!" they shouted as they lifted up their shirts to reveal their naked breasts with inscriptions such as rights and freedom written on their bare skins.

-But what is this? -Brenda asked herself increasingly annoyed. Stripping their bodies as giveaway merchandise didn't make them any more reasonable or feminist.

He was about to start complaining but couldn't even get to move when the women began to follow their leader like blind sheep.

-We are Amazons, Amazons, Amazons, Ahu, Ahu.

Rachel tried to stop them but Brenda grabbed her arm before she was run over.

-There is nothing we can do.

Both watched as the mass moved in an inseparable nebula as one of them, unseen by the others, drifted away like a rat on a sinking ship.

-It's her. She's leaving them! -Rachel started to run and Brenda closed her eyes, knowing there was only one thing she could do. Run with her friend while she thought about whether there was a sentence reduction for well-behaved psychologists.

The clock struck a quarter past nine and Akim shifted in his seat, trying not to fidget. It's still early, he said to himself with his hands sweating from nerves. When it was half past nine he got up and sat back down with his heartbeat getting more and more excited but it wasn't until the clock struck a quarter to ten and the waitress grumpily asked him if he was finally going to have something to eat that he got up in a fury. Brenda had stood him up. She hadn't shown up.

He got up without asking for anything but leaving a tip interesting enough to placate the evil look of the owner of the place.

How could that be? He swore that the night before she was convinced to give herself a chance. Okay, just to get to know each other better, but that was something, wasn't it? He walked lost while lighting a cigarette. Could it be that the unmentionable one had sent her more messages and claimed her in Paris? Could it be that he was on the island and they were together? No! He said to himself as he walked at full speed and without sense but curiously arriving at the door of his hotel.

-I need you to tell me if Esperanza is here or not. I won't ask you anymore," the young red-haired man threatened the poor receptionist who was nervously trying to adjust her uniform tie.

-Peter, I cannot provide you with private information.

-I just want to know if he came to work. She's not answering my cell phone and I fear the worst. That woman can't be trusted. They're all going to the slaughterhouse because of that harpy.

Akim listened to the conversation attentively. If they were talking about women and dangers, Brenda was sure to be there. His doctor had a special magnet for trouble. He moved closer to better listen to the conversation.

-They're all there Peter, but you know what will happen if they see you. Last time you almost didn't make it out alive.

-Where are the women? -Akim asked as if he were one more in the conversation, drawing the attention of the receptionist and the young man who looked at him suspiciously.

-And you are?

-My name is Akim and I'm afraid the woman I'm looking for is with that group you're talking about.

-Then I pity you. My girlfriend has been with these Amazons for a year and all she's been able to do is get herself into trouble. This is her fifth job and she's willing to give up everything for that crazy woman. We've even given up our tea shop to follow them.

-Where are they now? -He asked, not caring at all about the boy's story and his business.

He began to get very nervous. Brenda was all too willing to get into trouble to help.

-They're at some activist march, but my girlfriend hasn't told me where. Peter grumbled in annoyance.

-But you will tell us, won't you? -Akim spoke with a seductive tone while leaning his muscular arms highlighting his tattoos and dazzling the receptionist with the deep blue of his gaze.

She knew perfectly well the effect that the image of her body caused in certain women and that woman was perfectly in the group of those interested in bad boys, with wide bones and restless look, so she did not think twice if she could find out where her blessed doctor was.

-Well yes, I don't think there will be any problem. After all, you'll find out soon enough.

-Exactly, honey. You don't know how grateful I am. Akim smiled seductively and the young red-haired boy snorted in disbelief.

-They plan to sabotage the armed forces centennial mass.

-But that's in the center of the island! All the authorities will be there. Peter squeezed his forehead hard.

The young man ran for the door cursing loudly and Akim followed him at full speed.

-When they say sabotage, what exactly do they mean? -Akim shouted as he ran past the young man toward the exit.

-If your friend doesn't end up in jail, she'll end up getting groped by all the armed forces combined.

Akim blanched at that comment and shouted at the young man who was starting to get on his Vespino.

-No! Get in my car. We'll get there faster.

-Nice buga. Said the boy as he got into the pearl gray sports car.

-Rented," he answered reluctantly. Which way? -He asked between nervous and frightened as the young man pointed in the right direction with his hand.

God, I had no idea what it was all about but the moment was not ripe for questions. First he would find Brenda, make sure she was all right and then he would kiss her to death. Damn it, that woman was ready to kill him with a heart attack long before he reached thirty.

Every man for himself

I don't know how you do it but your sweet eyes collapses every corner of my impenetrable wall.

Akim

Brenda tried to find Rachel but it was a real mess. Before reaching their destination, the group was surrounded by an impassable line of huge men who didn't even look like law enforcement. The big guys with leather hats and not very legal looks spread out forming a large circle and at the shout of one of their leaders they pounced on the women like cavemen before a feast. The women were groped and insulted shamelessly.

Skinhers, shouted one of the attendees. Male chauvinist pigs, shouted others. The truth was that they hated these women and were willing to be the wildest. Some screamed trying to escape from their grip while others tore their shirts leaving the girls almost naked. Brenda desperately tried to rescue a poor girl who was barely able to defend herself against two men who cornered her against a wall with clear intentions. They intended to rape her. In desperation she looked for something to defend her with and spotted a stick from a tree on the ground but she didn't care, with a huge amount of fury she grabbed the twig and hit one of them in the head who turned around stroking his bald head that had barely turned red from the friction.

-Oops Rex look what we have here. Another Amazon wishing to join the party.

Rachel shouted at the girl to run. The latter, taking advantage of the distraction of the man who attacked her, kicked him in the crotch and ran away, but Brenda had no better luck. The big man she had hit when he saw his friend lying on the ground in pain became furious and grabbed her, pulling her long hair until she fell to her knees on the ground.

-You bitch. You want us to play with you alone? Well, honey, get ready. He said pulling her hair harder until she writhed in pain, pulling her closer to his crotch.

Brenda writhed on the ground trying to free herself but was only able to hurt her knees against the rough ground causing them to start bleeding.

The big guy started to unzip his fly while pushing her against the wall. Brenda looked around for help but it was chaos. Women running, men with shaved heads and nasty looks were kicking them like dogs. She tried to scream, hoping someone would hear her, but her captor, upon discovering her intention, slapped her so hard that she became unconscious and a little dizzy. Her ear was ringing like a bumblebee in front of a honeycomb, she was one click away from fainting. The savage, enjoying his work, brought his bulging crotch closer to her mouth while smiling triumphantly. He pulled down his briefs sticking the doctor's face to his hard, thick penis. Brenda could barely see out of one eye, the other was totally closed due to the force of the punch,

-Honey, I'm going to enjoy what's coming....

-I hope so." Akim replied angrily as he swung a right hand so hard that it knocked him down with a single blow.

Brenda fell backward as she felt free of his grip on her hair and grunted as her back hit the sidewalk full force.

-Son of a bitch. Get up! -Akim shouted uncontrollably as he slammed him to the ground again and again.

He was uncontrollable. He had seen from a distance how that asshole had hit Brenda and how he dragged her towards his filthy cock and he ran in desperation. He wanted to see blood flow. He needed to kill that asshole with his bare hands. He gave it a first stroke, a second and a third when he felt a trembling hand grab him from the man begging him to stop. He drew in a shaky breath and tried to regain control. He turned to look at her closely and as he saw her flushed face he felt the hatred begin to boil his blood again. The side of her face was swollen, her left eye could barely open and her lip was bleeding. Damn bastard, she felt like waking him up from unconsciousness so she could keep beating him to death.

-Brin... -He said as he lifted her in his arms with the utmost care. He wanted to die when he felt her moan in pain. He would have stopped time so as not to see her like this. Once and a thousand times he would receive the blows in her place. She was so soft, so delicate and such a good person that she didn't deserve even the rose of a delicate rose petal.

-Rachel... I have to find her. He said, barely able to move his lips because of the cut.

-She's fine. She's gone with a friend and his girlfriend.

Brenda looked at him curiously but Akim began to hurry up, elbowing his way through. He fled quickly at the sound of the police approaching.

-Honey, she's fine, but we have to go before the police show up and we get into more trouble.

Brenda nodded her head. Akim walked briskly, he didn't want to imagine how it would affect his reputation if the name of the famous Dr. Klein appeared in the media. Brenda's career would be seriously affected.

He held her tightly shielding her with his body as he ran to the car to flee from that hateful place.

In the evening light

You tell me to forget you, that you're not for me but tell me what is the way to forget you without dying in the attempt.

Akim

Brenda's head was spinning like a dizzy duck when Akim stopped the car and picked her up in his arms. She wanted to tell him she was fine, that she could walk but the words wouldn't come out. She felt disturbed and confused. Her life used to be quiet, maybe even somewhat predictable, from work to home and back again. Nothing used to break the monotony of her daily routine, but for a year now she was not getting any scares. What if a father bomb, what if a madwoman for love, what if some women shouting their rights loudly while showing their naked breasts, what if some savage skinheads tried to rape them, this was too much. She closed her eyes, rested her face on the broad torso and breathed exhausted. She was barely able to think. The ringing in her ear along with the dizziness and pain from the punch knocked her out. "If it wasn't for him..."

With the utmost gentleness Akim carried her up the hotel stairs and propped her up in her comfortable bed. Brenda felt terrible. Her face hurt and her head was splitting like a ripe melon.

-Lie down. He was angry and it was logical, she could no longer remember how much trouble she had gotten into and in all of them he always appeared to save her.

-I'm so sorry," she said apologetically.

Akim was looking back and forth across the room when he stopped when he heard her.

-What do you feel? -he asked with a frown.

-You are angry and I understand that. I always get you in trouble," she said with a dry voice, "but before being judged I would like to argue that this time I had nothing to do with it, I was influenced by the bad company of a delirious friend. She commented trying to give a touch of grace to the situation.

The man smiled unwillingly and fixed his deep gaze on her, making her shiver from head to toe. Would she ever stop feeling that uncontrolled throbbing every time she had him in front of her and he outlined her with the deep blue of his gaze?

-I'm not angry with you. It's never with you," he said, coming closer and kneeling on the floor and leaving their heads at the same height. I would have killed him for touching you...

Akim wrapped his rough hands around her face and caressed her swollen lip and she could feel his fingers trembling.

-I've never felt anything like it. I wanted to see him dead," he said as he leaned his forehead against hers.

-I'm fine. I'm fine.

-If I had...

-I'm fine and I have to thank you again. What number is it this time? The fourth, the fifth time?

Akim gently stroked her bruised cheek and shook his head as he stood up.

-You owe me nothing.

His voice sounded rough again and Brenda wondered what new mistake she had made now as Akim walked tensely toward the door.

-I'll go get some painkillers, absorbent cotton and some alcohol. In a few hours you will have a black eye and half of your face will be swollen," he said before leaving and carefully closing the door.

Brenda hurriedly got up to the bathroom mirror being aware for the first time of how hideous she would look. No one who knew her could say that she wasn't conceited and liked to always look impeccable but knowing that Akim had seen her in such a pitiful condition made her feel more vulnerable than usual.

-God... -He said as he looked at her face with one eye and half of the other.

The mark of the wretch's fist was a deep red that was beginning to turn purplish around the edges. The affected eye was barely visible and the left half of the lip had a deep scratch with blood already dried.

"I look dreadful." She thought annoyed. "If he doesn't forget about me after this.... For heaven's sake Brenda! What are you thinking? -She said to herself as she held the half of her forehead still intact.

-Sweet! O my god. Sweet. Sweet!

The door burst open and Rachel's screams echoed in his head like a mason's drill on a summer afternoon.

-I'm here... I'm here. Brenda responded as best she could by peeking out of the toilet door.

-Thank heaven," she said, hugging her disconsolately. The receptionist said you were here but I didn't believe her. Oh Sweet! I didn't see you anywhere and I got so crazy.

Brenda accepted his embrace with difficulty, her back still ached from the terrible blow she received when she lost her balance when Akim managed to free his grip on the human beast.

-She murmured in pain as Rachel pressed her body against her damaged face.

-But what... my god, my god... -She said hyperventilating at the sight of her friend's bruised face.

-What have they done to you? Oh, it's my fault... Oh that I'm dying, oh that I'll kill them. She commented nervously while she kept talking.

-I'm fine. Nothing happened to me. They saved me just in time.

Brenda did not want to confess how close she had come to rape.

-But who, how?

-It doesn't matter anymore. He replied as he sat on the edge of the bed and Rachel did her thing in a chair near the small desk, which was under the plasma TV that hung on the wall.

-What happened there, and why were we attacked by those hooligans?

Rachel slumped her shoulders in exhaustion and Brenda listened to her with great attention.

-As you know, the Amazons try to defend women's rights and freedoms," Rachel nodded, "Many times we have had to face Neanderthals who only see in us an ass and a pair of tits.

Brenda thought that giving away the naked views of their bodies as a sign of vindication was not a good way to seek respect either but she preferred to keep quiet and continue listening.

-In the last few months we have received threats from different groups and among them are these guys who laugh at us and insult us constantly.

-Who are they?

-Skinhead who, according to them, want to put us in our place.

-Imbeciles... -. The doctor replied angrily.

That there were groups of men who in this day and age still thought of women as mere brood mares drove her out of her mind.

-Yes, well, the truth is that someone called them and gave them the information about our plans.

-And you know who it was. That's why we ran to stop them. She assured confidently.

-Not exactly. I have a cop friend who called me to tell me what was going on. Apparently someone tipped them off.

-Cop friend? -Brenda asked without understanding. She knew all of his friends and didn't know any of them as cops.

Rachel ducked her head and hunched her back even more.

-Not exactly, my friend," he said, barely looking up.

-You're telling me that you, that he... but I thought you and George were fine. She replied, somewhat disturbed.

-And we are, you see, Hannibal and I are something like occasional lovers.

-Occasional?

-Yes, from time to time... if the case arises... you know what I mean....

-The case? No, not really.

-I mean that in some moments we vary, the monotony and those issues....

-Those issues?

-Fuck Brenda! That George and I invited third parties into our bed. There, I said it.

Rachel didn't finish speaking when she was already covering her mouth with both hands. Her wild eyes and the strength of her palms on her lips indicated that her nerves had betrayed her. Brenda tried to digest the confession and although she wanted to appear adult and liberal she could not. She felt the heat rising in her face. She knew her friend was a showbiz person, open and uninhibited, but from there to sharing a bed with two men at the same time, one of whom was her husband...Wow.... and Wow!

Without knowing why Brenda began to feel that during these years of friendship she had behaved like a real idiot. Did Rachel really think she was such a prude as to hide her membership in the Amazons or the threesomes in her marital bed? For God's sake, in her profession she had heard stories of the most colorful things, even her own life was upside down. That very morning she had been rescued by a man almost eighteen years her junior and for whom she was losing her panties at the mere sight of him.

-Are we no longer friends? Do I disgust you?

Brenda looked at her in concentration as she gave what at first appeared to be a smile but in two seconds turned into a colossal, somewhat ill-timed laugh.

-Rachel," he said, unable to hold back his tears from laughing so hard, "You're my idol. You're my idol, why were you hiding it? Did you think I wouldn't accept you? -Her friend smiled beside her as she nodded her head, "But why? I've always understood you. We have been friends for years. You know I stand up for people's rights above all things.

-Yes, I know, but not many people would understand, and since you've been with.... -She bit her lip to stop herself from continuing.

-You mean since I got married. She replied saddened.

-Swett you know I adore Max, he's the superest of the super and he loves you so much but he's so... so... so....

Brenda looked down. She already knew what came next after that sentence. Her friend Connor kept repeating it over and over, so uptight, uncomprehending, haughty, snobbish and a few other adjectives.

-Rachel, have I changed that much? -she asked confused.

-Maybe a little. You know, your friends were surprised you chose Max. After all, he's so much like...

Brenda watched her closely. Did they look alike? Who?

He was about to ask when a light bulb went off in his brain and he didn't need to know any more. His father. Max looked like his father. That man she respected but didn't love. The one who had looked down on her since she was a child for being of the fairer sex. The one who said she should find a man to protect her because she wouldn't be able to do anything on her own.

-God... -He said as he saw clearly for the first time.

-But Brenda, you're a sweetheart. We all know that," she answered so quickly that the words clashed in her mouth. Max may have tried to make you more like him but he didn't succeed, you're a piece of bread, you're always ready to help.

-And that's why you didn't tell me about the Amazons or your threesomes? -She said, observing that although she considered herself a fighter, a survivor and a tireless professional, others did not see her that way.

-Rachel, what have I done with my life? Who have I become?

-Sweet, you are a great friend and an even better psychologist. Maybe your father undermined your confidence and that's why you sought refuge in someone like Max.

-You think Max is my refuge?

-I don't know, don't get me into this mess," he said, fanning himself with his hand.

-You are right. I am the one who must face what is or is not.

-Max loves you, he has proven it many times.

-But you decided to bring me here. You thought I need space and solitude to discover who I am and what I have become.

-Well, let's just say that I sensed that someone had broken your patterns and freed my friend of years ago and I wanted to be by your side when you finally felt untethered.

-Thank you. He said with tears in his eyes.

-I may not be as smart as you but you will always have me by your side.

-Don't say anything like that again. The diploma of intelligence that you lead is the one granted by the experience of life and that is worth more than the one obtained by many psychologists of the well called respectable ones and that I know very well....

Rachel hugged her and cried gratefully. She could tell how important such a comparison was to an actress with little education. She felt appreciated.

-And speaking of sincerity... -She wiped her tears and pulled away from Brenda's embrace. You still haven't told me the name of that mysterious man who has you upside down. Do I know him? Is he handsome? A doctor, a designer, a lawyer maybe?

A small knock and the door to the room opened leaving both women with their mouths hanging open but for very different reasons.

Today or never

Mistress mistress of my dreams, I am your knight in hard armor. Come for me, use me as you wish, I am here because I am yours. I'll wait behind my door for your message, the one that will take me to your side.
because madam, I am that knight in dark armor that always waits for you.
Akim

Akim entered the room with great care. It took him longer than he thought, he thought she was asleep. At first he only intended to stop by the pharmacy but when he saw his shirt stained by the filthy blood of that asshole, he preferred to go to the hotel where he was staying and clean himself up. She hated to discover his wild side on the first day of her conquest, but just remembering the bastard slapping her, her veins swelled with the desire to hang him in slow motion.

A pair of worn but clean jeans, the best of his shirts, an attempt to comb his unruly hair and a strong mint chewing gum were enough work to return to the arms of his beloved. He arrived at the hotel agitated by so much paperwork, he looked at himself in the hotel reception mirror and the result was not bad at all, so why did the two women keep staring at him like two sea breams out of water?

-Permission." He said, entering with a slow step, trying to feel out the situation.

He looked at his shirt, which although rolled up above the elbows covered the rough tattoos, he continued down and the fly was closed, thank goodness, he thought almost gagging.

-He... He... Him? -Rachel was trying to say something different but seemed to have gone into a loop.

-Rachel, Akim is on the island and he is the one who helped me this morning. Brenda tried to break the state of catharsis in which her friend found herself, but nothing.

-He... He... He...

-Maybe you don't remember well, his name is Akim? -she said red with embarrassment.

Brenda did not finish the sentence. Rachel seemed to have changed her record and was now repeating a new phrase.

-Mason... bricklayer... bricklayer... bricklayer...

-And here we are. Akim closed the door and placed a pharmacy bag on the bed next to Brenda.

-Yes, I see you remember him," she said, trying to sound nonchalant even though her friend's classism was driving her crazy. Would you please allow us a few minutes?

Brenda spoke as she took her friend's arm to lift her out of the seat and lead her towards the door, but she barely walked. On her way to the exit she did not turn her head, her gaze remained fixed on Akim as if absorbed by his presence. She seemed to be living in a parallel reality from which she was unable to leave.

-It's the bricklayer... It's the bricklayer... It's the bricklayer...

-Yes Rachel, Akim is a bricklayer, now go and rest. We'll see you later.

-Mason... Bricklayer... -Rachel said over and over again as her voice was lost after Brenda slammed the door almost under her nose.

Akim took the medicines out of the wrapper fully concentrated and trying to conceal the tension reflected in the muscles of his neck. The way that hateful woman mentioned his job reminded him of what he wished to forget. A poor, unworthy worker for her.

-I bought you a cream. I've been told it's very good for bruises," he said, his voice thick and restrained.

Brenda remembered the state of her face and turned away so that he could not see her.

-Come here. Akim stood behind her and turned her by the shoulders so that he could better appreciate her face and apply the ointment. Her feminine modesties made him instantly forget about

Rachel's faint-heartedness, about social classes, about poverty in the world and about a life without it.

-I'm dreadful. The young man smiled sideways, reflecting a mischievous gleam in his deep eyes.

-A little." She said teasingly and loving the redness of her shyness. Watching Dr. Klein drop the barriers of formality was a sight to behold.

-I apply it to myself," he commented as he stroked his face, trying to cover his bruises.

-No way. You are going to sit down and let me take care of you.

Brenda resignedly accepted the order and sat down. He began to feel nervous again, was something wrong with her outfit? Why did she keep looking at him like that, so fixed and almost breathless? It was the best shirt he had but if she didn't like it he was willing to buy the whole store just to see her happy, even if she wanted him to, he could wear all white like the inhabitants of the island did, although he doubted very much that with his ample proportions he would look more like a thick hospital column than handsome.

Brenda let herself be cared for. The softness of his caresses were a refreshing balm on her skin. Akim's fingers tingled wherever they went. Unfamiliar sensations ran through her body. Wherever he touched her, she trembled under his warmth. She looked at him in ecstasy. A man to be admired. Deep blue eyes, hard, masculine body, strong, calloused hands, a wonderful sight. One that married women should not indulge in, she thought guiltily.

-That's it. He said closing the medicine bottle and leaving her with a bitter taste as he lost contact with her.

-I'm sorry," he commented regretfully.

-You are not to blame for anything. He said, saddened at the memory of that hateful Rachel.

-I stood you up," she commented regretfully.

-That's what you meant. No, I hadn't really noticed," he said wryly. But now that you mention it, it reminds me that it's almost noon and I'm starving..." he said, sliding his fingertip along the edge of his chin, spreading the remains of the cream. -he said, sliding his fingertip along the edge of his chin and spreading some of the cream.

Brenda felt guilty but at the same time cuddly at the delicate caress.

-Not even a coffee?

-I've been waiting for you to arrive.... -. He replied scratching the back of his neck and she wanted to eat it in bites.

Moved by reflex, she rose from her chair and moved to offer him the most tender and grateful kiss she had ever offered anyone. Her hands rested on the broad shoulders and she stretched out the tips of her toes to get her lips to rest on the incipient beard. It was a daring act and far too inappropriate for her, but lately her life was replete with inappropriate actions.

-Thank you... -she murmured softly.

They both looked into each other's eyes and the sparks released by their gazes could be distinguished from a hundred kilometers around and without binoculars. The young man quickly grabbed her by the wrist preventing her escape and pulling her even closer to his hard torso.

-For saving your life, for waiting for you, for not asking for coffee or for loving you to the point of madness? -He said, narrowing his eyes with extreme sweetness.

They both gazed at each other. Time stood still between them. The room did not exist. Her lips demanded him to come closer and kiss him. They asked him to feel what he felt that last day at her house when he kissed her beyond the allowed limits. Her exasperated mouth demanded to feel alive again, it demanded at least a moment of that fiery passion. Her heart was beating wildly and her hands wanted to slide down his neck and get lost in the softness of his neck. She wanted, she wanted a hundred things, but she couldn't, she wasn't free, she didn't feel free. Afraid of her most hidden emotions, she released her grip trying to deny the desperate signals her body was screaming at her, but Akim held her firmly. He extended his rough palm across her back, held her gently but insistently. He had no intention of letting her go. That light touch burned her instantly. A deep heat spread throughout her body awakening every nerve fiber of her being. The solid hand brushed the fabric of her dress until it touched the depths of her soul. Heaven help her because she didn't know if she could resist much longer.

-I'm not going to pressure you, but I won't deny what I feel. I never will.

-And what do you feel? -he asked, knowing he shouldn't have.

-I'll say it when you really want to hear it.

She looked down like an inexperienced young girl. She was wading into waters too deep and completely unknown to come out unscathed. Akim would not stop and she was forgetting the reasons why she should refuse him.

Taking advantage of her hesitation, the young man pressed her even closer to his body until they were completely pressed in each other's arms. He rested his face in that little hollow between neck and shoulder to breathe in the sweet scent of vanilla, jasmine and Brenda.

-God Brin... if we keep on... -He commented as he gave her a small kiss on the softness of her skin.

-I'm hungry. How about paella? -he said, almost without thinking about the stupid thing he had just said.

-Paella? -Brenda took advantage of the broken climax to pull away quickly. Paella," he said amused as he watched her walk nervously, "Sounds good to me.

Akim answered with a devilish smile and she preferred to ignore him. It was better to escape than to have to think about that bed of soft sheets that never ceased to incite her to sin. They marched together towards the exit without commenting again about kisses, caresses and empty beds and Brenda breathed a sigh of relief. After all, if she put her mind to it, she could behave like a grown-up woman. A serious, responsible and committed one. She didn't have to lose her lingerie in front of a beautiful body, some heart-stopping muscles, a gaze as deep as hell or as infinite as heaven itself. After all, she was a successful professional and a connoisseur of the secrets of reason, how could she resist? She said to herself with enthusiasm.

They both enjoyed a wonderful meal and an even better afternoon. They laughed, walked and enjoyed each other's company. Brenda could not remember when she had ever felt so free to enjoy herself. Rules and social conventions were not between them.

-How was your life? -She asked, sitting down on the sand and blushing when she noticed the man's smile.

-It's stronger than you. You can't hold him back.

-I... if you don't want to talk I understand but I thought you might like to....

Akim shook his head as he sat down next to her.

-When Lucien was born, I matured faster than any other young man. I held him in my arms and understood that he was my responsibility. The situation at home was not very good and I had to find a better world for him. That's all.

-Did you decide to emigrate because of him?

-It was the main reason.

-What about you?

-What about me? -he asked curiously.

-Once in London, what happened?

Akim wrinkled his forehead trying to remember.

-Nothing special," he said, lifting his shoulders. As long as we found a decent home and a job to support ourselves, I was happy.

Brenda was surprised to feel him so calm. On a daily basis Akim showed people he was the tough guy with shoulder tattoos and an angry face who never cared about anyone, but the more she got to know him, the faster she discovered his inner tenderness.

-You never thought about art as a way of life again?

Akim watched her curiously and Brenda felt herself blushing for being nosy.

-I say it because one day you told me that you liked music and you studied fine arts and I think that if you liked it you would be interested in it... but if you don't want to -. She said while averting her gaze so as not to seem so gossipy.

-I don't think about it much anymore.

-You were very brave. He said without waiting for the man's response. Your future, your career, you gave up everything.

-I wouldn't consider survival a heroic act," he commented with a reluctant smile.

Brenda accepted his conclusion and didn't ask again. She enjoyed the cool Mediterranean breeze caressing her face and let herself go. She was calm. With Akim it didn't matter if her smile was excessive or if her behavior was not appropriate for a woman of her age, it didn't matter if her hair was properly combed or if her cheek was a little bruised, with him life was simple. They walked together and he approached the water with his shoes in his hand. He was happy. Her feet touched the cool sea water and like a naughty girl who does not think of the consequences she could not restrain the temptation to lift her foot. Akim seemed surprised to see himself wet but instantly reciprocated her attack by doing the same but with more power. Brenda moved avoiding his attack while with loud laughter she started kicking the waves getting him completely soaked. The man's eyes sparkled with vengeance and she reacted in the least expected way. She ran fleeing down the beach hoping not to be caught while laughing unconcealed. He chased after her and with the length of her nearly six-foot legs it wasn't hard for him to give chase. Surprising her, he lifted her up in his arms and carried her over some sand dunes to lay her down on the sand. Brenda was breathing heavily as she laughed and tried to break free from his strong grip but it proved to be an impossible task. He held her under his body by the shoulders as he settled his knees on either side of her figure. He was soaking wet and small drops of sea water were trickling down his cheeks. Brenda was smiling in amusement. She was happy. Passion for life was flowing through her veins again. She felt like a young, beautiful, fun and desired woman. Very desired.

-What now, doctor? Are you giving up? -she asked smiling.

She shook her head and Akim's laughter sounded like heavenly music encouraging her to act as she never imagined doing. Without a second thought and dominated by the situation Brenda let herself be enveloped by that precious blue gaze that adored her and moved her hands quickly to wrap her wet face with them. With total impudence and like a shameless slut she brought her lips close to his, tasting the salt of the Mediterranean on his skin.

Eager lips moved over hers and she could feel him respond instantly. That made her feel on an even higher cloud than the previous ones.

Akim took control of that blessed kiss instantly and Brenda let her head fall on the sand, enjoying the sensation of being devoured by lips that were roaming the inside of her mouth with complete satisfaction. She could feel the male weight on hers as hands roamed her shamelessly. Rough, calloused and crazed they moved to her waist to hold her possessively. Her eyes closed dreaming of a thousand and one pleasures while her lips felt imprisoned by a passion impossible to compare with anything else in this world. Lip against lip, caresses of one tongue mercilessly conquering the other.

Akim accepted her completely. He kissed her, savored her and offered her his all. Brenda unabashedly licked his tongue so passionately that she almost felt like she would burn right there. His hands pressed her hips with excessive force to squeeze her against his body.

-I want you... -He whispered against her lips as he showered the skin of her neck with kisses.

-Me too, but... -Akim's mouth silenced her with a short kiss.

-I accept it. I accept everything. Anything. I accept it.

-How can you accept what even I don't understand? You don't know what you're saying... -She answered agitated by the passion under the heat of his wide body.

-I want everything, I've been dreaming of you for more than a year without having anything. Whatever it is will always be more than the emptiness of not having you. A little, a lot, I don't care. A drop of water for a thirsty person is a spring...

-Akim... look at me... Do you see these wrinkles? -He said pointing to the edge of his eyes, "It's one of the hundreds of reasons that separate us," he commented bitterly.

The young man smiled and licked each of those almost imperceptible creases she called wrinkles.

-If you plan to push me away, you'll have to do better than that. I love every detail of your body and every crazy thing that comes out of your head. I love that you are so sensitive, that you don't hesitate to take risks for those for whom no one would even look, I am crazy about the passion you hide, I am fascinated by your optimism for people and I am totally defenseless against the attack of your gaze.

-Akim...

-I accept. Everything, whatever you have to give me, I want it.

Brenda brought her mouth close to his and stopped thinking. She could no longer deny the undeniable. This man was awakening her to a sea of sensations that she wanted to navigate. Her sanity may have told her that this was wrong, that she was not old enough or free enough to feel what she felt, but her body refused to think and surrendered without hesitation.

The night began to envelop them in that hidden corner of the beach and Brenda knew she was awakening to the newest and most irrational thing she had ever known. Desire, longing, appetite? No, that was so much more. Her body was a reflection of passion at its greatest expression. She trembled where his lips kissed her. It burned where his fingers caressed her, and her heart.... Oh, devilish heart that kept jumping out of control, yearning to recover the past time.

-I've thought about this every night since I met you.

If Brenda felt she still had any walls up, it was these last words that made her the most defeated. Akim had fought and she no longer had the strength to resist.

The first caress on her breasts made her throw her head back to moan like a woman eager to feel. Tenderly but surely he surprised her by lifting her arms above her head and holding them by her wrists. His hands were so large compared to hers that one hand was enough to pin both wrists up high. Fearful of that position she wanted to break free from his grip but he wouldn't let her.

-You'll like it. I know, I promise," he said, his voice thick with desire as he kissed her neck.

Brenda went with the feeling but couldn't help but feel a little uncomfortable. Akim was assuming a control she wasn't sure she wanted to offer. In their marriage sex was a mutual relationship, no improvised or overly exaggerated concessions and for some reason she felt she was in too vulnerable a position to be accepted. Akim may have sensed this because he continued to whisper in her ear as his free hand roamed her body.

-I want you to let me love you. Think of me, feel me here with you, let me give you all that you need....

-And what do I need? -She asked almost speechless with desire as she noticed how he lifted the soft cotton dress and wrapped it around her waist.

-Trust, free yourself.... Close your eyes," he said as he leaned on his elbows to watch her with fire in his eyes.

-What if I don't want to? -she asked amused.

-Do it and I promise to wake you up. He responded by moving his lips over hers but without kissing her.

Brenda accepted the challenge and closed her eyes as she realized that the posture of the arms held above her head no longer bothered her.

-Okay, sweetheart, now enjoy. I want you to think only of you and only of you.

It was impossible for her that Akim was able to understand the depth that those words had for her. To think of her... to feel just for the sake of feeling... without thinking of anyone else but her, was that possible? did such a man really exist?

Brenda felt her suspenders being pulled down and the gentle Mediterranean breeze hit her breasts as the man kept murmuring compliments that went to the core of her very essence as a woman. Maybe all men at times like that tell the same honeyed lies but she didn't care. She hadn't heard them for so long that all she wanted to do was enjoy them. Max didn't talk, he never did, words weren't important, he said over and over again, he preferred the contact of their bodies without banal words and she always accepted it that way, though now, tonight, she was discovering that she did like words in the act and very much so, she thought as she felt the weight of the solid body on top of hers working its way over her. Astonished at herself for feeling so uninhibited she wanted him to let go so she could caress him but he wouldn't let her. Restlessly she moved up and down as she felt him smile in amusement.

-Impatient?

-Capullo. Oh, I... -She said, silencing herself instantly. It was clear that passion unleashed a very hidden side of her, even to herself.

-What doctor? -He replied amused. "Don't you say those things? With me, yes," he said confidently. I want you to do and say everything you feel? -He said as his body settled between her legs that opened expectantly to receive him and feel all those promises that he hoped he could fulfill.

Long fingers caressed her hips and her lingerie slowly fell below her ankles. Her chest heaved as she felt the warmth of his masculine body drive deep inside her. Hard, strong, demanding, Akim thrust into her as he snorted ecstatically. He kissed her hard, a wet, aggressive, possessive kiss, one that left no doubt of his intentions. He said he wanted to arouse her and he didn't know how well he was doing it. His vanished passion was making its presence known with devastating force. The real woman presented herself ardent and needy. She wanted to be touched, caressed, devoured. She needed to feel her potency, her primal desire possessing her relentlessly. To feel like a woman with all the letters without skipping any of them.

-You are a dream... -He murmured hoarsely as he pushed harder and harder on a body that would open up for him. God... I want you so much.

Akim embedded himself on her body, melting them both into one. The sea breeze was their only witness. The cool wet sand cooled their bodies as she stretched more and more eager to give him everything he asked of her. The young man moaned as if he were in heaven and she followed him every step of the way to bliss. He penetrated her again and again and again without rest. She bent her head and kissed his breasts while eager to feel him even more inside her, she wrapped her legs around his hips to assist him in the thrust. She was burning with need. Tension built up in her body waiting for a release that she recognized instantly although this time it was very different. That was not the prelude to an orgasm, that was passion itself made flesh. It was feeling the sky open up to hold her in his arms. The way he moved, the way his muscles tightened on her made her shudder with a moan that came from deep inside her. He parted their bodies and continued to move on her leg until he cursed aloud and emptied himself with three thick, hot spurts over her thigh.

They were both ecstatic and silent. The waves continued to give them their dance and Brenda began to feel her eyes close numbly under the warmth of his solid body. Akim caressed her breasts with an unearthly tenderness, murmuring how much he wanted her while she, satisfied in body and soul, whispered to Morpheus how special it was to feel like a woman from the top of her head to the bottom of her heart.

I accept you

> I admire you while you sleep and wonder if you remember me in your dreams as I do in every second of my days...
> Akim

Akim stroked the hair of the woman who was leaning sleepily on his chest in disbelief. She was there, with him. Both had loved each other desperately until they ended up exhausted on the sand wet with the night's dew. He felt plethoric. A complete man. The air did not fit in his chest. He tried to accept that he still had a long way to go, he wanted not to create false hopes, but damned if he didn't celebrate.

She was with her dress crumpled on her body after lovemaking totally surrendered to his caresses. Never in his best dreams would he have imagined such a passionate reaction. He knew Brenda would be affectionate, he had always known that, but the woman he had on his chest was a real firecracker. A woman made for pleasure. He knew that under her prissy woman's cloak she hid an indomitable being eager to get out but what he found, phew what he found, he thought smiling . If what just happened was only the first time she didn't want to imagine what the next ones would be like. Her body stiffened just imagining it. Brenda took a deep breath and knew she was asleep. Careful not to wake her and doing complete juggling he got up with her in his arms and walked to his wooden bungalow trying not to wake her. Their modest hotel was right in front of them. He smiled as he remembered that with all the bad intentions in the world he had taken her to that beach but never in his best dreams did he imagine having her in his arms and laying her down on his bed after having shared their passion on a sand bathed by the starlight.

Brenda opened her eyes as she felt herself propped up on a bed and smiled sleepily as she watched Akim lift up her dress and leave her totally naked.

-You're awake. He brazenly walked all over her as he removed his clothes and approached the bed to crawl over her body and cover her with tender caresses.

-And so do you, I see. He said stroking his manhood ready for a second round.

Akim did not respond, he just worshipped her like a goddess at a spring festival. His skin trembled at her touch and his breath hitched with each caress. His heart was pounding, claiming more and more of the soft body that was writhing and rising with desperation. She was heaven made flesh. The sweetest of his experiences. He craved every little millimeter of that fine skin. With utmost care his rough fingers traced the hollow of her neck that he was beginning to adore, followed along the fine collarbone and trembled with fear as they brushed over the mound of her breasts. The tips of her nipples tensed needily and she flattered them with the utmost delicacy fearing to hurt them. She was so soft, so exquisite and he was so rough, so rough, so... simple.

With his mouth open in desperation, he brought his wet lips close to her body and accompanied each caress with a string of ardent kisses that moistened wherever they passed. He traveled her body like a pirate navigating new seas. Brenda was his land, his treasure, the one he did not want to give up. The stars and the heavens knew that she did not deserve it, but who dictates the wrongness of what is due in the face of what the heart obtained by fighting with a closed fist? Pirate, robber or guilty of love, the sentence mattered little with her by his side. With a sweetness unknown even to himself, he caressed her tender lips and drank every fresh drop of her flavor, running through every little nook and cranny of his delicious palate.

He became intoxicated with her scent as he came alive with every sigh of her passion.

-Talk to me..." He whispered against her mouth to continue with a trail of kisses over her face. Tell me what you want me to do to you. I'll give you everything.

She rubbed upward seeking his touch but it wasn't enough. Her little chocolate eyes were closed and even though she knew she enjoyed Akim she needed more, she sought more. She wanted his surrender. He wanted to tattoo kisses on her body, he had to engrave the words surrendered by you on all her kisses.

-Ask for it... -He said hoarse with desire.

-Kiss me. He replied with his eyes still closed.

-Where? Here? -he said, nibbling on the white skin of her neck.

Then Brenda opened her eyes and he felt his heart leap out of his chest. Having her under his body with her legs spread wide and the patina of passion clouding her gaze was too much for a poor man like him.

-Where... -She repeated, challenging his restraint. She would break down those blissful walls and it would be with him.

Her gaze was confused and he knew that an important battle was raging inside him. The polite and accommodating doctor should unleash the woman she had taken it upon herself to hide and that he would bring to light. He wanted all of her, all of her. With her perfections and her desires, with her tantrums and her smiles, all of her one hundred percent.

-Here? -He encouraged her with fiery lips, pleasuring her until she moaned. Or here? -he said as he sucked on one of her nipples with the exaltation of his lips.

She moaned and shuddered under his body as he released her waiting for orders. She closed her eyes again. She knew what he expected. With a courage he came to think impossible she held his wrist with barely any strength. He took her strong hand to guide it to the mount of her womanhood and deposit it right there. On her sweet wetness. The center of her pleasure. Akim smiled thanking heaven. This was all he was looking for. A first step to eternity, a first step to feeling her surrender to him.

-My life... -He whispered hoarsely before leaving a trail of kisses down her body to where his hand was.

With each brush of his lips she moved restlessly upward but he held her glued to the mattress with the weight of his own body. When he took her with his mouth she purred a very low yes but loud enough to make Akim swell with pride. His fiery tongue licked her with pleasure enjoying a taste he never thought real. He may have known sex and there was no such thing as an unapproved lesson for him but this was so much more. The sensation of feeling her on the verge of explosion made him want to roar like the wildest of men. When she began to tremble his patience became impossible. With desperation he ascended her body like a snake enveloping its prey. He would devour her without permission. He reached his lips to catch every moan of passion that sprang from her mouth as he reached out his rough, broad hand to entwine it with hers. With a single stroke he entered that delicate body that enveloped him with its warmth and made him tremble with pleasure. She was an angel of heaven wrapped in the most sinful ardor of the seven hells. He desired her with desperation. He slid in again and again until he felt the blazing fire of her wetness burn him.

Brenda began to moan again and he bit her lips encouraging her to peak once more. He moved slowly to give her time. He would wait as long as it took to feel himself being squeezed by those wet walls. Again and again he entered her until he thought he would die at any moment when he felt her embrace him by the shoulders and stretch her neck back. She was about to come and it would be with him. Akim thrust again and again to give her all she needed when he felt a force squeeze his member deeper and deeper into her small body.

-God... It can't be real... -He said, knowing that he could no longer contain himself.

He intertwined his strong fingers tightly with hers as he rammed with the strongest of passions. Once and twice before burying himself and cursing under his breath before falling motionless into the adoring hollow of her shoulder.

When he managed to breathe again Akim broke away, put the condom in the wastebasket and hugged her with all his strength. Brenda was silently caressing him and he reached down to offer her his whole body. She began to draw circles on his male torso all the way down his abdomen and he warned her with amusement.

-That road is dangerous.

-A lot? -she asked in a mischievous voice, and he showed her until almost dawn.

Akim was the first to wake up and smile at the sight of the body next to him. He was not a man of sleeping with company but discovering Brenda as a bed companion was much more than any dream. It was caressing the clouds and locking them in his hands. The woman was literally glued to his body and her indiscreet breasts peeked out from between the sheets without any modesty. Unable to contain himself a second longer he caressed the softness of her delicate shoulder with the back of his fingers and thought how happy his life would be if every morning was like that one. Fate seemed to be smiling on him and although optimism was not usually his natural state, he could not hide an immense feeling of euphoria.

Brenda was not an easy piece to conquer and he knew perfectly well that one night of sex did not mean victory but he was too happy to think of anything but keeping her by his side forever. He wanted her before but now he adored her. She represented all the unattainable become reality, God, she's got me crazy, he thought perplexed at his own feelings. Her hair was disheveled on the pillow and although he could see the purple on one side of her face it didn't make her any less attractive in his eyes. On the contrary, it showed that there was a Brenda, a complete and overwhelming woman, a woman passionate about life and human beings, a woman willing to put herself on the line for what she believed in.

He combed her tangled hair gently and remembered that he had told her he would accept any crumb of her affection but now, here, naked and in her bed, he doubted he could bear to share her with anyone. No, Brenda Klein would be his full-time.

Careful not to wake her and like an indiscreet voyeur, he moved the sheets to her feet to observe her divine body. Wrinkles, Old Age? Had she really said that nonsense to scare him? The light peeked through the window and her gorgeous nakedness blinded him. Unable to contain himself and careful not to rest his weight on her numb body, he began to kiss her breasts with the utmost dedication. How could he not understand what she was capable of arousing in a man? She moaned in her sleep and he smiled wickedly. He would take her to the most glorious of pleasures. He would show her a world of sensations. He would awaken her passion, make her addicted to his body so that Brenda Klein would never be able to leave him.

-I want you. He whispered in her ear more to himself than with the intention of waking her up.

Gently and tenderly he caressed her cheeks guiding the rough hands through the coolness of the tender skin fearing to hurt her. She was so... so... so much and he so... so... so... little.

With a deep sense of dread he leaned back on his elbows. He never wanted her to wake up from the dream they were beginning to dream together. With a tender smile in his eyes, he took that little face in his broad hands and with his thumb, barely touching her, he ran his finger along that terrible and very deep wrinkle, which, according to her, he had around her sweet chocolate eyes. Brenda stirred in her sleep, and he sighed with a sigh of tenderness. Never in his best dreams could he have imagined that sleeping with a woman would be half as wonderful as it was with her. He kissed her slowly, slowly, wanting to drink in her vitality. He used his lips as a precise scanner to remember every detail of her body. Roundness, size, texture, everything was absorbed by lips that nibbled, licked and loved relentlessly. She opened her eyes as she felt him caressing her belly and he looked up to soak in that image. Her sleepy eyes, her desirous body and her lips inflamed by his caresses, that was an image that would never be erased from his tormented eyes. He adored that woman to the point of madness. What is different about her, Nikola had asked him, dear friend, if you saw what I am seeing right now you wouldn't ask me that question, he answered himself amused.

Brenda smiled as she met his gaze and knew he would tear down the universe if she asked him to. He climbed up to her mouth rubbing her body with every intention to make her feel him. Careful not to crush her with his weight he propped himself up on his elbows but did not kiss her. He wished she could see it. He needed her to also tax his face, to remember him during the day but also at night, to need him to breathe, to make her dawns unbearable without his presence, he wished she felt like she would die without him as it happened to him every time he didn't have her. She reached out her hand to caress his face trying to get a kiss but he denied her.

-He said with a deep voice and a twinkle in his eye.

His doctor looked at him between curious and disoriented and he smiled without being able to contain himself. He loved to break her schemes because when he did she became that woman that no one saw except him.

-I want to hear your voice in the morning begging..." He commented with ardor in his eyes.

-Do you want me to beg?

Akim smiled trying to reassure her. Of course he wanted to hear her beg but not in the context she imagined.

-Doctor, I want you to ask me for whatever you want," he said as he lowered his face to kiss her cheek. I want you not to hold back, I want you to ask me for what gives you pleasure, I want you to tell me about your dark appetites and ask me to make them come true," she said, her voice hoarse with desire. I want to awaken your desires and for you to tell me how....

Her voice was lost in a delicate neck stretching back to offer him more skin. Yes, she was understanding him and was surrendering.

-I want to feel your body under mine but I don't want just your tremors, I'm looking for more, I need you to wake up against my caresses," he babbled nervously with his lips pressed to hers. I want to satisfy you... I want to feel you... I want you to claim what belongs to you," he whispered as his tongue fiddled with hers. She moaned and rubbed against his hard body. Making a super human effort he restrained himself from possessing her, he wanted her to the point of pain but she would never be his unless he was able to awaken her social modesty.

-Please... -she whispered nervously and he smiled like a hungry wolf after prey. Without ceasing to caress with one hand that sexuality ready to be received, he spoke hoarsely.

-I don't understand, honey? Tell me what you want and I'll give it to you.

-Akim please... don't do this to me.... -she replied, squirming under the broad, muscular body that refused to release her.

For a moment he was tempted to give in. She was beginning to stir and he feared he was stretching the rope too tight, but if Brenda could not break down the barriers, if she would not do with him what she dared not do with others, then how could he be sure to keep her by his side?

-Try it, love... just let yourself go.... -His strong fingers delicately entered the sweetest of her wetness inciting her to express in words what her body was crying out for. Tell me what you want, whisper in my ear your desires and I promise I will fulfill them. Do it my love... please..." she said in something that although it seemed to sound like it was a little like a dream. -he said in something that although it seemed like a simple carnal desire for him symbolized a desperate plea.

-Akim...

-Yes, my life. He answered desperately looking for an answer.

-I want you inside," she said in a soft voice.

He smiled hopefully as he inserted a second finger inside her and gently and insistently rubbed her clitoris.

-So...? -he asked hoarsely and totally excited.

-No." He replied with his eyes closed tightly and his hips lifted high. "Don't play.... Akim

-I am here, my love. He said forgetting all prudence.

-I want you inside. Come inside me. I need you inside me," she said, reaching out to grasp his hard penis between her fingers. Put it inside me," he answered, agitated with desire.

Akim would have howled like a wolf to feel her speak like that but he was in too much of a hurry to satisfy her to cry out. With a single deep, strong movement he was inside her, bringing their bodies together in a way that was beyond natural.

-Better...? -He asked viciously as he stopped moving and felt her squeak through his teeth.

-Damn you, move, he wants to cum with you inside me. I want you to slam your body against mine with all your might and never stop." She screamed in exasperation from the need.

The man laid his head on his girl's neck trying to contain himself and not act like an animal. He knew that arousing Brenda's desires would be good for both of them but he never imagined that much.

He was about to become a wild beast with no control whatsoever. Her words had turned him on like never before.

He stretched out his hand and with his claw-like teeth broke the condom he had on the bedside table and, leaving her body but without moving too far away, put it on at a speed faster than the speed of light and penetrated her just as she asked him to. Hard, without restraint and without rest. He would die exhausted in that act but happy to be what she was looking for in a man.

Brenda made a hoarse sound as he thrust relentlessly into her again and again. Their lips pressed together madly. He had never felt anything like this before. No woman had ever driven him wild beyond control, and when her delicate hand rested on his shoulder to claw him hard as he climaxed, he knew heaven existed and it was inside that delicate body. Heat flooded him and the wetness of her small body enveloped him until he could take no more. He bit her soft shoulder careful not to hurt her as he released a first, a second and a third time before collapsing against the tenderness of her skin. This was definitely the best night of his life. He didn't have much to offer her but he had a lot to ask of her. He felt guilty but God have mercy on him because he didn't plan on ever walking away from her.

Kisses that kill

> You came into my life painting it with unknown colors, before you it was a canvas of dark without light, today I am happy to live because you taught me to paint.
>
> Akim

He woke up and went to the toilet being very careful not to wake her up when the vibrating sound of a cell phone erased that smile of a deeply satisfied man, which had been on his face all night and part of the morning. He was sure that even when he was asleep he was still smiling gawking. He tiptoed like a petty thief on his way to the phone. He knew it was wrong, that he shouldn't do it, he told himself hundreds of reasons to convince himself not to do it, but his hands didn't seem to listen to him. With great care not to be discovered, he rummaged through his jacket, feeling like the worst of men.

"You never cared for any of them and now you're acting like a jealous husband going through their pockets." He shook his head thinking that he was acting like a jerk even when he was scolding himself. "A jealous husband? Am I really such an idiot as to make such comparisons to myself?" he cursed himself under his breath but continued with the outrage of the blissful device. He felt like a traitor and for a moment thought about not intruding, but he couldn't. The overwhelming feeling of losing her, the feeling of feeling like shit again as in the last year by not having her, overpowered him and made him steal the demonic device. He pulled it out of his pocket and looked at the screen. "God, men don't do this stuff," he said to himself in alteration. He breathed a little more relaxed as he read the name on the screen. It wasn't the unmentionable one of her husband.

Brenda stirred on the bed as he would have his eyes, fearing to be caught red-handed, he approached with his hand in the air bringing the cell phone to her and speaking with absolute indifference.

-It's Rachel. He said as he offered her the phone and headed to the restroom as if nothing had happened.

She greeted her friend and Akim closed the restroom door trying to calm her nerves. She had a few days before the unmentionable thief would show up with his so-called rights to snatch what she wanted most. He had to act with caution but in haste. Time was not in her favor, she thought as she doused her face with ice water.

-But how? What are you saying?

Brenda asked nervously and Akim walked beside her startled to hear the tone of concern on her lips. He moved closer waiting for her to cut and explain herself but as he watched her sit up on the bed and leave her haughty, naked breasts in full view, he forgot all concern. He brought his mouth close to such a tender delight and began to nibble on them enjoying the glorious morning pleasure that only she was capable of offering.

-*Please* wait... -He said, covering the microphone and stroking his black hair. Akim smiled mischievously as he raised his shoulders in a sign of it's not my fault but yours. *It's all right. I'll go as soon as possible... No, I haven't slept at the hotel.... Yes, I'm fine... please Rachel, we can leave this conversation for later... In half an hour I'll meet you in the cafeteria at the entrance...*

Akim watched her somewhat angrily. Meeting Rachel was not in his plans. Maybe breakfast in bed and some more sex, lunch and sex, afternoon snack and sex, nap and sex, yes were the way he thought of how they should spend the rest of the day.

-I have to go. She said hurriedly as she rummaged through her clothes scattered on the floor.

-Go where? -What happened?

Brenda dressed nervously as if she didn't hear him and Akim feared the worst. She couldn't go to London. Not yet. Nikola had assured her she was booked for ten days and it had only been three. She couldn't leave. Damn it, he needed that time.

-Brin, wait... Stop. Brin... -He tried to sound calm, even though he was about to jump out of his nerves.

-Will you ever tell me why you call me that? -She said as she hurriedly put on her sandals.

-Akim spoke with his deep, thick voice and that typical accent that was even more pronounced when he was angry.

-It's Rachel. The police have been asking about her. They told her that she can't move from the island. She answered as she decided to put on her dress without a bra because despite looking for it around the room she couldn't find it.

-Police? What is she being charged with?

Of being the one who led the attack on a high-ranking military officer. They say that she led the Amazons and that.... -She stopped without continuing while she turned her head upside down to gather her long hair in a ponytail.

-So what... ?

-The truth is that I don't know what the alleged act of vandalism they are accusing her of is, but she was very nervous.

-That's silly, that woman is too repipi to do anything to spoil her designer clothes.

Brenda thought that although somewhat flippant, Akim's description was quite accurate.

-I'm leaving, I'll call you back.

-Shall I call you back? -Akim stopped her by the arm, looking at her with a raised eyebrow. Shall I call you back? I don't think so." Akim, who was also finishing putting on his sneakers, hurried to put on a black T-shirt and looked at her with a smile. I'll be damned if

I'm going to let you go alone. Your face is still a little bruised and God knows what other mess you'd be able to get into without me.

She smiled at him and he knew that this woman would be the death of him. He ate from her hand like a chicken. One that, although extremely big and tattooed, but a chick nonetheless.

-Come on, I'll give you a ride," he said, picking up the keys to the sports car.

-What about that? -he asked, pointing to his hand.

-I rented it when I arrived. He said without mentioning that it was the only thing available at the agency and that even if the rental cost him a kidney, he didn't mind if he could find it faster.

Brenda got into the car but didn't say much more. Akim deduced that she would be worried about Rachel. She had sounded very worried when she had cut the phone off.

-In less than ten minutes we will be there. The island is small. He said trying to relax her.

Brenda accepted the information with her head but did not answer with words. She was totally silent and he began to worry. He would have wanted to know how she felt, if she thought about it, if she still felt him inside her body, if she still remembered his pleas to have him inside her, because damn it, he did. He still had the salty taste of her skin on his lips and the scent of Jasmine and vanilla in his body. He could still hear her moans echoing in his ears as he penetrated her velvety wetness.

If Brenda did not wish to speak, he should shut up, but damn it, "With this woman when is the time?" he thought in disgust. He sped up trying to focus only on the road but could not. She was the center of his thoughts since the first day he met her. He was stunned and imbecilically in love. Yes, even if it was hard for him to admit it. Those excessive nerves, that irrational jealousy and that continuous fear of losing her represented that he was mortally in love. From head to toe.

"Last night you gave yourself away. I woke you up, I know it, I felt it, and I'm going to remind you a thousand times if I have to". Since when? How many women had he been with? How many of them did he remember? None, he said to himself cursing under his breath. "None except you…"

Brenda was worried but it wasn't about Rachel. Her friend was probably exaggerating, she always did. The real reason she wasn't talking was because she could still feel his mouth caressing every nook and cranny of her skin. She had. She had begged for every caress. She had begged to feel him inside hard and deep… I'm sick, she said to herself, covering her mouth with two fingers. How could I? Are years and experience of no use? She brought her hand to her forehead and sighed in shame.

She was not like that. She believed in trust, in sincerity, she was a specialist in these matters, how could she let herself get carried away? For heaven's sake! If she had behaved like a neighborhood whore on a night out, she thought upset. She had rolled on the beach with a man in some bushes and then got into bed to sprawl out without a hint of shame, I'm sure not even the whores in the village were so desperate. And had she screamed? Yes, she had, and moaned, and demanded, and demanded…. God… He closed his eyes trying not to remember but it was impossible. Images of their night of passion came up again and again. Memories of her nails digging into his broad back begging for more made her want to die of embarrassment. She was no naïf, she knew perfectly well that passion led to such scandalous situations but she had always been a fairly controlled woman when it came to sex. Max applauded her controlled behavior, he said those women who went all out were slumming and although he didn't judge them she knew she would never be like them, but last night…last night….

Akim had managed to awaken with just a touch what she thought was dead, gone, buried or whatever it was that was there.

The car parked in front of the hotel and she decided that she should get out and drive away as soon as possible. Maybe if she didn't look into his eyes, if she didn't meet that deep blue gaze of his, she could analyze everything that had happened from a more rational perspective and look for a solution to such a terrible mess. She was a professional of the psyche, she had to sit down and clear herself, surely in a few minutes she would have the perfect therapy that would guide her in the solution of her strong, young and tattooed problem, or not?

-They have taken her away. The girl named Esperanza, who worked at the hotel and was a current member of the Amazons, said in a loud and extremely nervous voice.

-Who? Where? -Brenda began to get really worried.

-I am El Peter, Espe's boyfriend. He said stretching out his hand and Brenda was speechless, wondering if this information was of any use to her, but the young man continued without further ado. The police took her away with charges.

-Why? -The doctor could not believe her eyes.

-They accuse her of being the propitiator, together with the skins, of the attack on the military mass.

-That's not true. We have to get her out of there. She said, ready to leave as soon as possible.

-I don't think it's possible.

-Why! -Brenda raised her voice in disgust and Akim smiled as he noticed her losing her temper. It was silly but seeing her unhinged and without the usual formalities brought her closer to him.

-She is incommunicado. Esperanza replied, fidgeting a little nervously.

-And why? -He asked again as he felt he was losing his strength.

-I'm not sure. Esperanza answered doubtfully and her boyfriend looked at her angrily which made Akim suspicious.

-Who filed the lawsuit? -He asked, extending the full width of his body and positioning himself next to Brenda to show that she was not alone.

Esperanza shifted nervously but said nothing. The man was about to ask again but this time with more energy when Peter bluntly confessed.

-It was Carol's harpy.

-Peter! You don't know that. The young man looked at her snorting and Esperanza squared herself in front of him.

-Yes, we know, fatty. It was the crazy one.

-And why? -Brenda asked again with the only sentence she was able to say and Akim felt sorry for her. She looked exhausted and was stroking her forehead as if her head was about to split in two.

-Who knows? She is crazy.

-Rachel is the only one who knew about the skin attack," Esperanza spat angrily. It's more than clear who sold us out.

-That's not true. Rachel has a... friend in the police," she commented nervously. friend in the police," she commented nervously. He informed her of the attack plans, that's why as soon as he found out he ran to warn them. If that were true, why would you have been there? She had to run away and I was almost killed in one blow. It's stupid to think she's the culprit.

Akim cursed under his breath as he remembered what might have happened if he hadn't arrived in time. Just remembering that wretch made him awaken his most caveman instincts. Those that for fear of losing her he always tried to hide from her.

-Carol is only looking for our good. Esperanza answered as if someone was attacking her and Akim felt a strange itch in his body.

He was about to ask a couple of questions to find out the reason for such an act of faith towards his leader when he was surprised by a Brenda who, without any explanation, turned around in a hurry and headed for the exit.

-Where are you supposed to go? -Akim firmly stopped her by the elbow. They said she's incommunicado. There's not much we can do.

Brenda smiled to herself and Akim saw trouble approaching. He was beginning to know her well enough to know that a new revolution was beginning.

-Something can always be done. I'm going to the consulate.

Amused but extremely haughty, he spoke with a broad chest of pride.

-That's my girl. He said without thinking and instantly regretted it when he noticed her frightened face.

"I scared her. Shit." He thought angrily at his lack of restraint. It was still too early for absurd macho bravado claims. idiot!

-I'm coming with you. Peter said confidently and Akim was grateful for the interruption.

-You're not going anywhere, Peter! -Hope issued a threatening order, but the young man did not accept it.

-I'm sorry, Gordi, but I'm going to help you. She doesn't deserve you and I'll prove it to you.

Peter gave her a resounding kiss on her rounded cheeks and hurried off after his new friends who were already about to get into the car.

Akim paced nervously in one of the consulate rooms. She did not show up. They spent the day going back and forth like a puppeteer's suitcase. Whether to convince the secretary to attend to them, whether to fill out forms and more forms, whether to ask for the assistant to the assistant, God, this was bureaucracy made flesh. Peter sat down next to her and handed her a paper cup of machine coffee, which she instantly appreciated. They hadn't eaten all day and it was almost time for dinner. He didn't want to imagine how Brenda was doing. She had been locked in the consul's office for hours without going out.

-Thank you. He said accepting the drink. You should leave. Your girlfriend didn't look very happy.

-I do it for us. Akim looked at him curiously as he took a sip of his horrifying coffee. That woman is not transparent. She has them fooled and I must unmask her.

-Don't you believe in the rights they fight for? -he asked with a hint of anger.

-Of course I do, it's that bitch I don't believe in.

Akim took another sip, interested in the story. Brenda was starting to get involved with those women and he didn't want to see her get into another danger. Again.

-Do you have proof?

-No, but I will. My fatty will have to accept reality.

-You are afraid for your girlfriend...

Peter stretched further and Akim smiled at the silly look on his face when he thought of his fatty. Would he also make those little puppy dog eyes when he thought of his doctor? Yes, he was convinced he would.

-My fatty is the only thing I have. We grew up in the same town, we had the same dreams, we were meant for each other until...

Akim waited for Peter to continue but didn't, he simply drank the last of his coffee and crushed the paper cup between his hands. The young man didn't look a day over twenty but his strapping body made him look even younger. Akim was really intrigued. Peter was hiding something.

-Did you grow up together? -he said, trying to get some useful information.

-Yes, she grew up with her grandmother. We were neighbors, classmates and pranksters. She's been my girlfriend since I was six. I asked her one afternoon at the door of her house and until now. We have never been apart. Where she is, there I go.

-Do they live on the island?

-No," he replied amused. When she heard about the Amazon annual meeting she looked online and got a job pretty quickly. She works at the hotel in the evenings and I do some odd jobs that we get for lunch, but we're finally going home in a little while. Our business is waiting for us.

-Entrepreneur. He commented interested.

-Something like that, fatty loves to cook and we are about to open our own tea shop, with the most delicious homemade cakes in all of London.

-I congratulate them.

Akim slowly sipped his coffee imagining why a young girl from the village and living with her longtime boyfriend with whom she was starting a promising future wanted to blindly follow a leader who according to Peter was totally unhinged. Brenda appeared behind the huge wooden door and Akim stood up completely forgetting about Peter, his girlfriend, the Amazons and the world in general. She had that power over him.

-How was it? -he asked nervously.

-They say they can't do much more. They have asked me to return to the hotel. If everything goes as expected in a couple of hours it will be free. She replied exhausted.

-That's very good news. He said caressing her cheek, "You don't have to worry....

Brenda looked him in the eyes between tired and somewhat distrustful and Akim wanted to eat her with kisses. His doctor was like that, she would not rest until she had everything under control and the problem solved.

-So do we know who accused her? -Peter asked with interest.

-It was Carol. He accuses her of being the instigator. She claims Rachel called the skins and provoked the attack.

-Disgraceful. Always blaming others and looking like a martyr.

-Yes, well, the truth is that she is the least of my worries. Now I just want my friend to be free and to be able to return home.

Brenda spoke with real exhaustion and without noticing the frozen state of the young worker who was unable to react. Nikola had assured that they would be on the island for a total of ten days, that left him a total of seven days to win her over. Returning to London, to her routine and to her unmentionable husband would make everything difficult. He assured that he would accept whatever she offered him, whether it was much or little but that was no longer feasible. He wanted it all and would fight for it all and nothing less. The three of them marched towards the hotel in silence, it seemed as if the tiredness of a whole day of worries had overcome them, although the reality for each one of them was very different.

Akim watched Peter in the rearview mirror, surely he was thinking about how to get his girlfriend away from the Amazon, Brenda however, had her eyes closed and although she would have liked to think that she was dreaming about him, the reality was that the woman was exhausted and as for him, his thoughts were more than clear, how to get the maximum time to conquer her while keeping the unmentionable away? He hated to admit it but one night at her side was not enough to compete with a man who had been in her life for too many years according to his taste.

Rachel sipped her tea after she had only had a bite of her small sandwich for dinner. She was somewhere between exhausted and furious. That wretch had accused her. Her! If anything she could be accused of trying to save them. She had always sensed that Carol was not entirely trustworthy, but to the point of accusing her and putting her in jail?

He sipped at his tea as he looked at Brenda, who sat directly across from him smiling sympathetically. "What a bad motherfucker, accusing me when it's her fault I had to confess my own bedroom secrets to my best friend!" he thought as he remembered how he found himself having to come clean about the cop's relationship. She thought as she remembered how she found it necessary to clarify the policeman's relationship. What would Brenda think now, she said to herself in horror. Or not! She thought as she realized for the first time that the bricklayer was sitting next to her without saying a word and typing a message on his cell phone.

-Are you better? -Brenda asked worriedly.

-Yes, much calmer. I have to thank you for saving me. As always. He said smiling.

-Don't be silly. You know I would move heaven and earth to set you free.

-Of course I know." Her words showed total conviction. She was his super Brenda, his best friend, his savior.

A call on the doctor's cell phone made her get up from the table and speak in whispers, covering the microphone as she answered.

-It's Murray, I called him this afternoon. It will be to know if you are already free. He said as he walked away to answer and Rachel smiled to see how Brenda had really moved Rome with Santiago in order to free her. Akim was about to get up from his chair when Rachel held him back with her words.

-We need to talk," he said in a threatening voice.

-Is that so? -he said mockingly and fixing his deep gaze on her.

-Yes, bricklayer, and don't get smart with me, we don't have much time," he said as he looked at Brenda in the distance talking to Murray on the phone.

Akim raised an expectant eyebrow. No good could come of that blissful braggart. Women like her hated men like him.

-I'm all ears. He replied mockingly as he stretched back in his chair.

-What are your intentions? -he threw out without anesthesia.

-I don't think I understand you." He froze for a few seconds when he finally shook his head with a fake smile on his face.

-Cut the crap, you know perfectly well what I'm talking about. I know guys like you and their intentions.

-I guess you're going to clarify them for me?

-How much?

-I beg your pardon?

-I say how much do you want. I can write you a check right now. I have plenty of money. You name the amount.

Akim closed and opened his eyes as he took a deep breath and Rachel began to feel a little worried. It was the first time she had stopped at the image of the worker and she could tell he had more muscle than she had anticipated. Tension was building in his broad neck and his deep gaze was transforming from sky blue to hellish blue. Maybe she hadn't been entirely correct in her assumptions, she thought, swallowing saliva.

Akim crossed his arms and moved his body slowly closer on the table making their faces almost collide. He spoke to her with his voice slow but so deep that it made her shake her socks off.

-Damn woman... Let's pretend that this conversation never existed, because otherwise I would have to hang you with my own hands and I wouldn't want Brenda to be upset.

Rachel swallowed slowly as she stroked her neck in an instinctive act.

-So you really like him," she said, almost trembling from the shock she had just gotten over.

Akim shook his head and regained his position in his seat.

-You may not be able to see her because you don't see beyond your nose, but Brenda is a woman hardly comparable. Rachel liked his words but she didn't want to interrupt him. She didn't have to justify her affection for her best friend to that bricklayer. She's wonderful, she's the best thing I've ever known in my life and although I know perfectly well that I don't deserve her, I'll never stop trying. I want her for myself. I want to see her smile, I want to feel her free. She is so much more than what everyone sees.

Not all of them, Rachel told herself, but without confessing it out loud. Connor and she did know what the real Brenda was like, they even got to know her long before they saw her married.

-It's not free. -You don't mind?

-I would be a fool if I didn't care. He replied angrily.

Rachel studied him in detail. This man was not the sort of man she would ever look at but one thing was very clear, the few moments she had seen them together, her Brenda smiled in a different way. More sincere. More uninhibited. The bricklayer managed to bring out the hidden woman.

-Will you be his mistress? -he asked bluntly.

-What do you care? He replied annoyed and Rachel laughed out loud.

-Dear, with me less teeth. I know your kind too well.

-My kind? Anyone would think so. A lady like you. He said contemptuously.

-You'd be surprised how alike we are, and that's why I want you to know that I'm not going to take my eyes off you. Brenda is my best friend, I adore her and I won't let you hurt her. If you love her I'll be on your side but if you hurt her you better be prepared because I can be the bitch of all bitches.

Akim was surprised to hear her speak, where was the sweet, crazy and all that nonsense she was talking about when she spoke?

-You're not going to tell on us? -He asked, knowing he shouldn't trust her.

-I'm not going to deny that I love Max very much. He is a fabulous man and if he would change some behaviors it would be best for her but I will do what Brenda asks me to do. If she chooses you I won't stand in the way.

Akim felt her pulse pounding. The best man for her. And there was the first of the many stabs she would receive if she continued to insist on obtaining what was forbidden to her. A thousand complexes began to gnaw at her insides. Damn it, he could also be an ideal man if the circumstances had been different. It was not he who chose to be born at the wrong time and in the wrong place.

Brenda approached once she cut the call and looked at them interested in the conversation but Rachel was quick enough to distract her. She did not wish to be discovered. Akim knew she would be watching him from the short distance.

-I'm going to rest. It's been a long day.

-Yes, we'd both better get some rest. Tomorrow we'll leave early.

Rachel looked at her curiously as she watched the bricklayer's face transform.

-What are you talking about?

-The consul advised me to leave as soon as possible. Better to be at home and face Carol on our own ground. We don't know why she accused you and what reason she has to want to see you away from the Amazons. Brenda answered seriously.

She spoke with conviction, but Rachel was not listening. The bricklayer's discomposed face had her engrossed. It was clear that he hadn't expected it. Akim may not have been the winning bet in her friend's heart, but something was beginning between them, that was indisputable, it was enough to see the gleam in their eyes to recognize it.

-We're not going anywhere.

-I think you misunderstood me. If that crazy woman decides to accuse you again and the police accept the complaint, I won't be able to take you out of Spain.

-Nonsense, you always could," she said amused, "besides Carol won't make another move. Something tells me she's just trying to scare me.

-Why do you say that?

-Call it instinct." Brenda shook her head in distrust.

-We can't risk it. We are leaving.

-Then you go alone, my dear sweet, because I'm staying.

Rachel thought she heard the bricklayer breathing again but didn't stop to look at him, she was too busy convincing her friend.

-We have paid reservations for ten days and we've only been here for three, one of which I spent behind bars, I'm not going anywhere. I'm going to enjoy the island, I'm going to go out, eat some tapas and drink a tinto de verano even though I have no idea what that is.

Brenda seemed to think about it for a few long minutes but then nodded.

-All right, we'll stay, but you're going to promise me that you won't go near the Amazons until we get back to London.

-I can promise you that," he said, smiling.

If she didn't think he hated her, Rachel would have sworn the bricklayer felt like kissing her. She said goodbye, assuring herself of a tiredness she didn't feel, and went up to her room. Whatever was going on between those two was a matter between them and one he didn't intend to meddle in, or at least not until it was absolutely necessary.

A matter of time

> Swear to me that you will always stay in me.
> Tell me that no matter how many springs leave me,
> you will always be here.
>
> Akim

Brenda was nervous and despite her best attempts to hide it, she was unable to do so. After all she had been through, it was the first time she was alone with Akim. She didn't quite know how she should act. To tell the truth he had no idea. It was the first time he had been in such a situation and although he had had many patients who had told him about similar circumstances, he did not remember any of his own advice. Should he talk about what had happened? Should he let it pass as a simple memory? What should he do? She asked herself over and over again, extremely nervous.

"You must go, you must leave as soon as possible," her conscience replied in haste. She was thinking and thinking a mile a minute and her brain seemed about to explode when she discovered that Akim was no longer sitting beside her but now behind her chair, he was holding her hand forcing her to get up. Silently, without a word, he led her up the stairs to his own room. Neither of them spoke. Maybe deep down she didn't want to either. They were in front of her door and the man opened it slowly, took her in his arms and led her to the bed. No words. No sentence, no explanation, no denial....

Akim responded with a delicate, rough caress on her cheek as he began to slide her dress down. She closed her eyes and waited for the inevitable. The young man's mouth closed over hers and time, regrets and her finger ring lost the battle to the stark reality.

-No Philippe, I don't need that much. Just one thousand pounds more will be enough... OK... when will you pay me the money?... on the card you gave me? So fast?... That's perfect. Thanks, I'll pay you back as agreed.

Akim hung up the phone happy with what he had obtained. With a small extension of his loan he could prepare for the farewell evening. The days were passing too fast, he thought as he watched her in the distance as she rested on the sand. So beautiful, so relaxed, it was too good to be real. In those few days he had experienced a kind of happiness that romantic composers sang about in their songs. She sighed and could feel her heart tearing into hundreds of pieces at the thought that this would be their last night together. No longer would they wake up together, no longer would he see her smile excitedly with her first coffee of the day, no longer would she be his.... She would be gone and he would have to share her. She hated to think of anything else but that night but the thought of the unmentionable one was proving unavoidable. She hadn't mentioned him, avoided any comment related to him but Akim discovered her doubts the night before. Brenda hadn't offered him any promises and he didn't have the courage to claim anything from her either. Not yet. He knew her well enough to recognize the hesitations in her moments of silence. She was confused, but how confused? Passion did not dominate what Brenda would call "her duties" or at least not for now and he wasn't about to lose her to his lack of patience. He would wait for her, drown her with his passion and wait for her to make the decision to be by his side herself. He hated every minute of doubt, he would have liked to tie her down if necessary until he convinced her that theirs was much more than a sweet summer dream but he couldn't, if Brenda felt the slightest bit cornered she would slip through his fingers like water through his fingers and he hadn't come this far to act so stupidly. He would swallow his pride, he would bite his tongue until it bled and he would unload all his impotence in bags of cement, he would do it all if he could get it. He approached her slowly so as not to wake her up.

She lay with her eyes closed and the orange sun bathed her golden body. Akim felt his throat go dry and his body tighten longingly. No, she wasn't the most beautiful woman in the world, maybe even to some she was just another one but to him she had him locked in the prison of her kisses, her caresses and her damned madness. Brenda Klein was a whirlwind, one cloistered in a cage that someone had built and from which he wished to free. The man bent down carefully and gently brushed aside her silky hair to kiss her in that little nook under her neck below her ear that had become her favorite place.

Brenda rested on her huge towel on a beach too far from any existing population. She needed to rest. The events of the last few days would overwhelm the most expert in matters of the heart. Her body was responding to a thousand longings she was beginning to discover and to a dream she never thought she had dreamed. At what point does life force you to go through that tunnel you have always refused to go through?

Her eyes closed, keeping the warmth in her eyelids from a sun that was beginning to orange in the distance. She took a deep breath and a small tear escaped from her eyes, still closed, trying to hold back the inevitable. The present and the future, reality and desires collided like a speeding train in an uncontrolled march that she was unable to hold back.

Ten days, it only took ten days for the construction of a life that she carefully pampered and that today would either survive or collapse under her nose.

Who says yes to the truth or to the lie? Who defines what is real or imaginary when it is the heart that directs each one of its acts?

Would it be that? She thought questioningly, is it the heart that is behind this deep emptiness that dominates me and completes me without letting me breathe or is it that we simply blame love for what we should simply call stupidity?

Brenda embraced her body dressed in just a simple swimsuit trying to give herself the worst of comforts. That of traitors.

A soft, warm breath came close to her ear and her body bristled with the simplest of touches. She knew it was wrong, it couldn't be. She thought of the twenty thousand reasons she would offer if that drama belonged to one of her patients, but her mind stopped imagining when his lips caressed her cheek, wiping away the second tear that was beginning to fall.

-Everything will be all right... -Said the deep voice trying to show understanding.

Well? She thought in a daze. Nothing is right, this is not right, I am not right. My body demands from me what my head rejects. I am unworthy, cruel, treacherous and weak. Weak to express what I feel. Unable to confess to you that I won't be able to continue. Unable and cowardly for not admitting that I won't be able to continue. Because no matter what my treacherous heart has sown, I will continue on my way trying to forget you. No matter how much you have engraved yourself on my skin or how sweet I find your perfume or that the blue of the sky is only a cheap copy of your gaze for me, I will forget you because my future and my destiny depends on it.

"She's a weak child." Her father's words said to her mother in a corner of the kitchen still echoed in her head and today they were more present than ever. She tried to deny it and get over each of her humiliations but today they drilled into her head more than ever. He was weak. Weak to start over, weak to face the uncertain future without thinking about the opinion of others, weak to take a risk without more, weak to recognize that the passion he was looking for came from the hand of the one he did not expect. A hard body stood over her body and began to kiss her with understanding tenderness and her lips as treacherous as the rest of her body surrendered to a list of sins too long.

Love, lust, passion, tenderness, truth, lie, all words without meaning when the heart dominates them.

A rough hand caressed her now naked breast that was refreshed by the sea breeze while fleshy lips kissed her neck that stretched back to enjoy his caresses. Closed eyelids never needed to be opened to discover who it was. Ten days proved to be enough time for her offending body to recognize him. Ten days... it only took ten days to erase what took a lifetime to build.

Strong arms lifted her up without question while passionate lips did not stop eating her in bites tasting the inside as if it were a real delicacy.

Brenda responded to every kiss and every caress by feeling like the most desired woman on the face of the earth. She never felt this way or maybe she did, who knows, but the reality was that if she had ever felt it she no longer remembered it.

With great care she was placed on a soft bed and for the first time she opened her eyes to recognize her refuge of the last week. A small wooden bungalow by the beach witnessed what she dared not name.

A fierce and penetrating gaze devoured her while her heart pounded like every time she felt him near.

"I swear I tried. I swear I tried..." She thought before losing consciousness in a sea of kisses and caresses that she didn't try to stop.

The sun of Hope shone brighter than ever before in his life.

Akim acted in silence. He managed the timing and the caresses with total intelligence. Brenda Klein was not just one more, she represented the greatest of his conquests and hopefully it would be the last. He was tired of strolling along the paths unattached and enjoying every flower that approached him. The path Brenda marked out for him was the one any man would want to settle on and he was no blind man. He may have lived twenty six years without her but now his life was no longer the same. He dreamed of what others had, adored what was to come and would fight for what did not belong to him.

The brown hair fell scattered on the white pillow and he stopped to contemplate them, thirsty for her image. He wanted this woman, he wanted her in his bed, in his life and in every minute of his sad existence.

Her heartbeat hammered trying to escape her chest but Akim held it back. Every moment he spent at her side would be his moment. He would make her feel beyond any limit, he would awaken her to the world of passions as she had awakened him. He would devote every second of his caresses to adoring her like a faithful vassal to his mistress. He stretched her out on the bed and kissed every hollow of her naked body. Brenda tried to move but he prevented her. Brenda's pleasure was his own pleasure. Watching her enjoy was the most blessed and erotic of his rewards. He tasted her mouth, traveled over the roof of her mouth and made her moan as he abandoned her to go down on her silky body. Hearing her sulk as he left her lips was the sweetest of songs to his needy ears. She was beginning to demand and he adored her. Brenda was asking just as he had taught her and he felt pleasurable. Every moment at her side she was leaving more of the reserved, conservative, responsible, committed woman behind to become what she truly was, a free, fiery, feisty, feisty and terribly sexy woman.

Intoxicated with her sweet fragrance of jasmine and vanilla he kissed her again and again until he reached the most intoxicating of feminine scents. He buried his head between her legs bewitched with her flavor. Nothing was enough with her, no matter how much he gave her, she would always want more. His lips moved possessively and his tongue pushed into a body that rose to welcome her. If he hadn't had his mouth occupied he would have grunted in pleasure.

Brenda squeezed his hair and then tugged hard but he didn't mind. Each tug on her head brought him to an even greater state of arousal. His lips devoured her uncontrollably and he felt her moan loudly before jerking on the mattress that tried to cushion her jerks.

Desperate to share those moments with her and with the taste of her body on his lips he climbed in and thrust with all his might without asking permission. She lifted her hips to receive him and he thrust again and again while he said aloud those words that he only encouraged himself to write in that little notebook and in the solitude of his room. Hundreds of feelings came flooding out of his lips as he rammed into her with all the strength that only men who are madly in love possess. And how could I not be in love with a woman like that, he said to himself as he nibbled on her neck.

-Yes...please don't stop...I need you so much..... -she whispered almost feebly.

She asked and demanded and Akim died of pleasure just listening to her. In a few days his Brenda had opened up to his needs and demanded what none of them should be silent about. God, how could I go on living without her, he thought as he pushed even harder. No, he would not leave her without a fight. He had come late to her life but he was in it now and he did not intend to leave. The past would not exist, they would write new chapters together.

He buried himself as deep as he could until he made her feel like he was there to stay when he felt her shudder and squeeze him in her warmth. They both moaned almost in tandem and Akim felt himself almost collapse over her body. They both panted for a few minutes until he was able to move to the side and hold her with all his might. He had almost no nights left to feel her by his side and that cold feeling made him freeze a heart that never wanted to die again.

Last day

I hold you in my arms and thousands are the unanswered questions. My mind tells me you'll leave like a sweet summer dream but I don't want to believe it. I hold you tight and kiss you hoping I'm wrong. Don't leave me, cries my desperate heart, don't abandon me, claim my yearning body, but my lips are only able to kiss you and beg you in silent agony, choose me....
Akim

If there was a vocabulary with which she felt that afternoon, it could be described as wonderful, spectacular, dazzling. She hadn't felt that way in years. She laughed with joy, with no qualms. She enjoyed a wonderful meal, she walked along the promenade with enthusiasm and now she was enjoying a refreshing evening in a bar. Nothing could be better. Akim went out of his way for her and although she wanted to feel a little guilty, she couldn't. She loved being the center of his attention. She loved being the center of his attention. Knowing him so young, so handsome and so attentive to her made her feel like a woman in many ways already forgotten. Desire was reflected in her deep gaze and pride flared on her lips filled with carmine red. Every smile of that man was vitamin for the most dormant of her feminine senses. With him she felt strong, enthusiastic, free? He didn't demand, he didn't ask, he only offered. He did not demand, he accepted...

-A thousand pounds for your thoughts," he said, sitting down next to her with two ice-cold beers.

-Nonsense... -He said downplaying the importance of the subject and returning to planet earth.

-Then five hundred, half of it. She looked at him curiously and he answered with that smile he only gave her. If it's nonsense, I'll have to pay less....

Brenda smiled and replied sadly.

-In my father. In everything I did to live up to him. Akim looked at him in surprise and Brenda felt the need to explain. He never wanted a daughter. He was very disappointed not to have his longed-for heir.

-Maybe they were your feelings. He said, thinking that no father could really think like that. He would have adored Lucien just as much as a boy as a girl.

-Not at all," he said with an unamused smile. He made sure to say it loud and clear so I wouldn't forget.

-It must have been very hard," he commented, leaning in tenderly.

-I'm afraid so. Even if you were to talk to a psychologist about it," she said, winking with amusement, "she would tell you that it marks you a lot. No matter how hard you try to overcome it, it's there, like a thorn that, even if you try to banish it, keeps pricking you and trying to hurt you.

-What does he look like? -he asked curiously.

-Arrogant, self-serving, aloof, classist," he said as he snorted the foam from his beer, "elitist and cold, very cold.

Akim reflected silently, thinking how many of her current self-imposed demands had to do with her father's rigidity. Now she understood his continuous quest for perfection and perpetual analysis of duties and obligations. She thought over and over again about the consequences of her actions, in fact she still could not understand how she had managed to break down his walls.

-It's your turn. She said enthusiastically and Akim watched her curiously.

She responded in amusement as he lost himself in that smile that drew him in like a little boy to a piece of candy. He was madly in love and didn't bother to hide it. These were no times to deny the undeniable.

-What do you want to know? I think I've told you everything. I ran away from a country that had too many tanks and too many bombs, I'm a single father because a woman thought I was small potatoes, my father still scolds me as if I were a child, and I have a friend who is like a brother, even though he's a bit of a fool. The rest is history. He said with a transparent smile.

-What about your mother? You never told me about her. She said interested.

-She... -Akim tried to look for a word that defined her but couldn't find one. It was not easy to talk about her, much less to Brenda. He should be very careful about what he should or should not tell. My mother loved my father very much," he said slowly analyzing each sentence. He was always her life, he loved us above all things. He said taking a long drink of beer.

In a few words, he gave an outstanding summary of his mother, even though his summary form omitted small details such as the fact that his father fell in love with another woman and wanted to leave her; his mother attempted suicide and his father returned home but nothing was as it had been before. The woman died with sorrow in her soul as she felt unable to win back the love of her life and the man never stopped feeling guilty.

He sipped a second drink hoping that the summary would be enough for him and he would not ask again. Not that he was ashamed of his mother, far from it, but he didn't want to talk about broken marriages with her. He adored his mother but it took him a long time to be able to understand and forgive his father, to tell the truth now that he recognized himself as the third in discord he understood him for the first time in all these years. You don't choose who you fall in love with and just like his father, today he was involved in a love triangle he never wanted to be a part of.

He smiled at the twists and turns of fate. For many years he hated the woman who had taken the love of his life from his mother and now he was the one fighting to take from another what he considered his by legal right. Akim smiled half-heartedly and somewhat disappointed in himself. If his mother saw him right now she would not be proud of him, in fact he was not. He looked straight ahead and bumped into those little chocolate eyes that drove him so crazy and nodded to himself. Brenda didn't need to know anything about that story. He wouldn't be the one to throw mud in his own path. He would fight for her with all his weapons and that meant little lies or big secrets for that was the way it would be.

-How old were you when he passed away?

-The worst. Sixteen. I guess that's why I rebelled and started making one mistake after another.

-You mean Lucien.

-No," he said, glad that the conversation turned away from the subject of his mother. Lucien is one of the few good things I've had in my life. Being his father is a gift of life.

Brenda smiled longingly and Akim asked interestedly.

-Have you thought about becoming a mother?

-Yes, but it was never a good time," she said sadly.

He decided not to ask again, that topic reminded him of the unmentionable one and if he did not want him in his life, much less in his thoughts.

The waitress approached Akim's call with a more than suggestive smile as she handed him the bill. The man tried to conceal the girl's clear intentions but could not help but be surprised to see a phone number written on the ticket. He offered the money and didn't make a big deal out of it.

-Brenda sounded too serial and although she tried to disguise it with a fake smile Akim was delighted. The waitress mattered little and nothing to him, but seeing her jealous was glory to his male senses.

-My heart is already committed," he said with a deep voice and his accent as always so marked.

-She is very pretty and very young. Akim...

-Or no, let's not start with that. You're going to have to try a little harder," he replied, interrupting his argument, "because for now you don't scare me.

Brenda closed her eyes and Akim could feel her head running as she made endless evaluations of shoulds and shouldn'ts and cursed under her breath. She needed time. She needed it. Time to understand what was starting between them and time to be able to prove it to him.

-Brin... my darling... -he said tenderly. This is my time. You have given it to me and I have accepted it, I refuse to lose you. I want your body and your thoughts here with me. Time will teach us the reality of our paths.

He stood up just as the waitress arrived to hand him his change and surely a reply to his suggestive invitation. Akim shook his head somewhat angrily and moving swiftly approached his doctor and without warning kissed her in the middle of the room and in front of a beautiful waitress who turned annoyed to another table.

Brenda closed her eyes at his touch and he smiled triumphantly. He adored watching her lose her composure, adored how she surrendered to his caresses and adored that little dimple under her cheek as she smiled.

-You drive me crazy," he said in a thick voice as he gave her one last kiss on the neck.

-Don't do it again," she replied, annoyed.

-But what? -He didn't know how to continue. Her reaction completely baffled him.

-I don't want you to kiss me in public again. I'm not the little girl you usually go out with. I'm not that Lola, or that silly waitress, or any other little girl.

Akim was stunned when he saw her walk out the door without looking back.

She was about to leave walking alone when he stopped her by the shoulders without any delicacy.

-Can you tell me what just happened?

-You don't understand! -she replied angrily.

-No, not really.

-For God's sake Akim, don't play dumb," she said angrily and trying to escape from his grip.

-I may be, and quite a lot, but I swear that even if I think I should apologize, I'm not quite sure why.

Brenda loosened her grip and moved so moodily that she dared not interrupt her.

-I'm not a child. -That tells you something! That... that... -She spat, looking at the bar they had left behind, "That one probably imagined I'm your mother. He replied with pain in his words.

-And you imagine that because? -He said trying to follow his reflection.

-Please Akim, don't laugh at me. You know very well why. I've been with you for too many years, too many.... People will only judge us and I can't cope with...

Brenda tried to continue but he wouldn't let her. Not again. At first he didn't imagine the cause of her displeasure but now that he was listening to her he wasn't about to let her go on with that little speech about the age difference. She had to recognize her worth and accept that any man would be crazy to have her. Any man.

-That waitress has a lot to envy you.

-Please don't make fun. She said trying to pull away but he held her by the waist.

-I'm not making fun. You are beautiful. Your body is wonderful and your age gives you a fabulous maturity. You awaken my emotions and feed my heart. Yes, my dear, that and many other young girls would envy what you are.

-Akim... please...

She looked stunned. He was sure that if he let her go she would abandon him at that very moment and all because of the damned rules of a society that put day and age on feelings.

-You are every man's dream. Don't trivialize what happened between us with some stupid wrinkles. I can't let you do that. You've given me reasons I never had. Talking to you is nourishment for my life and sex is.... -he choked on what he was about to say. Sex is much more than making love. It's feeling it, it's living it.... You deserve heaven and I'm only able to offer you my heart -. He said embarrassed to discover his feelings.

Akim -Akim is that you are not able to see?

-All I see is what's in front of me. A woman I die for every day," he said, stroking her chin and lifting her up to look at him. You ask me to justify what does not deserve to be justified. In these days you have given me what I never thought I could reach, don't you dare believe you have the right to erase with stupid rules what my heart cannot silence. I may have been slow to come into your life, you may have lived before me, but don't you dare belittle any of the kisses you give me, because they are the only thing worth living for.

He reached out and held her by the small of her back as he guided her to the car. She stopped talking and he didn't expect her to speak. He was too upset. The very thought that she was planning to leave him was driving his nerves crazy.

They were about to get into the car when Brenda unexpectedly threw herself into his arms and wrapped her hands behind his neck to offer him the most desperate and ardent of kisses. Surprised he accepted the challenge and held her tightly around the waist to press her against his body. If she needed it, he needed it even more. When their breaths calmed and Brenda parted her lips from his they were both dizzy with ecstasy. Akim didn't understand such a display in public let alone after what had just happened but he wouldn't complain. He was hot and needy. His body burned inside, he felt a compelling need to unburden himself in her, in her warmth and in her perfume. He was hard and desperate and his doctor was the only one capable of soothing him. Doubts and fears clouded him and her body was the only thing capable of calming him. The car is parked in a dark alley, he said to himself. That was crazy, Brenda was not a slut he was used to cavorting with, she had made that quite clear to him herself. He opened the back door of the car as best he could and without thinking pushed her into the seat. She looked at him intrigued when he asked hoarsely out of necessity.

-Tell me no and I'll stop.

She stretched out her arms in invitation and he jumped on her after closing the car door.

-I need to have you now. I can't wait... don't turn me away.... -he said as he kissed her full face.

-I won't do it. She replied as she stopped him with a hand on his chest.

Akim stopped his kisses thinking he had regretted it when he saw her try to pull her shirt off her shoulders. His heavy body on top of hers prevented him from doing so so so he left a little free space between them but without ceasing to devour her with his gaze.

Brenda slipped her head through the collar of her shirt and pulled it and her bra off as he watched her with his eyes dark with desire. She reached out her small hands and pulled his up and he helped her undress him. They were caressing their naked torsos and eating each other's kisses when Akim mad with need lifted her skirt with his hands. She was rubbing herself and he unzipped as best he could his jeans. That car was too small for his size and he was bumping into everything but he didn't care.

-I want to be with you... I want to do it here and now. I want to have you inside me and for you to kiss me and only me," she said with the glittering gleam of passion in her chocolate eyes.

Akim moaned wildly. She was begging like in the best of her dreams and that was a wonder to a heart as anguished as his. Maddened by the feel of her he held her buttocks and pulled her closer to his erect manhood as he thrust with all his might. He should be gentler, he thought trying to calm himself, but she aroused so many passions in him that his desires remained mere daydreams. His hands wrapped around that delicious ass as they urged her to rise to receive him. Their teeth clacked together in an attempt to possess each other and their hips matched each other impatiently to achieve the ultimate of glories. They both moaned regardless of the tightness of the car and the mirrors began to fog up amidst sighs and moans of pleasure. Akim shudderingly rummaged through his pocket but was unable to find the package, so he was about to pull away when she grabbed him by the hips.

-You are in no danger.

Akim looked at her trying to think about what she was saying but it was somewhat difficult as his blood was somewhere else and it wasn't exactly his brain.

-I can't have children. He said with deep sorrow.

-But I thought, you said.....

-That it was never the time... to adopt.... -He answered bitterly.

Akim rested his forehead on hers as he digested the information. With the utmost tenderness he spoke just millimeters from her lips.

-After Lucien I haven't done it again without protection. I'm clean, I swear.

-I believe you," she said, stretching her neck to kiss him gently.

Their tongues entwined and they both let themselves go. Akim slipped his hand between their bodies trying to reach that sensitive spot on her body as he continued to thrust relentlessly. They would come together if his life depended on it. With precise movements he caressed her again and again while she stretched her head trying to reach what he was offering her. Akim breathed in agitated breath as he did not lose any detail of her body tense with desire. Seeing her so aroused was a spectacle of gods. He buried himself deep feeling that velvety wetness caress him and had to bite his lips to restrain himself. He wished it would reach the clouds and go with him. Brenda moaned loudly as he felt her squeeze him inside her and he let go to fly beside her.

-I'm going to crush you. He said as he tried to move but she held him back.

Their bodies were pressed together, wetness ran down their legs and Akim was unable to put words to what he was feeling. Bliss was five letters too simple to express everything he felt.

Forgetting yesterday

I can't take it anymore, I'm burning up... Baby you're no angel, you corrupt with your sinful kisses a man who loves you to death.

Akim.

-Are you going to tell me something or are you already bored with me? -Brenda said with a little pout and enjoying seeing Akim doubting her departure.

-Never. He said holding her tightly in his arms and devouring her mouth with a kiss that took her breath away. Never doubt me. I may not deserve you and I may be an idiot, but never doubt how I feel about you. Akim brought her small hand wrapped in his over his chest so she could feel it beating. Ever since I held you in my arms for the first time it has been beating for you. You brought me back to life and you will take it....

Brenda had wanted to respond, to say that she did not want to see him suffer, that she too felt a before and an after. The day was clearer, the stars were more authentic, the wind sounded cheerful and everything had been brought by him. She wanted to say that those days at his side signaled a change that she was just beginning to accept, but she preferred to remain silent.

Akim bathed her body with his beautiful blue gaze and caressed her cheek with his thumb and lifting her chin with delicate gentleness deposited a tender kiss between her lips. This time without need and without desperation. He didn't need to listen to her to know her thoughts. How could that be possible? They were from different worlds, from different generations, from different countries and yet Akim knew and understood her as if he had known her forever.

They parted and he spoke as with a smile that radiated happiness he pushed her into his hotel.

-I'll pick you up at seven. You have a couple of hours to get ready. Not a minute more. I'm not going to be separated from you any longer than that. Do you understand?

Brenda nodded her head and Akim took off leaving her flying through the clouds.

-A bit possessive, isn't it?

Brenda was surprised to be caught but instantly took control of the conversation.

-Any news?

-Not really..." he said as they entered the hotel on their way to their rooms. In the last few days everything seems to have calmed down," he said with satisfaction. It seems incredible that a short time ago I was in jail and all that in days... days and days....

Brenda went into her room and sat on her bed leaving the door open for Rachel to enter. Her shoulders slumped and she knew she was well deserving of every hidden reproach from Rachel. In Akim's arms she forgot commitments, reality and time.

-I guess I owe you an explanation.

-After days of not hearing from you? No, I don't think so.

-Rachel... -She said pleadingly, "Don't make it harder for me.

-Don't be silly." Her friend looked at her curiously and she answered with her hand on her heart. I super promise you for Snoopy my sweet.

-Thank you.

-But even though we are super very friends doesn't mean I don't want to know everything in detail. Right now! -He said, taking up positions next to her on the bed.

Brenda smiled sheepishly. Rachel spoke to her without any judgment. She was simply being a good friend who was willing to listen and Brenda couldn't have been more grateful. So much for her own Jiminy Cricket saying over and over again that this was the craziest of her follies, or maybe the only one, she thought as she remembered that from her earliest youth, she had never taken too many risks.

Studying a career against her father's advice may have been the most daring thing she ever did, but after that, she simply complied with the conventions demanded by a very strict society. Her father, she thought amused, what face would he make if he knew that in addition to being a doctor for the insane, she was now a cradle robber? Yes, because twenty-six against almost forty was surely a jail sentence.

-Will you stop smiling at the wall? Sweet starts that I'm open my mind. How is the bricklayer? As fierce as he looks?

-Akim, his name is Akim," he said with a smile on his face, "Open mind?

Yeah, whatever you say, but what about under that flea market T-shirt? Are those tattooed arms real or did he go under the knife? Because I once knew a guy who had everything fake at the end. And when I say everything, I meant everything.

Brenda's eyes widened and then she started laughing with an amused Rachel following suit.

-Yes, it's all real.

-Of course the poor can't afford such luxuries, I'm so silly, I'm just curious.

Brenda shook her head as she kicked off her shoes to cross her legs on the mattress and began to speak bluntly.

-It was great. I don't know how it happened or how I was able to do it but I can just tell you that I feel in a way that I have never felt before.

-Was it that good?

-Too much," he said, covering his mouth with the back of his hand in an attempt to hide his embarrassment.

-Everything! Count everything.

-There is not much. We walked on the beach, we talked, we laughed, we told each other our dreams and we told each other about our past. But everything was so natural, so authentic, I don't know how to explain it, it's as if that's the way things should be. When I'm next to him I feel so good. You'll think I'm crazy...

-I don't," Rachel said firmly.

-Rachel, I don't know what to do.... I mean, I know this isn't right. I just committed infidelity and I should feel bad but I can't because if I close my eyes I think about it, if I breathe I think about it, if I talk it's about him. God Rachel what is wrong with me?

-It was never in your hands....

-You say that to console me. For heaven's sake, I am a married woman and he is much younger than me, and I have studies in psychology and I know cases like this, why am I not able to use my own advice?

Brenda leaned back on the mattress looking for some mercy to her reasoning and Rachel sat even closer to look into her eyes with complete tenderness.

-I think the bricklayer woke you up.

-What do you mean? -He asked as he leaned back on his elbows to listen more carefully.

-Since that fateful day you tried to be what you were not. You hid your true self to become what he wanted. The male child, the perfect wife, the educated professional, always fulfilling his ideal prototype mold.

Brenda knew what day he was referring to. The one when they both overheard her father in the kitchen ranting to her mother about the huge list of imperfections a female daughter had.

-He wanted me to study law," she said, trying to show her friend her apparent rebellion against her father. I'm a fraud..... In all these years I've tried to help people thinking I could do it when I haven't really been able to get my own life on track.

Brenda hurriedly compiled the highlights of the past twenty years and discovered something she didn't like at all. Everyone always expected of her, but did she ever worry about what she expected of herself?

The days and years went by one after the other and in all of them she saw herself as a freelancer always doing what she had to do without even allowing herself to think about whether that was what she really wanted.

-You are not. We are all survivors of our past and you are no better or worse than the rest of the mortals. You strived for perfection believing that order would be established in your life but the bricklayer showed you that there was a gap.

-What about Max?

-This is not about Max and you know it.

Brenda covered her eyes with her hands tightly.

-No. I hadn't felt it for a long time and I didn't want to accept it. Rachel looked at her curiously and Brenda clarified, "I'm not just talking about sex, I'm talking about life. The passion to smile, to be happy, to feel free?

-Rachel watched her for a few moments and then began to smile mischievously. She looked at her intrigued and the woman gave an amused laugh.

-And while we're on the subject of passion for life, how about it?

-I'm not talking," he said, standing up at full speed. I'd better shower soon because he'll be by to pick me up in no time.

-I already thought it was strange that he gave you a lot of time off. So we're talking about a beast?

-Rachel...

-Donkey or kitten? You look at him and those eyes sparkle with fire and those tattoos are creepy and of course you say foal, sure foal, but then he approaches his doctor and it seems that his character has fallen to his feet and then you say, well kitty....

Brenda stopped in front of the closet unhooking a black dress to look at it carefully.

-What are you talking about?

-I say Foal," he said moving his hips up and down with speed, "or sweet kitten.....

-I'll pretend I didn't hear anything. She shook her head and picked up her high heels to put them next to her dress.

-What a romantic dinner. That's kitty.

-That's because it's our last night.... -He answered with heavy sadness.

-Have you agreed that you are a summer fling? Maybe it's for the best, after all he's so... so...

-So what? -She asked somewhat annoyed with her friend's tone.

-Poor, foreign, little thing.... Sweet, you know I support you and I totally understand that you wanted a change in your life, I'm even glad to see you being yourself, but to change Max for a bricklayer? That's not for you. You can play with them but never get involved.

-We're not talking about any future." She replied annoyed, although she had to admit that Rachel was saying out loud what the whole of humanity would surely think.

-You're not thinking of continuing this, are you?

-I am a married woman. Why did she say that?

-And I do threesomes. That has nothing to do with it. What I'm saying is that you're not like that. You won't know how to deal with a lover and the thing with you baguette and chives isn't real.

-Bread and onions," Rachel looked at her with wide eyes and Brenda clarified, "With you bread and onions. That's the saying.

-I know, but it's cooler with French ingredients," Brenda lifted her shoulders as she shook her head in surrender. The important thing is that you realize that you and a bricklayer have nothing in common.

-You mean go back to Max like it's nothing?

-I mean if it's not Max there will be another one but one more in line with your... style.

-I'm going to take a shower. He said with a dry throat.

Brenda locked herself in the bathroom not wanting to hear much more. She waited for the bedroom door to close before sitting on the edge of the shower and crying like a little girl without her teddy bear. Rachel was wrong. Akim wasn't the simpleton she thought but there was no point in arguing, there was something about what her friend had said that she was very right about, she wasn't a woman of two men. With one she had been with half her life, they had built a world together and with the other... with the other she felt alive. She turned on the faucet deciding that a warm bath would be much better than a quick shower. She wiped away her tears and began to undress when she fell into a reflection she hadn't thought of until now.

"He hasn't asked you to stay by his side? " She thought as she immersed herself in the water with the jasmine salts courtesy of the hotel. "He never mentioned wanting anything more. What if what he's looking for is to be a one-time lover?"

Brenda couldn't help but feel a little annoyed that she thought he only desired her as a body but on the other hand that made her feel lustfully carnal.

She thought and thought until her head hurt. She came out of the bathroom, dried her hair, combed her hair, perfumed and chose the sexiest of her lingerie sets. She adjusted inside the delicate black dress and stepped into the heels taking care of every detail. She looked in the mirror and closed her eyes as she saw her reflection. She may not have been a girly girl but she was ready to offer the best of her visions.

"Liar." She said guiltily to herself. With a relationship proposal or as simple lovers, her body was screaming for her to be in Akim's arms again. She longed for this man. She adored how he made her feel and suffered just imagining that this would be their last night together. That was the reality, a dreaded one that she could not yet acknowledge out loud.

Forever and ever

The clock hastily marks the hours when you will no longer be there.
My soul trembles just to think that tomorrow I will not have you or
you won't even remember me. I am a man and like everyone else I cry in silence and between mute cries I beg you to look at me, to stay by my side, to give me the gift of your love tonight and destroy the cruelty of a destiny without you.

Akim

Akim waited at the entrance while taking big puffs on his cigarette. She didn't like it and he was ready to quit, but another day, today he wasn't in the mood for change. This was their last night together on the island. Tomorrow they would each return to their lives in the city and the distance separating them would be thousands of light years. She would work in his office and he would watch her behind the glass door without being able to caress her, like a distant star in a universe that you can admire but never belong to. He had to show her so many things and make her feel a few hundred more, but damn it, he only had one night left. Just one night. - Fuck... -He said when he saw her as he hurriedly crushed half of the cigarette in the ashtray by the door.

Brenda stared at him as she walked at a slow pace like an angel descended from heaven, or at least that's what it seemed to him. An angel floating in the air and smiling at him. Only to him.

"I'm not going to let you leave." He thought as he opened the door for her to step out and they stood face to face.

-You look beautiful. He commented, giving her a delicate kiss on the cheek and caressing the softness of her dress around her waist.

-You're not bad yourself.

-Are you flirting with me doctor? -he said, raising a dark eyebrow in amusement.

-What if I say yes? - she answered, tempting him with a mischievous look.

-I would tell you not to. He said seriously and surprising Brenda, who instantly tensed up.

Akim, delighted with his doubts, slowly approached her ear so that he could feel that delicate aroma of jasmine, vanilla and skin so typical of her. His body responded to the mere touch of that woman but he was not frightened, he knew he was lost to her and it was foolish to deny it. He lifted his hand and trembled as he caressed the soft skin of her neck beneath his rough fingers. She was so soft, so real, so warm. His voice low with tension and desire, he brought his lips close to whisper in her ear with clarity, passion and a quota of sincere reality.

-Before I met you I was already yours. You don't need to conquer me.

Akim placed a crude kiss on her neck and sucked gently on that swollen vein that was throbbing harder and harder. She leaned against his chest as if trying to seek refuge and he moaned in bliss. That's what he was looking for and that's what he wanted. His doctor thought too much, studied and pondered things too much, and he needed her like that. Overcome by passion. That was the only way he could keep her. Gently he finished his caresses and pulled her away, holding her by the arms. She still had her eyes closed and Akim would have liked to take her in his arms, take her up to the room and walk her from beginning to end but that was not the plan.

-We're leaving," he said as he guided her with his hand on the small of her back toward the car.

-And that place is? -He commented with a small thread of voice.
-All in good time, my Brin. All in good time.

Brenda got out of the car guided by the hand of a real gentleman, or at least that's what she hoped to be that night because otherwise it would be of little use to have to endure the damn tie and his blissful obsession to hang him. He was wearing one of those suits the actors wore at the Oscars, a pristine Prussian blue. He doubted very much whether the suit was exactly Prussian blue and whether the tie was a delicate burgundy but he trusted the clerk. He knew he would have to sell his father to pay off his debt to Philip but he was delighted with the result. She looked at him with longing desire and he couldn't think of anything else to do but satisfy her. Life could be a real shit and in most cases it sucked but now he understood perfectly well the rich, in love and happy people because at times like this the air was less thick and the nights much warmer.

They walked together to the reserved table on the beach. The views were simply spectacular, hiding none of the wonders of the island. Set in a small, secluded cove to the north, they sat enjoying the cool sea breeze. The sun was no longer visible on the horizon and the orange light of its almost hidden reflections illuminated a dark blue and calm sea.

Akim pulled his chair closer to hers to cover her small hand with his. If the world stopped at that very moment and he was told that this was where his existence ended, he wouldn't bother to argue because he had known the meaning of life. She was so focused on enjoying the horizon that she didn't want to interrupt it. Her profile was outlined by the light of the burning torches and her hair caressed his shoulders thanks to the delicate movement of the sea breeze. Yes, she was an attractive, beautiful woman, but her essence did not lie in her long hair or her cherry lips, no, Brenda was the energy of a transparent gaze, the sage of strong ideals, the loyalty of friendship, the warmth of her sinless smile. With total indiscretion he observed every detail of her face, understanding the perfect combination that made her so different from the others. She didn't know it but she was a jewel in short supply. He shifted in his seat and had to smile as he saw himself uncovered in his detailed analysis.

-What is it? -she said curiously, but he didn't answer. He just looked at her and let the fire in her eyes speak for him.

The waiter approached at that very moment and Akim smiled as he saw her puzzled face. She hadn't answered him and he knew Brenda well enough to know that at this moment she would be eating her elbows in intrigue.

-I can advise you a starter of honeyed croquettes of ham one hundred percent Iberian with a farmer's salad that you can share. It is a real delicacy. Said the waiter proudly.

He waited for her to shake her head before accepting the proposal.

-For the second course and if you allow me, the Bullit de peix and arroz banda is a specialty that will bring you back to Ibiza on the first flight. He commented amused.

Akim nodded as he tried not to focus on the prices. The place was as wonderful and unique as the euros in each of their dishes. He closed his eyes and nodded again when they advised a soft, refreshing Catalan white wine although he didn't comment that he had no idea where exactly that region was located.

They talked, dined and laughed like a real couple and their chests stretched wider and wider with unique pride. Inside the restaurant, a soft melody began to play and Brenda smiled as she turned and saw the lights of the lounge come into view through the glass walls.

-Do you want to come in? We can ask for dessert to be served inside," he said, completely devoted to his smile.

-It's a beautiful place, it looks like a paradise hidden between the sky and the sea...

-I'm so glad you like it. How are you taking care of them?

A tall man dressed in cream-colored pants and a white shirt approached smiling as he rested his hands firmly behind the back of Brenda's chair. They both looked at him curiously and the man smiled, revealing perfect white teeth.

-Sorry for my clumsiness. I am Rafa Sabater and I am the owner of this humble place.

Brenda smiled delightedly at him and was about to get up to accept his greeting when the man responded with the same charm with which he had approached her.

-No, please don't get up. He said with a confidence that Akim found excessive. I just saw that you were in the vip area farthest away and I thought that whenever you wanted you could come in and enjoy the piano music session that will start in just a few minutes.

-Yes, of course. Thank you very much. Brenda answered too quickly and Akim felt a small pang of disappointment. The truth was that he had no plans to share her with anyone.

-Then I'll be happy to see her again. The man winked at her, making her delicate skin redden and Akim stirred in annoyance. Young man, let me congratulate you," he said, dropping his perfect sensual and Latin gaze on Brenda, "for your good taste.

"Young man, was that guy trying to play to his advantage of incipient gray hair in front of her?" Akim was about to reply when the man walked away without further ado. "Fucking prick," he thought angrily.

-How kind of you.

-He likes you. He replied, taking a sip of the smooth, cool Spanish wine, although to tell the truth, the Spanish were starting to kick him in the liver.

-Nonsense, he is the owner and his duty is to be nice to everyone.

-Whatever you say." He drained his glass in one gulp and stood up, trying to control a temper that did not always work in his favor.

-Let's go. Let's see what this fabulous pianist is like. He said offering her his hand to get up from the seat although he hoped she would refuse.

-If you want, we can leave. He said with a sorrow that made him curse silently. Damn him. He had to be more careful. Brenda wasn't just any girl. She was a woman with brains and she could see where many could barely see.

-No." He replied as he pulled her to his body and kissed her possessively. He needed to show her that he was there for her. Their mouths caressed each other timidly at first but after a few seconds the passion that always existed between them ignited like a dry log. He squeezed her buttocks to imprison her even more against his body as he smiled victoriously. He was delighted with her reaction and her happiness had nothing to do with the Spanish latin lover watching them from the living room.

The evening, although most pleasant, was turning out to be too long, or at least that's how it seemed to him when the pianist began the third song. Brenda was enjoying sitting on a single wide-winged sofa and he was sitting on the armrest without leaving her side for a minute.

-Shall we leave...? I want to have you all to myself," he whispered in her ear.

Brenda looked into his eyes and melted under his gaze. He wanted to get her to the hotel as soon as possible.

-Just a moment. I'll be right back. She got up on her way to the toilet and Akim smiled like a child with a bag full of sweets. The perfect Spaniard came to her side and her sweetness disappeared in an instant.

-Everything to your liking?
-Yes, thank you. He said curtly.
-Tourists?
-Yes.
-Will they stay long?
"Don't you get tired of asking? he thought more and more irritated.
-Tomorrow.
-A pity...
-I'm sorry? -Akim didn't quite know what those words meant, but he sensed that he wouldn't like the explanation.
-I want to say that the woman is charming. Elegant, impeccable, beautiful, qualities that have been in short supply lately.

Akim began to choke on his own saliva. He didn't want to answer, he knew himself and his lack of self-control too well. Could it be that the guy wanted him to smash his face in just like that?

I'm forty-five and I could tell you that I can tell a complete woman from head to toe.

-Are you trying to tell me something? -He said as he clenched and unclenched his fists to restrain himself.

-Not at all, you strike me as a very astute young man.

Akim began to stretch and stiffen his arms. He wasn't looking for a fight but if that guy kept talking he'd punch him in the mouth and to hell with the dim lighting, the Italian leather sofas and the piano player straight out of the sixties.

-I'm not going to deny that she caught my attention. At first I didn't pay much attention to you, but seeing the way she looks at you, it's clear that she doesn't mind your lack of... etiquette. She said looking him up and down.

-Etiquette... -Akim stammered in a low voice, searching the floor for the patience he was losing.

-Let's see boy, that woman is not in your league and you know it. How's that? Good, isn't she?

Akim knew his patience had been broken the moment he heard the insinuation of the words garter and good. Rage coursed through his blood and overpowered his fist much faster than his reason. The left hand hit him straight in the jaw causing the man to fall like a tower of cards. He looked down at the ground with all the hatred he could muster waiting for a response when her voice brought him back to reality.

-What's going on? -She spoke in annoyance.

-We are leaving.

He grabbed her by the elbow and practically dragged her toward the door. He had to get out of there before he showed her more of what he didn't want to show her. That was one Akim he didn't want to show. Not to her. He did not wish to be the man who first struck and then asked questions. The one who had to defend his position with his fists. The one who had escaped a war without looking back. The one who accused his father again and again for possessing a forbidden love and whom he never knew how to understand... the one who always judged without thinking of his pain, never, until now.

-I'm sorry... -. He pulled the car to the side in the darkness of the road knowing he had ruined the evening. She wasn't talking and that made him feel worse than he already did.

-Are you going to tell me what happened? You're not like that.

-You don't know anything about me. He shook his head

-Why don't you tell me what I don't know? Don't you think I've earned your trust?

Akim turned off the engine and pressed his forehead against the steering wheel.

-You would run away.

-Try it.

-No.
-I'm not going anywhere. Trust me.
Akim was denying more and more strongly.
-Why akim, why did you hit him?
He did not answer. He felt their questions like an interrogation drilling into his brain. In a few seconds he felt like a teenager and being berated by the cops as they dropped him off at his house in front of his parents' disappointed gaze. No, it wasn't right, nothing was right. For a moment did he believe that an expensive suit and a rented car would make him into someone different? That jerk had pegged him the first time around. "She doesn't play in your league." No, of course she didn't. No matter how much he spent on his clothes or how well he hid his tattoos, their worlds didn't intersect.

-I was diagnosed as violent," he said, knowing that his honesty would cost him the end of his dream with her. Unstable emotions to be more exact.

-How?

-EITD. Emotional instability personality disorder. Emotionally unstable with displays of self-destructive behavior. You alternate rapidly between different emotions and can go from despair to euphoric joy in a very short period of time.

-I know what TIE means, but who diagnosed you?

-At the age of fifteen. After several entries to the barracks my parents were forced to take me for some kind of treatment, which of course didn't do much good.

-And those fights were where?

-Neighborhood, school, wherever. I would strike first and then it would be seen. Attack was always my best tactic.

She stroked her chin as if she was thinking and Akim felt his nerves were killing him. She was thinking but she didn't seem upset, why wasn't she?

-Do you fight very often now? -she asked interested.

"What! How, why is he asking instead of running for help?" he thought in confusion.

-I don't remember. No, I think I've been controlling myself lately," he said, puzzled.

-Then it must be a long time ago, I mean, not counting tonight. Akim looked at her with his eyes out of their sockets. What was going on? -Now tell me what exactly that man said to you.

-Are you analyzing me? -he said incredulously.

-That's not what I asked. She answered like a serious doctor to a patient.

-I appreciate it, but I don't think...

-What did she say? - He sentenced with an emphaticness that Akim would have laughed out loud if it wasn't because he was afraid of losing her. That man provoked you, what were his exact words?

-That we belonged to different leagues. He confessed, feeling somewhat humiliated.

-I understand.

-What do you understand? What is this all about? And why aren't you calling the police to rescue you? I'm a fucking psycho.

-Don't be silly. You're not that." He said, playing down her words.

-Dumb? -That woman would have to be out of her mind to provoke him after what she confessed, just like that.

I don't know what studies this so-called professional had, but I had no idea.

-Woman, it was a woman. He said, holding back his laughter when he saw his doctor's indignant face.

-Well, whatever it was, I had no idea. A teenager in a country at war and trying to survive is normal to use anger as a protection mechanism. These are normal and totally understandable behaviors. Supposedly healthy people would react exactly the same way in similar circumstances," he said as if he were reading a very accurate diagnosis. When you left that place and sought refuge for yourself and your family, the episodes of fighting stopped. Otherwise you would remember. You may have a strong temper that you must master but that has nothing to do with an identity disorder....

Akim was beginning to think she was the real good kind but he didn't say so, but just listened to every word that described him perfectly. His childhood, his fears, his defensive strokes, all had perfect explanation under Dr. Klein's prism. His Dr. Klein, he thought every minute more in love.

-... that man removed a complex that although based on an absolute reality, you will have to assume. He called you little case and that hurt you, I would have hit him too -. she said amused.

Akim wrinkled his nose at the word complexes and Brenda grinned

-I can imagine what you are thinking, and yes, there are some complexes besides the typical ones of I'm fat, I have a big nose or my breasts are too small. Women are not the only ones with complexes. She said amused.

Akim smiled with her and walked over as he held her by the shoulders to speak to her with the most adorable sincerity.

-Does this mean you are not afraid of me?

-Akim I fear you very much but it has nothing to do with violence or anything like that. I fear you and very much but it's not your fists that scare me.

-Oh no? -He asked, enveloping her in his gaze, "And what are you afraid of, doctor?

Brenda didn't answer and Akim didn't wait for her to make up her mind. He kissed her like a man possessed. She offered him a confidence that even his own parents had never offered him. Blessed was his psychology that offered him a second chance. If she was right, and he hoped she was right, he would leap from his world into hers to unite their destinies.

With his skin burning with desire he let go with very little willpower from those lips that made him feel like the most tender of poets. He started the car and accelerated with determination. The night was beginning. He would take her to that special hotel he had booked for his last night on the island and pounce on her naked body. Tomorrow might not be very clear between them but tonight he would play all his cards on a winning horse. He could afford no other choice. Brenda had confessed to him the lack of passion she felt in many things in her daily life and he was willing to show her all the passion that existed in this world and beyond.

The last night

Stretch out your hands and gather in your warmth this heart that beats only for you.

Akim

Brenda wanted to ask why they were in a different hotel from the previous nights but Akim did not give her time to inquire. She was carried almost on her back to a small wooden house that was located on the beach in a place far from civilization. The lights were dimly lit but it was clear that everything was ready for their arrival. They made their way with the simple light of the stars guiding their steps. Akim walked fast as he held her hand trying to hurry her along. She tried but it would have been better if he allowed her to take off her heels that dug into the sand, she thought amused.

-Wait... -she said, pointing to her buried shoes, but he ignored her. He just took her in his arms and entered the house through a huge glass door that opened wide.

-Where are we?

Akim deposited her in the middle of the large bed as he threw her clothes on the floor one by one. He was in a hurry, as if the clothes were burning and she felt her skin starting to burn as well and not exactly from the heat of the summer night.

The tie and shirt flew aside and his libido ignited. He had that power. He would arouse her without even touching her. His gaze darkened into an ever deepening sea blue and Brenda felt like the most desired woman of all women. That man exuded sensuality and desire from every pore and all for her. Her female hormones clapped ecstatically as he undid his pants and showed her the potency of his desire.

-So we're spending the night here? -She said somewhat nervously as she felt the center of his undivided attention.

He shook his head as he approached slowly and gloriously naked.

-No? Shall we go?

Akim crawled across the bed as he positioned himself on top of her who was still dressed.

-We've already talked too much," he said, caressing her neck with his lips until he reached her shoulders and dragged the straps of her dress with his teeth. No more diagnoses for today. From now on, I'll rule the night," he said, making her forget about anything else but his caresses on her skin.

XXX

The whole night, one could not be more exhausted and happier. To say satisfied was a very, very understatement. The light of dawn illuminated the large window of the room and the sound of the waves of the sea together with her soft breathing were angelic music to his ears.

Everything ends

I'll be your lover, your master or your destiny, tell me what you desire
and I will give it to you, give me your love and I will always protect it.

Akim

He woke up with some tiredness in his body. He had barely slept a few hours, he thought happily as he opened his eyes and recognized where he was. With complete parsimony he reached out his arms to wrap them around the soft, warm body next to him but did not find it. The sheets beside her were stretched out and cold. Abruptly and without finishing waking up she sat up in bed trying to calm herself. She couldn't have left him. Not after the night they had spent together. He opened and closed his eyes trying to look for her around the room when he heard barely a murmur coming from the bathroom. Breath filled his lungs again. She was there, she hadn't left him. He closed his eyes feeling like an idiot for feeling so insecure but he couldn't help it. Brenda aroused doubts and a lack of confidence that upset him to the core. The women he barely knew always labeled him as cold, indifferent and even insensitive, if they saw him now, trembling with fear at the mere thought of losing her.

Brenda was talking on the phone and although he initially thought it would be a conversation with Rachel now her barely audible tone made him doubt it. He pulled on the boxer shorts he found over the night lamp and stealthily approached the door trying to listen. He could barely hear anything. He tried to get a little closer but the weight of his burly body made a floorboard creak a little too loudly.

"Shit," he thought as he felt a splinter dig into the sole of his foot. He lifted it up trying to remove it. With one hand he leaned against the wall to keep his balance while with the other he tried to remove the splinter but always with his ear as close to the door as possible. Brenda on the other side stopped talking and became extremely nervous. Seeing his pathetic image reflected in the mirror made him feel even more stupid than usual. Half naked, with one foot in his hand and one ear pressed against the door like a neighbor in flip-flops did not leave him in a good position. He tried to get away before being caught, but when fate is not on your side, it is not on your side. Without knowing very well how, he slipped, dropping his full eighty kilos in the middle of the room. The wood creaked under his body and his buttocks hit the perfectly polished wood.

"Fuck." He thought as damaged more morally than physically, he threw himself head first onto the bed. If he looked like an asshole he'd rather be one on the bed and not bawled out on the floor for gossiping.

Brenda opened the door in surprise. She was sure she had heard the noises. The nightstand was somewhat moved and the bedside lamp was lying on its side as it was knocked over when his body landed on the bed but he preferred to ignore the facts. He was lying on the bed with his arms under his neck in a relatively dignified position.

-All right?

She was dressed, her hair was pulled back in a high ponytail and her gaze was darting around the room as if searching for something. She wasn't looking at him and that stoked all his fears. The conversation on the phone wasn't with Rachel.... He was sure now.

Akim dragged his hand over his tousled hair trying not to let jealousy get the better of him.

-What's wrong? -She still didn't answer. She found her second shoe in the corner of the room and began to put it on. You're not going to talk to me? You're just going to walk away? Is that how you want to end it with me?

The woman with her sandals on and sitting on the small sofa, put her cell phone in her purse and let her body fall forward.

-I can't. I can't. I can't," her shoulders heaved. I'm not a liar.

Akim swallowed dryly. There was the conversation he knew was coming. No, Brenda was no liar and that led them down only two paths. Either she'd leave the unmentionable or she'd leave him. Seven days versus almost twenty years. You didn't have to do a lot of math to know who was winning and who was losing. He took a deep breath choked with grief. He had thought about this many times, even before sharing his bed and even though it hurt and he knew it was a decision he didn't know if he could bear he said in plain words what his heart didn't feel.

-I can wait. He said clenching his fists to avoid hitting the blissful lamp still lying down and denying his own lie.

-What are you saying?

Brenda looked into his eyes for the first time and found them shining. She had been crying. She cursed herself a thousand times for being the one to put her through that, but what about him? He hadn't asked to fall in love with the wrong person either. Society may have told him over and over again what his place was, but his heart didn't want to hear about positions and obligations signed on sad papers.

Brenda showed him a way of life where he could wake up with a smile and that was enough for a spirit as thirsty as his. He would lie, cheat and say everything he didn't feel if with her he could get the time he needed because otherwise he would die in that bed.

-I understand that your life did not begin with me. Fate played a trick on me. Let's just say I was too late for the race, but I'm not going to let myself be beaten.

Akim walked over to the couch and stroked her hair gently. He curled his fingers into the softness of her hair and shivered lost in the memories of the happiest night of his life. He was sure those images would never fade from his memory.

-I shouldn't have let it happen....

Akim felt his heart tearing inside. Hearing her regret about what he considered the most beautiful thing in his life was not a good thing.

-You regret it... -she said in a whisper more for him than for her,

-No, that's the worst of it, that I don't regret anything that has happened.

Brenda lifted her head to look at him as a tear rolled down her cheek. She stroked it away and wiped it away with a finger as she squatted down to be on the same level. His confession offered her a thread of hope she wanted to cling to with her teeth.

-I don't either," he said, placing a soft kiss on her lips and resting his forehead on hers. God knows you're the best thing that's happened to me in years.

-And you are what I thought would no longer exist.

-Brin, I'm so sorry, I swear that if I could have let you go, but I can't, you are engraved in fire. I can't let you go because if you leave with me I'll lose the oxygen to breathe. With you pain doesn't exist and hope is so real....

-I have to go. He said unwillingly.

-I am not going to lose you, not without a fight. He confessed with full sincerity.

-What do you want from me?

-Whatever you decide.

-And you? Are you sure of what you are asking for?

-From the first moment I saw you.

-Why are you doing this to me? -she said, shedding a second tear.

-You already know that," he said slowly.

-It is impossible, such a short time ago....

Akim grabbed her by the shoulders and pulled her close to his body. Yes it was possible and he knew it firsthand.

-You're here," he said, pointing to his heart.

-But I can't...

-You just have to let it out... Brin... -he said, knowing that he would say what he had never said to anyone before. I love you.

She pulled her body away from his to look into his face. Her heart skipped a beat as she watched those little chocolate eyes melt for him. She had started to come clean and she wasn't going to stop. It was now or never.

-From the first moment I saw you. I love you senselessly and without reason. I'm not able to think of anything else but having you with me. I know that the differences separate us and that we have more things against us than for us but I can't deny it one more minute. I want you so much that my chest tightens and my hands shake from caressing you. I want you so much that you hurt. Not having you is agony without consolation, losing you rips my heart out with my hands.

Brenda shed salty tears that reached her lips and he lifted her chin to wipe them away with his lips. Never in her life had she expressed her feelings so clearly and loudly to anyone. Her lips reached his and their tongues intertwined at first shyly and then became a desperate act. Her small fingers entwined behind his neck and he tightened his grip around her waist to lift her from the chair and lay her down on the bed. He wanted her, needed her. He had to feel her again. He had to penetrate her and feel that peace her body offered him as it enveloped him. No, he would not let her go.

Reality

You leave and my sight is lost after a few minutes. memories that will soon kill me. Love returns and let us begin together what should never have ended.

Akim

Brenda arrived at the airport accompanied by Akim, who even though he was leaving on a much later flight, insisted on accompanying them. Rachel chatted away and she felt grateful to her friend. Her head was already in too many tangles to have to explain herself to an uncomprehending friend. She sat on the waiting bench while Akim wandered off to buy some refreshments and Rachel some perfumes at the duty free store. She was going home. She had told Max on the phone and he had replied that it was time. He sounded angry. He was still in Paris but his voice showed his displeasure. She tried to calm him down but hiding in the restroom after spending the night with your lover was not a very good time.

"Lover..." He thought as he squeezed his forehead. Can this be real? Is this happening to me?

-My father was right. I am a fraud of a woman.

-What was I right about? -Rachel asked as she sat down with a bag full of perfume.

-Did I say it out loud?

Rachel looked at her with saucer-like eyes and Brenda smiled half-heartedly.

-I'm not crazy if that's what you think, or maybe I am? -She said to herself trying to psychoanalyze herself looking for an explanation to so much insanity.

-You are not crazy.

-So what would you call him? - He said pointing with his eyes at Akim.

-Human, sweet, I would call you human. That... that worker, he may not be my kind of guy at all but I can't deny that the boy is ready to dunk the whole baguette.

-Rachel! -Brenda was surprised by the comment, which in someone like her was a huge compliment to Akim.

-What! I am not blind and I understand you perfectly well.

-Well, I don't and I have no idea what I'm going to do.

-You're not thinking of talking to Max?

-Of course I have to talk to him. She said with conviction.

-Look sweet, you may be a little confused. This is your first time but it's a lot less serious than you think.

-Are you telling me I have to cheat on my husband?

-Baby, my George and I are a little more varied in bed and that doesn't mean we don't love each other. I understand that having bland Max as your only lover for a long time would do that to you.

-I respect your lifestyle and sex," she said in a tired voice, "but I can't cheat on Max with a lover. I would feel like a liar.

-Then don't rush your decisions. Take your time. Fresh sex is always the best.

Akim approached with the refreshments and they both fell silent instantly. Ideas were bubbling in their brains at a thousand degrees Celsius. Rachel was not at all misguided. Passion with Akim was a fire that consumed her inside but that was perfectly natural. Young, handsome and virile he was a living flame to her senses but that flame could be extinguished when the novelty wore off. The feelings could be mere confused sexual passion. If that were so he would be destroying a life and a marriage for something that would symbolize nothing more than a romp? She looked at Akim who smiled at her instantly and felt again that heat that burned her whenever he focused on her with the fire of his gaze. No, that didn't look like anything passing but she needed to hold on to a nail even if it was burning.

-It looks like we're all going home.

Brenda looked up to find Esperanza and Peter each dragging a small suitcase.

The three of them stood up and merged in a strange greeting. On vacation, three-day acquaintances feel like friends for years, but as is well known, friendships are magnified on vacation, she thought amused.

The women talked non-stop. Esperanza was telling Rachel the latest news about the Amazons and although her friend should feel annoyed by the amount of problems she had had because of the leader of the group, the truth was that she seemed interested. The lady at the microphone announced the last warning message to board and Peter approached the women to say goodbye and remind them aloud.

-So we'll see you at the opening of our tearoom?

-Do you have a tea room? -He said, listening to the information for the first time.

-Yes, and we open it in three days. Esperanza said happily, "You have to come.

-Of course they will. Akim just promised me that they will go together. Said the Peter as he led his girl by the elbow.

Brenda raised her eyebrows waiting for an explanation but the man raised his shoulders in a can't-do sign.

They all walked toward the tunnel up to the plane but she lagged behind. She wished to say goodbye to Akim without witnesses. He would be traveling on another flight and although she considered herself a most independent woman she couldn't feel a small twinge of sorrow at having to part. Rachel and the couple boarded the plane. She paused to say goodbye when he held her tightly around the waist and in one motion turned her around to face her against his body.

-He whispered before giving her a kiss she would remember for the rest of her life.

Her heels rose to better reach his lips as Akim pressed her back against his body. They kissed like a pair of teenagers in need of intimacy and Brenda felt a little embarrassed as they broke apart and noticed how the stewardess smiled at them and ticked her watch in warning.

-I have to go." He did not answer. He just looked at her with some sadness in his eyes. He wanted to tell her that everything would be all right, that she shouldn't worry, that something good should come out of it, but the words wouldn't come out. Everything he promised or said could be lies.

He walked as if his feet were full of lead. She did not want to leave him. Something inside her stirred her insides. She stopped and did something unthinkable even for her. She turned and was about to run to his side to give him one last kiss when she collided with a broad, hard torso that held her by the waist.

-If you didn't come, I was going to look for you. He said biting her mouth in a possessive kiss.

The stewardess coughed and the two parted in a lethargic mood.

-What time do you arrive? -she asked interestedly as she walked backwards.

-Around twelve o'clock. He answered without taking his eyes off her.

-Will we see each other?

-No doubt about it. She said giving him what for her was the most sensual of smiles.

-Ma'am, you have to go upstairs. The stewardess commented, showing her the watch.

She walked down the corridor but not without glancing sidelong each time back at Akim who refused to leave. She raised her hand in farewell and he responded with the sweetest of smiles. He boarded the plane and collapsed into the seat next to Rachel.

-All right?

-No, nothing's right, I'm not right, this is not right.... Oh Rachel, what's wrong with me? Everything I think or explain to myself blurs when I'm next to her. I want to die... -she said while leaning her head on her friend's shoulder.

Rachel did not respond. He had already given her plenty of advice. Everything was in her hands. Truth or sadness, passion or marriage, fidelity or lies, cards that were mixed trying to win a game that was already started.

Brenda closed her eyes and began to fall asleep. She had had practically no rest. The night was a continuous whisper of kisses and caresses. She had never experienced anything like it. If she breathed slowly she was still able to feel Akim's hands on her body. The hairs on her skin stood on end at the memory. In his arms she felt like a woman. A plain and simple woman. One who was not beholden to commitments or the needs of others. One who could be herself without fear of making mistakes. One who didn't need to apologize for what she wasn't.....

Return to the truth

There will be no other love like you, there will be no one else but you,
neither in this life nor in the next. I will carry you tattooed in my soul
from here to eternity.
Akim

Akim walked around his house like a caged dog. Her jaw tightened as she wrote the message number ... she couldn't even remember them anymore. She didn't answer any of them. The plane was delayed and arrived in the middle of the morning, he tried to talk to her as soon as he could, but nothing. He arrived home around four in the morning and did not have the courage to go and wake her up. The truth is that he had wanted to go and get her out of bed or rather lay her down again, but reason was stronger. He got up at the crack of dawn, he had barely rested but he wanted to talk to her. He tried again and again but nothing. It was after eleven o'clock and she still did not answer any of his messages. Angry, he checked that he had no answer and threw the cell phone on the sofa.

-Dad! -Lucien appeared with open arms.

-Hi, little one. How are you?

-I'm fine, in spite of Grandpa," said the little boy as he climbed onto his father's shoulders.

-No way, kiddo. You know you had to take a shower. Said the defamed grandfather.

-It was not dirty!

Akim kissed his son on the cheeks and placed him back on the ground.

-Some equally serious news. He replied amused.

The boy closed his mouth moving his lips downward in a sign of not that I remember and his grandfather laughed out loud.

-His grandfather looked at him curiously, but the boy was kicking the toes of his own sneakers, pretending to be distracted.

-I see... So you think he deserves what I brought back from my trip for him? -He commented with apparent intrigue to his father and causing the boy to open his eyes wide towards his grandfather waiting for an opinion.

-I think so.

-He's in my bed." He didn't finish saying it when Lucien bolted for his father's room.

They both smiled in amusement as they watched him speed off.

-Has it been very difficult?

-How was your trip? Did you find what you were looking for?

Akim ducked his head and at that moment felt just as embarrassed as his son had a few minutes earlier. He had run away without much explanation and his father seemed willing to listen to what he wasn't sure he wanted to explain.

-I had to leave... -He said, thinking that this sentence explained everything.

-And that's a good summary power. The man with as much experience as gray hair smiled as he tapped him on the shoulder.

-You know I'm not very good at talking. He said thinking that with Brenda it was totally different. He confessed to her feelings and fears that he didn't express to anyone. Would that be one of the many consequences when you become an idiot in love?

-I'm afraid that's partly my fault. I guess it's all about genes and their consequences," he commented with a touch of guilt. His son didn't speak and his father felt sorry for him. You were away for a few days, I guess you found her. He said with a mischievous smile.

-What exactly do you know? -Akim looked at him quizzically and his father sat down on the couch to talk calmly.

-Son, I'd have to be stupid not to realize that this is all about skirts.

The young man scratched his forehead trying to find the right words. The worst thing was not to confess to being foolishly in love, but to acknowledge to his father what he had thrown in his father's face for so many years. He looked at him with sweaty hands. The situation would be far from easy. How many times did he rant about his love for a woman other than his mother? How many times did he take the opposite side, accepting that he was an insensitive jerk for allowing himself to be taken in by a woman he never spared in insults?

"God..." She thought dragging her fingers tightly over her black hair. So many accusations, so many reproaches that he regretted enormously. In those years he had behaved like a capricious adolescent without once thinking about the hell his father would be going through. Today he was not an ignorant youngster and understood the variety of shades between black and white.

His father waited but Akim just looked at him. Words were always better for him to write them than to express them.

-Has she made any decision? -The son looked at him with wild eyes.

-Do you know who that is? -He asked, shaking his head as he leaned back on the wide sofa next to his father.

-I'll tell you again that I'm not an idiot. New t-shirts, clean-shaven beard, four-pound deodorant," he said amused as if he was smelling around him, "And all that to go to work? Yeah, I think I know who that is. Either that or you and Nikola have decided to come out of the closet. he commented with a chuckle.

-Don't make fun... I'm lost." He replied, stretching his legs and back on the soft sofa.

-I think you're right. He said now with a little more seriousness.

-Thanks for the encouragement. He mumbled in reply.

-Possibilities? -he asked interested.

-Few. This week was the first week that she and I... you know. He commented, ignoring the details. But everything was different there, but here. I don't know, I feel like it's slipping through my fingers and I can't stand it. He said as he scratched his head hard trying to clear his head. I should... I should... but I can't. I want her for myself. I want her for myself. No matter the differences or... I don't care about anything. I don't want to think, I can't think..... God, I'm a mess and I'm talking like a fool.

-No, you don't, and I understand you perfectly.

Akim studied his father's gestures and discovered the sadness in his gaze and felt himself dying inside. He was partly responsible for his grief.

-You loved her... -. He commented with pain.

-That's in the past.

-I forced you to go back to our mother. You could have been happy but I didn't care. He commented, dropping his shoulders and looking at the floor.

-You didn't force me to do anything.

-It's not true! -He shouted as he jumped out of the seat and walked nervously. When I heard about that woman I went crazy. I felt you were betraying me and my mother. I hated you with all my might. I went looking for you and insulted you with very harsh words. I behaved like an imbecilic and capricious child, I never thought about you. I only saw my mother's tears and I held you responsible for all our sorrows.

Her father sniffled loudly, probably trying to swallow the tears that were beginning to shine in his eyes.

-You were not responsible. It had to end. Your mother needed me and I would never have let her die alone. In spite of what you might think, I loved her.... -He said, his voice choking.

-But didn't I love her?

-To want, to love, simple nuances of the heart and its entanglements. I loved your mother and that's what you should keep.
-You never thought of looking for her?
His father looked at the wall and Akim knew that remembering her still hurt.
-I owed him his freedom. Often love hurts more than it heals.
Akim stopped and rested his hands on the back of the sofa where his father was sitting and said in a soft voice.
-I'm sorry...
The words reflected true feeling and understanding. Akim for the first time saw his father as a man as human as himself. He now understood his pain at having to abandon the woman he loved to fulfill his so-called duties.
-How many years were you with her?
-Why do you ask that question? He replied, shifting uncomfortably in his seat.
-Come on, I'm not a kid anymore. I need to know. I think it's time you told me everything. How did you meet her?
Her father closed his eyes and smiled mirthlessly.
-It was unexpected. She walked through the factory door and I gasped. You know, the usual "what a woman" and things like that. I instantly looked down and tried to go about my business," he commented, amused, showing that he hadn't been able to. The boss sat her down next to me and asked me to show her my section. At first I didn't think it was a good idea, but I didn't say anything, after all what could I say to old Nathan," he snorted resignedly, "excuse me, but does that woman intoxicate? I told myself that if my heart was beating wildly it was simply because of the reaction of being in front of a beautiful woman. Something normal and out of danger.
-The same thing happened to me," he said, interrupting his father who paused to look at him before continuing.

-You can imagine the rest. She was so smiling, she was always so happy and looked at me that way.... With her I felt that the world was less harsh. I couldn't stop myself. I tried harder than you can imagine. Many times I left her house saying that I would never come back but I never did. I always came back. Just a few hours by her side was enough to make me dream for days on end.

-How long was she your lover?

-Eight.

Akim tightened his grip on the backrest. Eight years? Now he wasn't exactly thinking about his father. Could he be a lover of the woman he loved for eight years? Was love so crazy and absurd?

-Did my mother know? She never suspected?

-I knew it," he said ruefully. I tried to explain, but he was starting to go crazy with jealousy. He never accepted it. He preferred my crumbs. And when he had finally made up his mind....

-He attempted suicide and then became ill.

-Yes. The doctors gave her a couple of years at the most. I couldn't abandon her. Believe it or not, I loved her.

-I believe you... Now I believe you.

-Thank you. He said, lifting his glasses to wipe away a tear that was beginning to fall down his cheek.

Akim coughed to contain his emotion and not cry like a child. When his mother died, his girlfriend became pregnant, Lucien arrived, they left his country and father and son never spoke about it again. He had always felt a thorn of anger against his father. He had never fully understood until today, that as a result of his own decisions, he too was imprisoned by an immoral love according to the norms of a strict society.

The boy appeared playing with his plane and both moved nervously as if trying to leave the past where it belonged.

-Dad, isn't that your phone jumping on the shelf?

Akim rushed over to the device trying to catch the call but couldn't reach it in time. Talking to his father he had forgotten that he had it on vibrate function.

-Fuck... -He mumbled as he saw three missed calls from his doctor. I have to call. He said wanting to walk to his room but his son stopped him by his legs.

-It's Saturday. You said you'd take me to the park on Saturday.

-Eh, yeah well, you see, sure I'll have to go out but I promise the next one we'll go wherever you want.

-No, you promised! -he shouted indignantly.

Akim was about to answer his son with the same energy when his father spoke with his usual calmness.

-It might not be such a bad idea. The boy smiled and Grandpa ruffled his hair, making it even more tangled than usual.

-I have to see her... -He said hoping that his father would understand his short and concise message.

-Let's see how I see it," Akim paused to listen carefully. His father might be a humble man but he was no fool. As I understand it, there is a certain lady who loves our - he thought for the right word - cake.

The boy in the middle of the two raised his head and looked at one and the other trying to understand the conversation.

-If you bring her our... cake you could win a lot of points. She doesn't have cake and from what I saw she really likes it. You were alone but I'm sure you were only engaged in? -he said remembering that his grandson was in front- eating... but it would be very nice if you could show yourself as something more than a -he thought again- eggplant. Anyway, if you show him your ability as a pastry chef, he'll like it for sure.

Grandfather was beginning to sweat and Akim smiled with him. The boy was looking at them most intrigued.

-So are we going to the park or not? -The boy asked, intrigued by whether they would bring cream or eggplant cake.

The young man thought about his father's idea and it didn't seem entirely far-fetched. That Brenda knew more than just his ability in bed pleased him very much. In a conquest getting plus points never hurt.

-Yes, let's go to the park. He replied as he watched his father's silent affirmation.

The phone rang again and Akim urgently picked it up without looking to see who it was and instantly regretted it.

-Lola, it's you... I can't... yes, I had to leave... I'm sorry I didn't cancel... yes, of course I understand you but you see... Lola I... I thank you for your understanding but I think we should talk... no I don't... no today I can't... tomorrow I can't... tomorrow either... it's ok we'll talk during the week. I'll see you...

-That girl won't take no." Her father snorted.

-Her voice sounded too harsh and made him feel bad instantly. After all, Lola was just a poor girl he used when he needed her most and discarded without any remorse. I will talk to her personally. I will explain to her that we can no longer see each other.

His father accepted his reflection. The phone rang again and Akim rushed to answer it.

-Yes, yes, I'm here... you didn't answer my messages... Sleeping? Dreaming about me...?...

His son locked himself in the room and the man went to the kitchen to make himself some tea. He hadn't wanted to show it, but his hands were still shaking. Remembering Clara stirred up feelings that despite the years were still too fresh. He had never forgotten her. He may not have been entirely honest with his son but what was the point of hurting him. He was his mother's son, why confess to him that his heart died the day he had to say goodbye to his true love? Clara was never the other. People may have seen it that way but to him she would always be the first and only one. The owner of his heart and the last of his memories when he left this world.

He put the cup in the microwave, dialed two and leaned against the shelf absorbed in his sorrows. He sincerely hoped his son would have better luck than he had because he didn't want her to suffer half the pain he still retained at the memory of her.

Walking among clouds

I love you by day, I love you by night, I love you when I sleep and when I wake up.
I love you when I look at you and when you smile at me. I love you today when you are mine, I loved you when I didn't know you yet and I will love you till there where the rainbow never ends.

Akim

Akim lifted the little boy up, gave him a loud kiss and placed him back on the grass. He ran around the park with the ball between his legs and his father lay down next to him. Brenda had been enjoying the two of them all morning, and she was overjoyed. She could never have imagined the complicit and fun way Akim acted with Lucien. He thought he was cold and distant but he was not like that, maybe the definition was reserved and rather surly but not at all aggressive or indifferent. If he had that doctor who diagnosed him with emotional instability disorder in front of him, he would tell her a couple of things.

-A pound for your thoughts?

-I was thinking of kicking a person's ass twice. Brenda covered her mouth with both hands as soon as she finished speaking and Akim laughed in her face.

-Oops, oops, looks like the doctor is getting out of her stiff upper lip. Do you know any more swear words?

-Don't be an asshole. He said smiling and covering his lips once again.

Akim let out a laugh and leaned back a little more to bring his face closer to hers.

-Are you sure he didn't bother you? -Akim spoke softly near her ear and she could feel the wetness of his words on her neck. The short distance reminded her of nights she wished she could relive again.

-Of course not, Lucien is a sweetheart.

-Like his father. She answered while slowly moving her long hair back with her hands, clearing her neck. Here, it's right here. He said with a soft and short kiss. This is the exact place," he commented again as he gave her a couple more caresses. Maybe here too...

The man's kisses began a short trail down her neck while his finger caressed where her lips passed.

-Please... -She whispered trying to stop him.

-Please what? -He asked as he continued his trail of kisses that began to move away from her neck and up her chin.

-We can't... we are in a public place... they might see us. Brenda instantly regretted her words. Akim's tension was more than evident and although he offered her one more kiss before pulling away it was clear that the moment was broken.

-I'm sorry, but I can't behave like it's nothing. It's not just our age difference anymore," she commented embarrassed. I owe her some respect, at least until I'm back in town and we can talk.

-Are you going to tell him? -he asked with a hint of hope.

-Yes. I'm not like that. I can't lie to her. Do you think I'm not right? -she asked doubtfully. Akim never claimed anything from her and she might even have thought this was a way to cajole him but nothing could be further from the truth. She had been thinking it through, and despite Rachel's advice, she had to come clean with Max.

-No." He replied quickly. Not at all," he said, calming his anxiety, "It's just that the other night you made me think you would need more time and I thought....

-I need it, but that doesn't mean I don't come clean.

Akim looked at her interested for her to continue but Lucien's arrival silenced her.

-Dad, are we going to eat the cake?

-Cake? -Brenda asked as she was helped to her feet by a smiling Akim.

-Yes, eggplants, I think? -he answered, lifting his small shoulders.

-No son, I think it's time we had one of those double cheeseburgers you like so much.

-Yes," the boy shouted as he held Brenda by the hand to tell her the ingredients of his favorite hamburger.

The young father stood a few steps behind watching them walk hand in hand as he tried to calm his elation. If Brenda talked to her husband, if they parted ways, his path would be totally clear and the destination would be much clearer, at least for him. She smiled with some remorse for her husband's unmentionable but shook her head instantly. He was very sorry but he was only able to think of his happiness and a life beside the woman he adored, the rest of the world could sink into the same hell he cared little for.

The day passed amidst laughter and merriment. The two men escorted her to the doors of her house and Brenda smiled naturally and without reserve. So many times she had smiled out of commitment and expressed her opinion out of duty that she no longer remembered what it meant to behave with total naturalness. Her patients listened to thoughtful advice, with her friends she was patient and supportive, while with Max... with him she learned to be understanding and tolerant. Everyone knew her but none of them understood her, she thought as she felt the warmth of those little arms that said their most effusive goodbyes.

-Thank you. She said, half bending down to receive the tender embrace.

The little boy broke away and she tried to turn to open the door when strong hands imprisoned her around the waist. Akim held her for a few seconds and she felt herself trembling like a flan. That young man made her feel like a schoolgirl where problems and doubts ceased to exist. Fears dissipated in his arms. He only needed to look at her to feel her blood boil like an erupting volcano. The heat ran through her in a way that only dreamers are capable of guessing.

-You won't say goodbye to me? -He whispered under his breath, burning her with the blue fire of his gaze.

He was about to excuse himself for the boy's presence but his father didn't seem to mind. Her lips settled on his gently. It was a short kiss and although it turned out to be nothing possessive it was enough to surprise Lucien.

-Dad! -Akim smiled, resting his forehead against hers and smiled, explaining himself in the funniest way.

-He has never seen me with a woman. He said smiling.

Brenda felt the colors rise in her face. That didn't mean just a kiss. Akim was making clear to her his reality and her meaning in his life. Her heart began to beat a mile a minute. An adorable boy, a fiery man and a freedom to be discovered, was this the true meaning of life? were these the sensations sought and never found? what was it about her now that made her yearn so much for the new?

Thoughts swarmed in her thousands as the door opened. He immediately let go of Akim's arms fearing the worst. Rachel looked at them shaking her head while mumbling phrases like unconscious or something similar but she couldn't justify herself because at that same instant and without consulting he dragged her into the house .

-Max and George are here. They wanted to surprise us. I told them you had a consultation with Murray.

-Murray? -she asked quizzically.

-Yes," she stammered nervously, "Didn't you tell me he was devastated by his wife's death?

-Yes.

-Well, it was the first thing that came to my mind," she said, upset. Now get inside before they come to the door and hang us both.

She ducked her shoulders ready to enter when a strong, rough hand grabbed her wrist. She looked at him and felt the pain in his gaze. He didn't speak, only pierced her with the glare of his gaze but she didn't quite know what to say to him. Both were cold in their places wishing for words from the other that neither dared to utter.

-You have to go in. Whatever happens tomorrow, you have to go in now. Rachel spoke as she tugged on his other arm.

Brenda nodded. Akim let go of her wrist and she went inside without looking back. She knew she couldn't do that because if he showed her that future by her side again she would run along with him without caring about anything or anyone, and of course, she wasn't like that....

Male voices sounded approaching and Rachel slammed the door, leaving the frames shaking.

-How did you do that? -He said as he thought of Akim's reaction on the other side.

-He will understand. Now you have other little problems to solve. He commented as he saw a smiling Max opening his arms to place her inside him.

Rachel stayed home for dinner with George and Brenda thanked her. Every time she thought about how she should talk to Max the words got stuck in her throat. He wasn't a bad man, he always tried to do what was best for both of them. Max loved her. He had always tried to polish her imperfections and impose his visions but she couldn't hold it against him, after all she always let him.

How many times for the sake of not arguing did she assume desires she didn't want without knowing that her inner self was drowning in repression? Every time he bowed his head in denial of his nature, that cord that bound them together as a couple weakened. Akim's arrival only accelerated a reality that had long been denied. The rope had been broken long ago.

-You're distracted, is something wrong? -Max sat down next to her on the couch with a drink in his hand, and his eyes instantly watered.

The passion may have been dead and the truth may have hit her face like the midnight chill but that didn't mean the affection was gone. She loved Max and knew how much she would suffer in his absence.

-We need to talk. He said with barely a voice.

-No doubt about it," he commented amused. We've been separated for weeks and I need to "talk"... alone - Max used to use that double meaning in his words with her, always getting a smile on her face, but this time it wasn't the case -. I understand that you had to accompany Rachel to see her aunt but now that you're here you're going to have to work hard to make her forgive you for standing me up.

Max spoke so calmly and understandingly that Brenda felt like the dirtiest of women. He brought her redemption when she sought punishment. Her heart felt torn. Max shouldn't smile at her. He should be furious, angry, screaming, anything that would get in his way. Max should know the truth and he would tell her. The lies were piling up and she couldn't stand them anymore.

-When we are alone I have to talk to you. I would tell him the truth of his days in Ibiza trying to hurt him as little as possible.

-George! -Rachel's pierced cry made them jump out of their seats. They ran into the kitchen where the couple was supposed to be preparing a second round of drinks when they found George lying on the floor and Rachel screaming his name beside him.

Max approached, feeling for a pulse in his neck as he shouted loudly.

-Call the emergency room!

Brenda ran for the phone and dialed 112 with her hands shaking. George was not only Rachel's husband, he was Max's partner and best friend. The two were inseparable. If anything happened to him...

-Yes, *please, I need an ambulance, it's urgent....*

Do not leave me

I saw you for the first time and it was enough for me to know that it was you, the one I always waited for.

Akim

Akim walked nervously on the green lawn between grassy headstones and leafy trees that hid him from the view of passersby. People dressed in black and with looks reddened by grief were approaching to offer a last farewell to the deceased. He hardly knew him and was not there for the deceased but for the woman who arrived holding the hand of a friend torn by grief. He heard the sad news from his boss who had explained the situation to them. "One of the bosses had died of a heart attack while having dinner with friends," he said sadly. At first Akim thought of the unmentionable one and although he didn't wish him dead, he couldn't deny that a selfish part of his heart didn't dislike the idea. Brenda had barely answered one of his hundreds of messages.

-I'll call you when I can," he said without explaining the second day after dropping her off at her house.

He walked nervously, at first he wanted to be there. He wanted her to see him in the distance and know that he was by her side, that he supported her in her pain but all his good intentions went to the dump when he saw him. The unnamable one, the perfect man was there, with his impeccable suit and his hands on shoulders that no longer belonged to him.

They sat on the wooden chairs and Akim facing them but hidden behind the trees could see the redness in her eyes. He would have jumped from his hiding place, run to her side and tell her how sorry he was for her loss but he could not. That was no place for a lover. He scratched his chin over and over thinking what he should do. What if she had talked to him? Would she have given him time? A thousand questions piled up in her head when she saw the last thing she expected. He hugged her tightly and she leaned against his chest to cry. Wait, wait... she said trying to calm herself but she couldn't, her clenched fist slammed against the tree almost automatically. Rage and pain gnawed at him in equal measure. He hated her with the same intensity with which he loved her. He wanted to rip her from those arms and tell her that he was there for her. He walked a few steps backwards and then walked a few steps forwards. Insecurity overpowered him. Damn it, that woman had settled in his heart more than a year ago and there was no human way to tear her away.

Why... why... why... what? He wondered as he watched her cry in his arms. Don't do this. Not after what we've been through... Don't hold him...

-It's not what you think. Nikola said, approaching from behind with an open umbrella.

The drops were beginning to fall but he had hardly noticed, indeed, he thought that the water sliding down his face was the result of a pain that cruel life was giving him again.

-What do you know what I think," he said with a thick accent and harshness in his words.

-I know you too well to know that you are not the most positive being on earth.

-He answered, looking at her from a distance like a thief waiting for an oversight.

Akim smiled to himself in torment. He did wish the name on the tombstone were another....

-The secretaries say they were like brothers. He is broken with grief. They both are. They're just consoling each other. Nikola commented, trying to make his friend see beyond his heartbreaking jealousy.

-She said she would talk to him, but clearly she has not.

-And you know all this because you see her crying for a dead friend? Don't be an asshole...

The young man smiled half-heartedly and affirmed with his eyes. He could not deny it. Ever since he first saw that woman his brain had been atrophied. He was writing more than ever, he started playing the guitar again, he even had some papers to resume his art studies. He came to think that maybe at night and with the help of his father... maybe... maybe... she...

-We'd better get going. He said as he watched her in the distance one more time. One last one, just one.

Brenda seemed to hear his grief because she looked up and found him. Her little eyes were heavy with tears and Akim was unable to think. He forgot all his inner rages and furies. He forgot how much he hated her to remember how much he loved her. He watched her telling her with his eyes everything that words and distance would not allow and she seemed to understand. He said something to the hatred of the unmentionable and got up opening a tiny umbrella he had in his lap. She was in the front row, walked down the aisle leaving behind all the wooden chairs arranged on the lawn and headed towards the main entrance. Akim ran towards her leaving behind a Nikola who said nothing. He didn't mind getting wet. He had to be by her side no matter what.

Brenda entered the main building while shaking the water out of her jacket. She still couldn't believe it. George was gone. Tears began to well up in her eyes again. She was broken with grief listening to the pastor's words when a strange feeling ran through her body and she met Akim's gaze in the distance. She excused herself saying she needed a moment and escaped from the place. She saw him hide behind the trees and then run to meet her and smiled longingly at him. She longed to see him too. Day by day Akim was taking root in her heart like winter moss.

-I'm sorry," he said as he stood in front of her and wiped away her wet tears with his calloused fingers.

-You have come... -She answered between curious and excited.

-I couldn't be anywhere else. You needed me...

She threw herself into his arms and he hugged her tightly as he kissed her soft hair. No matter how much nonsense she thought or how much jealous rage roared from her insides, one of his sweet caresses was enough for her to forget everything.

They both stayed like that for a few minutes until Brenda let go to look him in the eyes with sorrow in her gaze.

-Please don't cry any more.... You're tearing me apart. She said wiping her face.

-I look awful. She replied, remembering that she wasn't wearing any makeup and that those small incipient wrinkles around her eyes would be deeper because of grief and lack of sleep.

-You look beautiful... -He said, sliding the back of his hand under her delicate chin.

Brenda was about to throw herself back into his arms when she saw Max approaching in the distance at a rapid pace. She tried to say goodbye quickly so her husband wouldn't see him, but to no avail. Max's nearly six feet gave her too long and too fast steps.

Akim turned and the two exchanged glances. Brenda felt her heart stop. She thought about clarifying the situation with Max, but this was neither the right place nor the right time.

-You?

Akim squared his shoulders as if deep down he was glad they were caught together.

-We came to offer condolences to his widow. We are representing all the crews under her care." Nikola said, standing between the architect and his friend.

The man continued for a few minutes with his eyes fixed on Akim's as if he wanted to warn him about something, but his friend intervened again. We are really sorry. We know you were close friends...

-Yes, thank you.

Max replied politely as he reached out to wrap her hand in his and lead her back to the group of friends who were beginning to rise from their seats.

-Honey, Rachel is waiting for us. She nodded as she said goodbye to the two men with cordial politeness as she again had to leave, abandoning the one she did not want to leave.

-You're definitely crazy," Nikola grumbled as they headed for the exit. Did you see the look on his face?

-He's just trying to make it clear to me to stay away.

-Only? That guy is not only a man of power, it turns out that for those little things in life, he's our boss!

-Yes, I've thought about it.

Nikola sighed hopefully. Maybe his friend wasn't completely oblivious. He had realized all that madness and had come to his senses.

-I start looking for a job today.

-Fuck... -His friend whispered in disappointment. That was not the expected conclusion.

Wait for me

My heart awaits you in every step, in every silence and at every arrival and I am unable to tell you that you will not come,
that you are no longer waiting for me and that you will never come back.

Akim

He had been waiting all day to see her but nothing. That seemed to be the routine of his life lately, him waiting and her not showing up. He changed his clothes as he angrily picked up his helmet. He was tired of waiting for what never came. Always waiting for a door to open or a car to park to see her. He didn't think he could stand this situation much longer but he had no choice. She had asked for time and he had given it to her. They were lovers now because she had accepted it. I accept it, he said, as he kissed her desperately that afternoon after the funeral. He hated feeling like this, a beggar for his crumbs. Barely two days had passed since their agreement and already he was mad with rage. Would they be together? Had she been able to talk to him? Would they have made love?

God, he should stop thinking or he would go crazier than he already felt. He was about to close the main entrance and leave for home when someone hugged him around the waist, pressing his face into his back. He took a breath and instantly knew. Vanilla and jasmine...

-I should go. He said clasping his hands against his stomach and knowing that his words said the opposite of what his heart felt.

-I'm so sorry, but Rachel needed me. She's at home.

-You're cold. He commented hoarsely as he felt her nose pressed against his neck.

"Rachel, I was with Rachel, thank goodness," he thought trying to quell his fears.

-Max has gone to Paris to sort out all the projects George was working on and Rachel has moved in with me. I didn't want to leave her alone.

-I get it," he said as he was thinking a mile a minute. Max was out again? That left more time for them.

Brenda reached into her pants pocket mischievously as she pulled out her keys and unlocked the door to the offices again.

-I've had nothing for three days, too, and I need you," he said as he pulled her hand into the building on the way to his office.

Had he heard correctly? His beloved, respected and so well educated Dr. Klein was coming on to him? was she coming on to him? Something wasn't right, he thought amused, as he let himself be dragged into her office without any resistance. By the way she had said three days of nothing, no sex, that meant she and Max were not....

Unable to hide his joy, he pulled her hand tightly until he pulled her to his body and instantly grabbed her below the knees and lifted her onto his shoulders. With one kick he opened the office and with another he closed it while she giggled like a teenager. Akim felt that that sound was music to his ears and told himself that it would not be the first time he would hear it.

Without further ado, he released her on the red couch, knowing that he would fulfill one of the many sinful dreams that that couch had provoked in him since the first day he saw it.

She stretched out her arms and he needed no further invitation. He threw himself like a wolf in front of his prey. He wanted to devour her. He had also been three days without sex but mainly without her. Their mouths intertwined raging with desire Brenda asks him to touch her, makes her feel like a woman, desired...thoughts of BrendaXXXXXXX

The cell phone began to ring but they were both too busy to answer. It rang again a second and a third time as Brenda sighed resignedly trying to push away a man who growled angrily.

-I have to get this. She said as he refused to let go of the nipple in her mouth. Please..." She commented with barely a whisper and overcome with desire.

Angry but accepting her wishes he released her from his embrace and Brenda reached out to reach into her purse to pick up the cell phone that was ringing again.

-Hope? I'm sorry but I don't remember,... yes... Hope. Brenda spoke with barely a voice and Akim smiled proudly while he continued kissing her body lying on the couch as if it was nothing -Yes...yes...yes...of course how are you?...Yes I remember and allow me to apologize but I couldn't go, you see a very dear friend passed away and it was impossible for me...What! But what are you doing there?.... It can't be...

Brenda jumped up and Akim stood kissing the leather couch not understanding what was going on around her. He was about to pull her arm to lay her back on the couch when she said in a worried voice.

-I will be *there as soon as I arrive....*

-Not at all. He said earnestly as he reached out to embrace her delicate, half-naked body.

The woman released herself from his embrace and began to hurriedly fasten her bra behind his surprised gaze. Akim watched her trying to calm his passion as he wondered what was going on. She hurriedly got dressed but it was when she turned and looked into his eyes that it became clear.

-Trouble. That look means we are in trouble.

-Are we? -Akim lifted his shoulders as he too began to dress.

-Where are we going?

-It's Rachel, she's at Carol's house.

-Isn't that the president of the Amazons?

-Yes.

-And what is he doing there?

-I'll tell you on the way," she said, picking up her purse, which had fallen to the ground in her haste.

-All right, all right, but pick up your helmet. We'll get there faster on my bike.

-What helmet? -She said as she noticed for the first time that on the desk was a super cute new helmet with a gift ribbon on the front. Is it for me? -she asked excitedly.

-Yes. Let me adjust it for you.

-It suits me perfectly," he said as he put his head in.

-I know. I ordered it with your exact measurements.

Brenda wrapped her arms around him and blew him a kiss under his helmet and he melted. Seeing her like this made him feel like she was his life partner. His co-pilot. His road companion. That filled him with pride and he hoped she knew what that silly gift meant to him. He would have said a few words if she had allowed him to but if it was already difficult for him to express his thoughts out loud, it was much more so having a woman as dusty as his. Could it be that she kept going back and forth without getting into trouble? He thought amused as he let himself get dragged away again. That woman would end up killing him.

They arrived at the woman's house and Akim was surprised but said nothing. Brenda ran to the door and rang the bell. Esperanza opened it worriedly as she led them inside where by the screaming at the top of her lungs, a fight was going on and a good one at that. When they got to the living room she couldn't help but stare at the place. That was a most luxurious house. I was not impressed by that, in fact Brenda's own house was a waste of architectural beauty but there everything was very different. The woman who lived there looked like a nouveau riche. One who let herself be enveloped by expensive objects without thinking about whether they matched or not. For heaven's sake, that figure of who knows what and almost a meter high might be one hundred percent ivory but it was the most hideous contraption he had ever seen. He may have been of humble origins but his interrupted studies in the arts made him perfectly able to recognize a work of art from a piece of crap. And that statue was it.

-You bitch! You're a fucking bitch! -Rachel screamed uncontrollably and in tears.

Everyone was stunned on the spot except Brenda who came to her side trying to calm her down.

-Rachel, we'd better get out of here. He said softly.

-No! She killed him. It's her fault." She shouted again in despair.

-She's crazy! - said the Amazon leader.

-What are you talking about? -Brenda asked as he held her by the shoulders and ignored the assailant who was ranting like an angry mare.

-It's her fault... She killed him, Brenda... she killed him. She said with a thousand tears streaming down her face.

-Her friend responded as heartbroken as her own. Rachel was shattered and totally out of control with grief and pain.

-He knew, he knew what this bitch did to me. He knew about the prison and he got very nervous, and that's why he had a heart attack! -He shouted, losing control again and trying to pounce on the woman who hid behind Esperanza.

Peter was in a corner and Akim stood next to him. He didn't plan to intervene. As long as she was in no danger.

-Get her out of my house. Take her out or I'll call the police.

The woman shouted and pushed Esperanza to get the young woman to comply with her orders but Peter stopped her.

-You don't send her. And don't touch her again.

-You wretched wretch, are you going to do what this useless man says? You're useless," he shouted at the top of his lungs.

-Don't insult her or I won't answer. Peter replied, interposing his muscular body as muscular as a stick bug.

Akim smiled at the image. The woman was twice his size in length and width, but the young man was not afraid to defend his girl. That was love, he thought amused.

-She's like that. A bitch who doesn't mind hurting anyone. She accused me and took me to jail without proof. She lied like the bitch she is, and that's why my George is dead.... -she said sobbing. It's my fault, if I hadn't upset him so much....

-Rachel, it wasn't your fault. Brenda commented sympathetically.

-Yes, it is. Mine and this bitch's. That's why I'm going to pull out all her hair.

Rachel lunged at the woman. Carol instantly pushed Esperanza to the front line to hide behind the girl.

-Mom, no! -The young woman cried out in fright as she saw the madness reflected in Rachel's eyes.

-Mom? -Rachel, Akim and Brenda asked at the same time.

-Defend me. Useless for nothing. I shouldn't have had you. I should have drowned you in the river.

-But you'll be miserable, you abandoned her at birth! I don't know how she even lets you stand next to her." Peter shouted angrily.

-Peter, please... -Esperanza was trying to hold her boyfriend's arm to placate him.

-Mom? Liar... You're a liar! -Rachel shouted. You spoke to those women with airs of superiority when you yourself had abandoned your daughter whom you treat like an old rag. You insult politicians and then go around being a friend. You are a fake. I will kill you.

Brenda tried to hold her down but could not. She fell to the ground and then Akim decided to intervene. In two strides he reached Rachel and lifted her into the air hoping she would stop kicking hysterically. When the woman calmed down the young man deposited her in a chair and spoke to her tenderly.

-I know the pain you are going through. I've experienced firsthand how heavy the remorse of mistakes weighs on you, but you'll have to live with it. George is gone and there is nothing you can do to get him back. No matter how much you beat her, he won't come back, this from someone who made many faces bleed before giving up.

Rachel burst into tears and Brenda reached over to grab her by the shoulders and guide her toward the door.

-You fucking bitch. Carol was about to shout a few more expletives but Akim stood in front of her and let her eyes roam over his tense muscles before he spoke in that accent of his with deadly coldness.

-He will not file a complaint, in fact, he plans to ask for forgiveness and tell the lady that he understands her pain... if he appreciates her life.

Akim smiled at the pallor that instantly dominated the woman's face. Sometimes being the bad guy paid off.

-I... I, I understand your pain and I feel your loss," he said, looking at the tattoos peeking through the sleeves of his T-shirt.

Rachel walked at a slow pace toward the door and did not stop to listen to the woman and Akim walked behind them silently to the sidewalk.

-We will go in a cab. She said hoping he would understand her.

-I will follow them with the motorcycle.

Brenda nodded her head as she guided a Rachel who seemed to walk as if through the clouds. The poor woman was defeated and barely conscious of moving her legs. Akim waited for them to get into the cab and followed them into the house. He waited in the living room until Brenda offered her a painkiller and settled her on her bed.

-She fell asleep," she said, dropping exhausted at his side as he hugged her tenderly. The poor thing insists it's her fault.

-It will pass. It's the grief that speaks for her. In time she will understand that it was not.

-Do you mean your mother?

-Yes, I always thought I should have done more for her.

-What made you change your mind?

-Let's say that a talk with my father made me see things from a different point of view.

-I understand," he said, yawning loudly and not really understanding much.

-I'll take you home.

-No thanks, I'll stay with her. I wanted her to go back to mine but she refused. I think she needed to be among her things to feel protected. I'll sleep on the couch.

-Then we'll sleep together. He said with a mischievous tone and she looked at him strangely.

-You don't think I'll leave you alone to get into more trouble.

-But you will be uncomfortable and you work tomorrow.

-If you are by my side nothing can be bad," he said as he kissed her. It was not his intention to go further, but whenever he was with Brenda things changed course. XXX

-Brin, what does this woman do for a living?

-Nothing. He has been out of work for years.

Akim thought without answering and Brenda asked again.

-What's wrong?

-Don't you think it's strange that a woman with no family and no job lives in a neighborhood like that and has such a car parked outside her door?

Brenda did not answer. Akim came closer and pressed his body to hers, seeking her warmth.

-It's silly, but I thought it was funny," he said with barely a whisper before falling asleep against her back.

The woman did not fall asleep. She kept thinking. It might not be so silly, she said to herself, trying to connect the dots. After all, that was her job.

-Brin, honey, I have to go home. I have to shower and take Lucien to school.

Brenda nodded as he turned and found her to be the loveliest woman he had ever met. Truth be told, she had little experience waking up with any. She didn't usually complete the night in the bed of her lovers. He would enjoy himself and leave. Life without compromise was a better life. He remembered her phrase and laughed at his own stupidity. Life without her was not peaceful, it simply wasn't life. He said it with total conviction. Brenda drove him to madness, lifted him to the heavens and plunged him into despair, weakened him and freed him. It was the craziest and most maddening of situations but that was what love was all about and now he understood it because he was madly in love.

Weather

Since I met you I have been living the most wonderful madness. Your name runs through my veins, my blood is altered, my heart is racing and I feel myself flying, the clouds don't weep and the heat is no longer suffocating, welcome love into my life by you I have known the most beautiful of all my torments

Akim

Akim went about his work trying not to think. He arranged the cleaned brushes near the paint cans while the rest of the crew prepared for lunch. He looked at the time again and made calculations. The minutes seemed not to pass and the seconds were slow steps of giants that crushed his hopes more and more.

-Trouble in paradise? -Nikola asked as she walked over to lean against the wall next to him.

-He's here. He said as if that explained everything.

Nikola looked at him with a pitying face and Akim felt his guts churn. He did not want to be where he was. He felt weak and vulnerable and those were feelings that although new he did not like in the least.

-They must be talking right now," he commented, trying to explain his unfriendly face.

-Will you tell him?

-She thought as she remembered that in the last ten days it was the second time Brenda had come back saying that she had tried but nothing. The unmentionable one seemed to be dodging her and even though it was a most bizarre situation he didn't want to doubt her. If Brenda said she had asked him to talk but he was dodging it was because that was the truth. He refused to disbelieve her. She's tried a couple of times but he's barely home. He says he's too busy, that he has to take care of all the projects that George left pending and he's just leaving. He commented as he walked towards the exit door to wait for her.

-You know that... -Nikola affirmed while his friend, already on the sidewalk, lit a cigarette.

-What do you mean?

-I say when a woman says we need to talk we all know what's next. It's always trouble for us. It's clear that the man is trying to wriggle out of it.

Akim took a long drag on his cigarette thinking seriously about his friend's opinion as he nodded his head.

-You're not going to be so brainless after all," he said amused.

Ha, and this from the guy who fell in love like an idiot with a married woman and an architect with at least a seven-figure bank account.

Akim gave a small, reluctant smile. His friend was right. In a brainless race he would lose because of low intelligence.

-I'd better go.

Nikola sped off and Akim stomped his cigar on the ground as he saw the reason for Nikola's cowardly flight.

-You're still here. Connor spat in annoyance.

-It seems so. He answered unwillingly. The Scotsman kept provoking him whenever he could.

-Tell me how much you want and you'll get it.

The young man felt his veins swelling. It wasn't the first time he had been offered money to get away from Brenda and he was beginning to get fed up with those damned bastards who evaluated his feelings with a checkbook.

-Do you appreciate her so little as to believe that I have fallen in love with her without any attachments?

-I know her too well to know how much she's worth, but it's not guys like you who appreciate those virtues," he said. He replied with fury in his eyes.

Akim was trying to control himself. He had promised her that he would not attack the artist. He was a brother to her and she didn't want to hurt him but every patience has a limit and hers was on the edge of the precipice.

-Go away, find another job. I can help you.

-Yes? -Now he was offering her a job? What would be next? A new house?

-You'll cheat on her, you'll make her suffer and I'll kill you for it. Bastards like you don't care how much damage they do as long as they get what they want. Tell me, what made you fall in love with her? The beach villa? The sports car? The parties? Her bank account?

Akim began to breathe harder and harder. His fists were clenching for vengeance and his veins were swelling for blood.

-I'd better go. He said in a low voice, trying to keep his word and not kill the stupid Scotsman.

Connor grabbed him by the shoulder trying to stop him but Akim let go with a sharp jerk.

-Don't touch me again," he snarled, glowing with fire in his eyes.

Connor stood up to it. He was not afraid of him. Both were two specimens ready for a fight. Tall, strong and eager to fight for what they felt belonged to him.

-That's you," he said, smiling sideways like a dog about to attack. Has she seen you like this? Have you shown her the shit you hide inside?

Akim moved quickly to grab him by the neck and pin him against the glass door leading into the building.

-You are a wretch incapable of seeing beyond your own nose.

The Scotsman opened both arms in the air, releasing his grip with fury in his eyes. Akim was strong but he was a man of no mean size and strength.

-If you want to make me believe that he cares about you, then leave and don't come back. Don't destroy her life." He shouted angrily, blowing his breath on Akim's face, which was only millimeters away from his.

The young man tried to contain himself, how could he explain to that stupid man that he had already tried but had not been able to? Connor was her friend and was simply trying to protect her, she couldn't blame him, after all he would do the same in a similar situation.

-I love her... -He said defeated.

-Then it disappears.

-That marriage was already dead," he commented, slamming his fist against the wall so as not to shoot straight into the face of that man who didn't seem to want to shut up.

-She can, but you're not for her. You'll never give her what she needs. When the novelty wears off you'll drop her in the first puddle. Brenda is a special being, she trusts people. She may sometimes try to give the image of an overachiever, but those of us who really know her know perfectly well that it's a mask.

-You say you love her but you ask her to live in a world of lies. What a shitty friend you are.

-I didn't say that. I'm just saying that you're not the one.

-And why not? -he said, biting his tongue to avoid insulting.

-Because your world and hers don't collide. They never will. I'm not a classicist but I'm not stupid either. If you stay by her side she will lose her relationships, her position. You will embarrass her and she will fall without being able to get up and you will be responsible.

Akim cursed loudly and entered the building without looking back. Connor's words this time had hurt him far more than he would like to admit.

She left for work, trying to stop listening to the cretin's words, but she couldn't. The Scotsman's thick voice was drilling into her brain. The thick voice of the Scotsman was drilling into her brain. Damn shit! He would never hurt her. That guy had to be wrong.

He would do his best to keep up with her. He wasn't an architect or anything but he could try to be someone better for her. Akim looked at his calloused hands holding the wheelbarrow of sand and felt a dagger stab into his heart ripping it in two. He threw the hated artifact across the room with all his might as he took a shaky breath.

Brenda turned on the lights to enter her office. It was late and everyone had left. She sat at her desk holding her head trying to clear her thoughts. Max had returned from one of his trips, she tried to talk to him but just watched him pace nervously as he explained that he had to leave again. George had some important work to do and Max had to take on all his commitments. In part she understood this as well as the pain he clearly felt at the loss of his partner and friend.

-We need to talk... -she told him as he arranged some papers.

-Please, honey, I can't now. He answered her as he hugged her tightly. Without George all this seems impossible, I need you to understand.

-I understand perfectly, but we need some time for ourselves. I need to talk about something important.

-Then speak. He replied angrily while holding a briefcase.

-No, not like that," Max approached her regretfully and hugged her warmly.

-I'm sorry, I didn't mean to yell at you. But I'm really swamped. I have to be in Paris more than I should and then there are the projects here. I have to travel a lot and I don't want to leave you but I can't find another solution. I promise that when I have everything under control I will dedicate a whole week just for you.

Brenda ducked her head. She was only pretending for a couple of hours but she couldn't be so ungrateful. Max needed her and she was asking for understanding. She may no longer feel the passion for him that she should but that didn't mean she didn't love him and very much so. He represented an important part of her life and she would always love him. She closed her eyes as she scratched them hard when a voice startled the solitude of her consulting room.

-You didn't tell him.

-I couldn't." He said without looking at the figure leaning against the wall.

-Try to buy time," he commented, biting his tongue in anger.

-That's not true. He wouldn't do that," she said exhausted.

-Don't defend him! I can't stand it." He replied with barely controlled fury.

-And I don't! But you're talking nonsense. How can you try to buy time on what you don't know? -Brenda was not used to losing her temper, but she felt pressured. Akim used to tell her that he understood her, that he accepted her situation, but at the first opportunity he would start with little reproaches that began to tire her. Did he think she liked that situation? God! She hated lying to Max, she hated feeling like a scumbag but he knew it, she was married when he did everything to conquer her, now what did he pretend? That she would get rid of more than fifteen years just like that? -You don't think about your words. She said annoyed.

-Are you calling me an idiot? -He replied as he approached her desk to look her in the eye.

-I didn't say that.

-What's the matter, have you realized by looking at him that I'm nothing more than a bricklayer with a short brain? Is that it, doctor? -He spoke as he approached his chair and lowered his face to be face to face, "Could it be that the so attentive and polite Dr. Klein does not dare to tell me that she is sorry?

-What's wrong with you? -He said as he got up from his seat to try to understand why he was so angry.

-Is that it? Max gave you a new sports car? Tell me, how did he convince you? Did he lay you down on the bed and make you scream louder than me?

Akim regretted it the very instant he felt the force of her five fingers on his face. He scratched his cheek to relieve the stinging as she tried to step aside to get away. He held her by the wrist to restrain her.

-I'm sorry. The muffled voice was barely out of his throat. She was right, he was an idiot, but one who was afraid of losing her. One who was dying of jealousy every minute she wasn't by his side.

Her phone was ringing off the hook and Brenda was annoyed, angry and in a very bad mood. Without listening to him she reached into her jacket pocket to pull out her cell phone. If he didn't answer it, she would answer it for him. She could no longer stand Max's running away, Connor's recriminations, Akim's reproaches or the sound of his damn phone.

-No wait...

-Brenda didn't do it until she saw on the screen the number of calls from that woman. Ten in the last two hours.

-Take it. He said stretching out the artifact and picking up the bag to leave.

I was bursting at the seams. Akim deigned to demand when she was still talking to that little girl with the huge tits. She felt stupid, old and jealous, very jealous.

Akim cut the call without answering to explain himself but she wouldn't let him.

-Go away. She told him, overcome with rage and jealousy.

-No." He replied, hugging her back tightly and preventing her from leaving.

-He didn't want this argument, he hadn't even planned it, but since the talk with Connor he hadn't been able to recover from it. She hadn't communicated all afternoon and he was desperate. He waited for her for hours and when the sky darkened the doubts began to attack him as they always did when she was not by his side. When he saw her sit down and hide her face in her hands without even noticing his presence, he thought that the ground would have buried him alive. Thousands of situations went through his head, after all Max was in town and that man was the only one who could take away the only thing he wanted in this life. Well him and that annoying Lola who didn't seem to understand that he would never have anything to do with her again.

-I didn't mean to...

-You lied to me. You said you would accept whatever I could give you and you accepted it. I told you I needed time to talk to him and you said you understood but you keep insisting and pressuring me and now on top of that..." He said pointing to the phone without being able to say Lola's name out loud.

-I'm not pressuring you," he said, knowing that he was and completely ignoring the call. She tried to control herself but jealousy always got the better of her. He thought he could be her lover until he conquered her heart but it was a mistake. He wanted her all to himself and did not want to share her. I've been here all afternoon... It's been a bad day and when you arrive you don't look for me and when I ask you you tell me that you haven't spoken and I thought the worst. I try to be patient but it's not easy for me.

-For you? And do you think it is for me? Do you think that if I could choose I would be involved in this? Do you think I'm not also overwhelmed and tired of thinking about the harm I can do to you or to him? I'm tired of always being asked to think of others and never of myself. Do you think I don't feel terrible?

-Brin... -He reached out his hand, trying to caress her, but she pulled away.

-I want to be alone.

-No, don't ask me that.... -. He said trying to hug her in spite of her tightness.

-I need to be alone. She answered seriously. I'm asking you, please. Go away.

Akim rested his face on top of her head and placed a delicate kiss on her hair.

-She doesn't mean anything. It's not what you think...

-Please leave. Brenda didn't plan to break down in front of him. If she felt shitty it was better alone than by his side.

-We'll talk tomorrow.

-I think the same...

-No, don't you dare say it," he said, his voice trembling. I'll see you tomorrow when we're both calmer.

The young man left, closing the door very slowly as he walked towards the exit. Her explosive character and her continuous doubts had managed to put him on the ropes. She had been on the verge of asking him to distance himself from her and his breath had been taken away at that very moment. Did he really think he could go on with his life without her? At this point that was unthinkable. Brenda was the forbidden fruit he could not give up. For years he felt alone and abandoned. Fortune was a cookie that he never got to taste and now, that he finally had it, that he had tasted it with his lips and his body, now it would not be possible for him to continue without it.

"Idiot," he thought to himself as he remembered the way he had pushed her and damn my luck he said to himself as he remembered Lola's ill-timed call. Brenda's face had blurred and he wanted to die. All he needed was for her to doubt his feelings. He put on his helmet and accelerated at full throttle, thinking of a way to get her back. This afternoon he had felt her driving away without being able to stop her and his blood had frozen in his veins. He had to show her that he understood and supported her. He had to conquer her like a man does with a woman and not like a damn jealous

Neanderthal. Could he be a bigger idiot? Was she looking to talk to the unmentionable one to explain that she had fallen in love with someone else and he still doubted?

Akim stopped at a traffic light feeling increasingly ridiculous as his own thoughts once again created the eternal doubts. He never said he had fallen in love? He thought as the traffic light blinked yellow. Passion was evident between them but love and passion were games that many participants used to confuse. Maybe therein lies my answer and my salvation, he thought hopefully for the first time all day. The car behind him blew its horn loudly demanding that he move and the young man smiled with real pleasure. His girl was looking for passion and she had given it to him, now she would make him discover something else. He adored her and was completely sure of his feelings, time to awaken hers.

Lies

No one like you to wake me up in the morning. Your body says good morning to me and my heart says to you that will always be so as long as you are by my side.

Akim

Brenda waited in the office even though she didn't feel like it. The moment Akim left her office she felt guilty. Pressure and jealousy had gotten the better of her. She needed a little understanding and not a sack of reproaches, and on top of that call....

If anything had awakened her from her sad life, it was Max's lack of understanding. He always dictated and she complied, whether it was out of duty, understanding or not arguing, she always gave in and she was really tired. Akim's words put her up against the wall and she did not want to feel that way again. She no longer wanted to act as she should, but as she felt.

Someone knocked on the door and she gave them permission to enter. She was waiting for them. Peter had asked her for an urgent meeting and sensing her trembling voice, she summoned them to her office as a matter of urgency.

-Go ahead. He said as he saw the fearful couple at the door. That didn't look too good, he thought as he offered them a couple of chairs to sit on.

-Dr. Klein, forgive this assault, but we urgently needed to see you. Esperanza spoke in fear and the psychologist felt a shiver run through her body.

-Please call me Brenda. He commented, breaking one of his strict professional rules. How can I help you?

-It's because of my mother.

-That harpy is not your mother, she never was. You don't call a crazy woman who leaves you lying in a hospital your mother. Peter spat out each of her statements.

Brenda listened attentively, she understood the young woman's story and Esperanza's need for psychological treatment, but why such urgency?

Esperanza spoke but Peter continually interrupted her so she could not stand it anymore and stood up with all the authority her position offered and politely asked Peter to leave.

-But... -He answered between surprised and annoyed.

-Esperanza is intelligent enough to tell me about her concerns, so I ask you to wait for us outside.

-But you don't know. She... needs you.

-I know and I understand your concern. Don't be afraid, I will be able to help her.

-Doctor," he said almost whispering so his girlfriend wouldn't hear, "You see, we can't, I mean with the opening of the store we are a little tight.

-Don't worry. Now go have a cup of coffee. I think your girlfriend and I have a lot to talk about.

The doctor closed the door with determination and asked Esperanza to sit on the beautiful red couch.

-Hope, why exactly did you come here?

-Peter says...

-No, no, forget about Peter. We are alone in this room. I need you to be the one talking to me and not your boyfriend's conscience. Now I ask again," he said with a broad smile to give confidence, "What attracted you to me?

The girl shifted nervously. She was very young, Brenda imagined she was in her early twenties and felt sorry for her. The short, wide-hipped girl was biting her nails, searching her fingers for the courage that had definitely deserted her.

-You can trust me. Whatever it is, I'm here to help you, you know that, don't you?

-Yes, yes," she said with determination. I trust you. You've always been very polite and very good to me... and that's why I can't let her hurt you. You've been so good to me, always speaking to me with love. And your friend, you looked for her and didn't stop until you saw her free. I can tell you love her very much and the way you hugged when you met tells me that you are good people. I wanted a family, I didn't ask for much more...I thought that in time she would love me but Peter is right. She doesn't love me, if she did she would talk to me like you do but she doesn't like me, she never did....

The doctor, although she only saw unconnected ends, let her talk. In therapy, many people needed to start with a lot of relief and then, yes, get into the problem itself.

Esperanza was speaking without commercial breaks when Brenda felt her skin begin to crawl.

-Did you say harm Rachel? Why would your mother do something like that? That doesn't make sense." She asked nervously.

Esperanza, who felt more and more comfortable as the minutes passed, sat down on the couch to look into her eyes.

-You see, my mother is a little.... -The poor girl fell silent in shame.

-Selfish?

-Yes, to put it politely.

-Go on. Brenda was beginning to feel really uneasy.

-I don't know much. I overheard her talking to someone on the phone. She was telling her not to worry, that the contracts were not in jeopardy. That if necessary she would throw the stupid stone out of the way herself. Then she cut off, cursing loudly and shouting that no one would stand in her way on the way up.

Brenda breathed a relaxed breath. Esperanza had simply heard one of the many phrases that people say when they are sulking.

-I understand your concern, but you don't have to worry. I imagine your mother was just angry. When we lose our temper we often say what we don't mean. Brenda looked at her notes and saw how she had inadvertently written Akim's name about five times in a row. She continued trying to stay on topic.

-Human beings are temperamental. Words spoken in moments of anger do not always reflect our true feelings. She said, thinking how she herself had to apply her own lessons hundreds of times. A few hours before she had felt angry and pressured, but there were no embers left of that fire. She behaved with Akim in a way she didn't deserve and she was sorry.

-You see, doctor. Doctor? -He asked as if looking for her.

-Yes, yes, sorry. I was thinking." He said, clearing his throat and trying to hide it.

-You don't know her. My mother does not threaten, she acts. I am the living example that she cares little for others. He spoke with so much pain that Brenda knew she should help her come to terms with those feelings of abandonment, but now the urgency was different.

-Are you sure?

-Yes, my mother doesn't like to lose. Ever since we came back from the island she's been nervous. I don't understand why, but I don't like it.

Brenda relaxed again. The young woman's fears were simply reflections of an insecure personality. There was nothing solid behind her fears.

-She won't stop until she sees that stupid stone out of the way. Esperanza repeated again.

-Honey, that's just a simple way of talking, you see when we are angry....

-He has always called Rachel a stupid rock. She said with conviction while the doctor was getting whiter and whiter. She hasn't said it once. There have been many conversations I've been able to eavesdrop on. She commented with regret.

-And does he always speak with the same firmness?

-Always, and she doesn't know how many hours she spends on the phone. There are days when she hardly eats. I even made her one of those cakes that Peter likes so much to see if I could tempt her and win some of her time but nothing. I made those apple and cinnamon tartlets with sugar but nothing.

-You said a lot. Brenda was trying to think a mile a minute.

-The tartlets? No, none, he didn't even try them.

-I mean the calls. He said smiling for the first time.

That young girl was pure sweetness and her plump, rosy cheeks made her look even more tender. You would have to be a really bad woman not to fall for the charms of such a daughter.

-Oh yes, he spends hours and hours. And since we got back from the trip, even more.

-Do you know who he's talking to?

-Politicians and businessmen. People with a lot of power. Brenda wrinkled her forehead in surprise.

-Do you know what he works on?

-He doesn't work. She answered confidently.

-Renowned family?

-No, his father was a waiter and his mother a teacher.

-Herencias... -Brenda was getting more and more scared. Her suspicions did not sit well with her.

-No, his parents didn't even have a house. They lived on rent.

-But then how does she do it?

-You mean the house and cars?

-Do you have several cars?

-Yes, three, and all in your name. The truth is that Peter asked me the same question and I couldn't answer him. He said as if for the first time he was listening to the evidence.

The Amazons is a non-profit group, isn't it?

-That's right doctor, but I don't understand where...?

-And you don't pay a salary or any fees or anything like that, am I right?

Esperanza became very nervous. She didn't like the doctor's conjectures, after all, that woman may have been an ill-born viper, but she was still her biological mother, the one she had been looking for for years and had found only a couple of years ago. He remembered the happiness he felt when he got her back and the desire he had to tell her that he forgave her and wanted to be part of her life. He threw himself into her arms excitedly with a nostalgic kiss and hoping to find her affection but he never found it.

-No doctor, she may not be the best of women but you can't accuse her of.... doctor?

Brenda was already on her feet gathering her coat at full speed as he took her by the hand to lead her to the door.

-Let's go, I have to introduce you to a friend. Maybe between the three of us we can find out something. If my suspicions are true, your mother may try to hurt my friend and any of the Amazons.

Esperanza's eyes widened as she let herself be dragged towards the exit.

-But Peter...

The groom appeared so quickly when he saw them leave that he almost knocked over his second cup of coffee.

-Peter, we don't have time. We must leave and it is essential that Esperanza accompanies me.

-I'll take them." He said resolutely as he tossed the caffeine-laden paper cup into the wastebasket.

Brenda paused as she reached into her purse for her car keys.

-Peter, this is something we have to do on our own. Esperanza knows how to protect herself and I will not leave her alone, you understand that, don't you?

Dr. Klein's words sounded more like an order than permission so the man scrunched his brow.

-But it's late and I don't like her walking alone. We are from the village and this city is a jungle, I would be more relaxed if I or Akim went with you.

-He won't go. She answered confidently.

-Yes. Said a voice that spoke loud and clear behind the door.

Brenda looked at him and felt her heart pounding. She had asked him to leave but she was totally remorseful. Every minute without him by her side was becoming an impossible punishment to bear. With that tousled jet-black hair, his black leather jacket and that fire-blue gaze, he looked like a perfect angel just fallen from heaven fruit of some very deep sins.

She closed her eyes trying to control herself. She couldn't behave like a little girl in love. She wanted to rush into his arms and tell him she was sorry. Explain to him that confusion dominated her day and night. That she wanted to feel free to love him without restraint but heaven knew she couldn't do that. First there was Max, she owed him.

-No, as I told you, this is something we have to do on our own. We know how to act on our own. We don't need bodyguards. She said looking at Akim and making her position very clear. He looked at her with a look that Brenda would have thought seemed funny, but she didn't quite understand why.

-We'll be fine, Dr. Klein will walk me home. Don't worry.

Esperanza approached her boyfriend and gave him a sweet caress on his face. Peter embraced her and melted in an effusive kiss that made the doctor uncomfortable. Those two looked as if they would never see each other again and Brenda cursed herself for being in this situation with her god of sin. She was about to leave for the car when a familiar strong calloused hand held her by the wrist while the deep voice whispered in her ear....

-I'll wait for you at my house.

-I..." He turned and their faces were facing each other separated by barely a rose petal's length.

-Don't ask me to stay away from you again. I can't do that.

His lips came close to hers but he did not kiss her. He simply let them brush as he spoke slowly.

-Do what you have to do and come to me. I can't bear to have you away. He told her with his eyes glowing with desire.

Brenda forgot the argument, the place where they were, the presence of the other couple and the thousand reasons that separated them. She stretched her hands to cross them behind his neck as she kissed him with a passion she didn't know she knew. He embraced her with possessive strength. His fingers tightened around her waist as strong arms clutched her to his body. When they managed to separate they were both dizzy with desire.

-Wait for me... -She whispered softly.

-Always.

Brenda looked behind the broad shoulders and saw the amusement in Peter and Esperanza's looks that made her want to die of embarrassment. She opened the street door with urgency and the young woman walked with her smiling.

-The doctor is a woman to be reckoned with. Young Peter spoke aloud as he watched them drive away in the sports car.

-That's my wife. He said without thinking and surprising himself by the possessiveness of his words.

"My wife." He thought smiling bitterly. "First time I've ever felt anything like that and it had to be for someone else's wife."

She'd better go home and put Lucien to bed soon because she didn't even want to think what would happen if the little boy saw Brenda. He would surely throw himself into her arms and have to share her with him all night long.

"Ah no. No way." He said to himself amused as he gave the nervous boyfriend two gentle slaps on the back.

-They'll be fine. Go home. They'll be back soon." "If not, I'll hang that harpy myself," he thought to himself.

The young man nodded as he walked with leaden-footed steps out the door.

Late and early

> You call my name with your eyes but turn around when you see me.
> You call me with your body but ignore me with words.
> Sometimes you move me with your actions but others...others you disappear leaving me without a destination.
> Woman, watch out for the game because you may not know the rules yet.
> Akim

Brenda parked, sorry for the hour. The conversation with her former patient and current friend Murray had been most enlightening but very long. The politician had made a few calls in her presence and between them they were able to tie up a lot of the loose ends of Esperanza and her devilish mother.

The young woman was right, her friend Rachel could be in danger but nothing like that would happen, she told herself smiling knowing that she herself would be in charge of dismantling that feminist do-gooder. The Amazons didn't deserve a leader like that harpy. As she locked the car she thought it would not be easy to unmask that she-wolf disguised as a lamb but for her friend she would do it. She had to catch that beast with her claws ready to attack so that there would be no doubt. She walked hesitantly towards the house looking at her watch and checking that it was already ten minutes past two in the morning. Surely Akim would be asleep by now. She'd better leave. She would explain tomorrow. She was about to turn around when a thick voice emerged as the door of the humble house opened.

-Are you leaving?

She looked up and their gazes met. The most attractive of his sins leaned against the doorframe waiting for her decision. Did he really think he could leave when he was tempting her like that? His broad arms crossed expectantly over his hard chest. Determined she stood in front of him to rest her small hand on that broad torso. Akim's heart was pounding and Brenda knew what she had to do. She brought her lips to his torso and kissed him gently where the heartbeat rode madly. The man stroked her long hair as he tugged her gently to force her to meet him with his gaze. She lifted her head and said tenderly.

-I have to explain... -Akim kissed her with pure desire while he lifted her up, provoking in her a small cry of astonishment.

-Not now," he said, hoarse with passion.

Brenda felt transported to the scene of a romantic novel where the most wonderful man on earth took the protagonist to a bed where kisses and caresses would be the preliminary to the sweetest endings. Akim may not have been as perfect as many fairytale princes or as sweet as many Romeos with their Juliet. His imperfections were obvious and their worlds were totally exclusive but that didn't stop her from feeling like the sexiest and most adoring woman on the planet in his arms.

XXX

-Sh, they're all asleep. You don't want to wake them up. Akim said amused as he nibbled on her delicate toes.

-All of them? -she answered confused.

-My father and Lucien," he replied as his mouth caressed her legs and ran up her white thighs.

-Is your father at home? -She said trying to run away from the bed but Akim held her back with the weight of his body on top of hers.

-Where did you think they would be? We live together.

-I... I... I... I don't know. She commented as she felt Akim's kisses approaching her most intimate place causing her to lose her mind. I have to go before she wakes up.

The man smiled in amusement as he fondled her breasts one by one with the utmost dedication.

-You're not going anywhere.

Akim's hands were truly miraculous, she thought as she watched him lose consciousness in a sea of sensations impossible to compare.

XXXX Explanation of tattoos

Both exhausted and satiated they fell asleep. Akim embraced her possessively and Brenda could not help but feel an enormous regret. Every day that passed by his side, guilt filled her a little more. She had to come clean with Max as soon as possible. He didn't deserve her betrayal and Akim didn't deserve her waiting. As soon as she returned she would talk to him, regardless of the consequences. Their marriage could not continue. Her feelings screamed Akim's name from every pore.

The light began to brighten and Brenda woke up somewhat confused. This was not her room. She sat up in bed and slowly remembered the longest and most wonderful night of her entire history. She woke up and noticed Akim sticking his head out of the door to bring her a towel. He was smiling and dressed in just jeans. He saw that broad naked torso and felt himself blush as he remembered the maddening bites he had given her only a few hours before. He looked at her tattooed shoulder and recognized a small scratch that still glistened reddened. He sat down beside her and she stroked his wound with her finger in apology.

-My doctor turned out to be a beast. I'm full of marks. He said amused while pointing to another redness on his other shoulder. I was about to call the police. He commented smiling.

-Idiot.

-Stretch.

-Handsome.

-I love you.

They were both silent for about five more minutes of eternity when at last she was able to say something.

-I have no freedom. I can't, I mustn't... Not until I talk to him.

He looked at her with eyes shining with love and Brenda felt herself dying. She had to resolve her situation as soon as possible.

-I accept it, but don't ask me to understand. I want you in my bed, in my home and in all the days I have left to live. Every moment that I don't feel you as mine something breaks inside me. I loved you from the first moment I saw you and that feeling grew until it became this madness that doesn't allow me to breathe if you are not there.

Akim rested his forehead on hers. He looked exhausted. He could feel the immense effort it took for someone like him to express so many feelings out loud.

-I'll wait for you in the kitchen. He said giving her a kiss on the head.

-Won't you shower with me? -she asked eagerly.

Akim whispered a curse under his breath and then burned it with his passionate voice.

-I can't... Lucien is awake and...

-Doesn't the door have a lock? -she asked hopefully.

-He said as he wrapped her naked body in the towel and carried her to the bathroom almost in his arms.

XXX shower

Brenda was just finishing drying her hair and starting to get dressed while Akim was preparing breakfast when she saw him. There it was again. That notebook she often carried in her backpack.

"No, you mustn't," she said to herself trying to stop being her usual curious self. "It's not right, it's part of your privacy. It wasn't right," she repeated herself again as she stretched out her arm and moved closer and closer to the notebook.

"Lately I don't do anything that I should," he thought trying to justify his indiscretion.

She opened it almost unintentionally when she saw that the pages were covered with phrases, lyrics of something that looked like songs and on the side of some of them there were some charcoal drawings. She leafed through them, trying not to look too gossipy, but at one she stopped, struck by the image. That drawing was her in her office. Every detail of her face, her long hair, the brown of her eyes, every detail was captured to perfection. More than a drawing, it looked like a black and white photo. In the portrait she looked concentrated but the most striking thing was how the drawing captured the distance of the observer. As if spying on her from a distance. She read the words written underneath and felt tears begin to flood her eyes.

Tell me if this is love because I don't understand it. I watch you dreaming of belonging to you but you're not there. You don't listen to me. I need you and you don't appear, I look for you but you don't find me. I whisper to the wind to bring you closer to my side but it doesn't do it.

I'll be your friend, your lover or both, on your lips is the decision. Darling, run to my arms, come to me, let me embrace you and you will know that no one has whispered your name as I do. I wait for you in the distance and I beg you in the privacy of a deserted room to be the reality of my lonely evenings. Tattoo my name next to yours, there next to the chest of your love. Write in your heart the words, surrendered for you, as long ago I wrote in mine, surrendered only for you.

Brin...Brin...Brin...Brin... no one has whispered your name like me...

Brenda wiped away her tears and walked out into the small kitchen. Akim was smiling amusedly at his son when he saw her appear. When he saw her he smiled at her but instantly tensed when he noticed the gleam in her eye.

-Is something wrong?

-Why do you call me Brin? I want to know. You always hide the answer but today I need it. She asked excitedly.

-Because it's only yours and mine," he said confidently with no intention of hiding anything from her.

He had not finished speaking when he found himself wrapped between two arms that grabbed him by the back of the neck to hang on to him and drag him into an effusive kiss. He responded instantly, forgetting about breakfast, the kitchen and the little boy who was watching them laughing his head off.

-Ejem... Good morning. I didn't know we had a visitor." Father cleared his throat in amusement as he saw their faces flushed with embarrassment.

-Good morning. She responded like a child caught with a stolen candy.

When Lucien saw Brenda out of his father's arms, he jumped out to be hugged and Akim had to give him room so she could lift him up. The four of them had breakfast as if it were any other morning but the doctor was no fool and noticed the mischievous glances of the father towards his son so she decided to go to the room to gather their belongings and give them space to talk. Lucien accompanied her as she told him about her new advances in the world of biology and her ant house.

-Don't you have anything to tell me?

-I am not a child.

-I'm not attacking you, it's just that I was surprised to see a woman so early in the morning and in our kitchen.

-I am not gay. He said seriously.

-Even I'm not an idiot," he said, trying to cut his bad temper, "it's the first time you've brought a woman home to sleep with you. Does this mean you're together?

-If you mean has he told her, not yet," he said, annoyed at being cornered, "but he will soon.

Her father made a strange gesture and Akim suddenly felt furious. He did not wish him to doubt her.

-He is on a trip. They'll talk when he gets back. He said gruffly. His father did not answer and Akim felt even more annoyed. She will, you don't have to doubt her.

-And I don't." He said as he picked up the breakfast cups. It's him I'm afraid of.

-What do you mean? -He asked, trying not to sound so interested.

-From my own experience I know what a couple is capable of doing to keep someone who wants to leave.

-You mean because of my mother? -He stammered regretfully, knowing that he had also been part of his mother's plans to keep him.

-Yes. She cried, begged, threatened and lied. You have to be careful with that man. I'm not sure but something tells me he won't let her go just like that.

-You're not the first person to tell me that. He replied annoyed.

-And what do you plan to do?

-Fight with all my strength," he answered confidently. I can't lose her.

-Then do not allow yourself to be separated from her.

His father looked down sadly and Akim understood that his father knew perfectly well what it meant to lose the one he loved.

One who was not his mother. He would be vigilant, he would not be like them.

Days go by

> You are by my side and I find that the days are clearer,
> the sun shines cloudless and the moon smiles brazenly.
> I embrace you and close my eyes under the stars
> that dance happily for our love.
>
> Akim

Impossible to work, impossible to stop looking at the woman behind the glass of her office. To say wonderful would be to insult her with simple words. His Brin was a dream from which he was seriously afraid of waking up. She elevated him to a world where differences did not exist. She transformed him into the good man he longed to become. Nights at her side were peace. The caresses of her hands represented the hopes of a better life.

Brenda looked up as if called by his thoughts and smiled at him with so much love that he almost threw the damn materials on the floor and kidnapped her to an unknown place. One where she was his and no one could ever take her away from him. Rarely had the wheel of fortune stopped on her number and today she possessed the prize, held it in her hands and did not intend to let it go. Now he understood his mother's constant complaints when he was little, telling him that he was a hard head. Yes, he was. Brenda had come into his life and he planned to close the door on her. Someone like him didn't usually get second chances. Surviving in a society marked by the footsteps of ruthless elephants had left him too scarred not to fight back. He loved her, he was in love and he would do anything to wake up every morning by her side. This last month he had had her full time and he wanted to keep it that way.

The phone rang just as Nikola approached with a bottle of water, so he raised his hand as a signal to wait for a moment. The friend leaned against the wall. The morning had been a busy one amidst sandbags and boxes of gleaming floors.

-...*Yes Philips I understand...yes you don't have to worry, you will get your payment...no, it's not like that, I just had a little inconvenience but everything will be fine, I promise...I won't be late again....*

Nikola was beginning to transform his cheerful face into a thoroughly disgusted one and Akim cursed himself for his bad luck. A few minutes earlier and he wouldn't have been there to hear his pitiful plea. He didn't get to cut off the call when he felt his friend's accusing gaze drilling into his brain.

-It's not what you think. He said, pre-empting the accusations as soon as he cut off the call.

-I told you it was dangerous. What the fuck have you gotten yourself into!

-I've got it under control," he lied with little conviction.

-Yes? It's not what it looked like. How much? -Nikola asked angrily but willing to help him with his savings. After all, they were almost brothers.

-It's not necessary. I'll sort it out. He replied in disgust at her intrusion.

-How much fuck!

-Ten thousand," he said arrogantly, trying to restrain a friend who was too much of a busybody.

-What! What have you done!

Akim reached out to steal the bottle of water from his hand as he drank nervously.

-The idiot of the unmentionable one has been gone for a month and...

-You spent it all on her...? Damn you Akim," Nikola kicked an empty bucket in disgust.

-To tell the truth, it was both of us. And stop fussing or he'll see us and I don't want him to know.... -he commented embarrassed.

-But what have you done? Theater and dinner at the Ritz every day? -He asked just as angry as before, but whispering so as not to be discovered.

-Something similar...

-You're crazy. You're an idiot...

-And what did you want me to do!

-Everybody's thing, damn it. A movie on the couch and a pizza with onion rings.

-That's not his world! -I needed this month to be special. I needed her to...

-Did not discover the differences...

Akim shifted nervously. When it came to his Brin logic was never on his side. He wanted to be someone different for her but reality crushed him by telling him what he wished to bury but couldn't. Different worlds, unequal opportunities....

-Look at me! I'm a fucking bricklayer who barely earns enough to survive! I have a shitty job and no chance of ever getting better. I come from a country of which I can only remember pain and sorrows. I've been trying to enroll in arts but I have to start from scratch because everything I studied abroad here is useless. Do you think if I tell her my reality she'll choose me over him? -She spat with disgust and anger at his every word and Nikola lowered her tone a little more relaxed.

-She knows who you are. She knows you better than you know yourself.

-Are you sure? I've taken her to a different place every night and she's taken it as normal. She hasn't noticed... That's her world and she's not able to see anything different... -. He answered doubtful that Brenda really understood the reality of her limitations.

-Are you calling her cold and calculating? You? -Akim slumped against the wall, overwhelmed and defeated.

-Don't be stupid. Brenda is the most sensitive woman I've ever met. Nikola lifted his shoulders in incomprehension and he answered unwillingly. The money we've spent, the places we've visited are so normal in her life that she didn't even realize that I'm not part of it.

-And you asked Philiphs for more money?

-Only until the unmentionable one returned and spoke to him.

-And then what were you going to do? Tell him to bring you flowers to the cemetery? That guy is dangerous. If you don't pay him you're dead.

-Fuck I know, I know.... You wouldn't happen to have the address of a plastic surgeon, would you? -He said trying to break the tension.

Nikola walked back and forth until he stopped in place.

-I have something better. You'll have to work nights.

-I don't care about that. He replied hopeful and intrigued. His friend was a box of surprises.

-They pay well and they need a strong guy. I'm a friend of the owner, I'm sure he wants you to start tonight.

-Today... -He stammered thinking he would no longer enjoy her in the evenings but Nikola was right, the debt had gotten out of control and Philips was a lender to be had.

He was about to agree when he saw behind the glass as Connor entered his doctor's office.

-Will you tell him? -Nikola asked, interested to know.

-Never.

-And where did you say the job is? What do you need me for? -He asked, deflecting the subject of his sincerity, but without looking away from the office.

-In Inferno. They need a sturdy guy with a bad face. You know how to keep order, take care of the visitors, guide them around the place... You're a perfect fit.

-Isn't that the trendy place in the center of town?

-Same.

-And the one where Lola works as a waitress? -He mumbled.

-Is that a problem? -Nikola asked, arching an interested eyebrow.

-I hope not. The last time I saw her, she wasn't very happy. He replied as he recalled the series of insults Lola hurled at him as he left.

-Okay, I'll send you a message with the details. Those London night jobs pay very well. I'll talk to you right now and...

Nikola kept talking but Akim didn't hear him. Connor was moving around the office like crazy and Brenda was facing him with her face up. He had been watching them argue behind the glass for a while now and it was getting harder and harder for him not to intervene. That Scotsman had him between his eyebrows and he imagined the discussion and the reason for so many arm movements. In one of those replies the man grabbed her by the shoulder and she could not contain herself. He bolted for the office. If that big guy was looking for a war, he'd better look for it with someone his own size because if he didn't let her go before she entered his office, she'd slam him against the wall with a single punch.

Failures

Your eyes frighten me, your caresses frighten me but here I am, telling you that you have me inebriated in your power and without any intention of escaping.

Akim

-Stop yelling or I'll have to throw you out of my office.

-What was I missing? Are you planning to separate from your friends too? What else is that nobody going to take from you?

-Don't call it that!

-And what do you want me to call him! -he shouted angrily. You're crazy if you think you'll get any good out of all this ridiculousness. He has nothing to do with your world. You plan to leave Max and go with him where? To eat bread and onions together?

-When you're like this, I can't talk to you. You talk nonsense.

-I'm not saying them, you must reconsider....

-If I remember correctly, it was you who encouraged me to live life. Wasn't that exactly what you were saying? -Connor looked at her angrily and the woman smiled victoriously. Max was supposed to have me wrapped up in his world and not let me give free rein to my personality and now that I'm doing what you proposed and my chains are released, it turns out that you don't agree with what I'm doing. I'm sorry but I don't understand you.

Brenda took a shaky breath. She had been arguing with her friend for almost an hour and the fight had no end in sight. She couldn't understand Connor's petty attitude.

-That guy's no good for you. Have you seen him? Tough, tattooed, lowlife and much younger than you. He'll use you, step on you and dump you in a ditch before you know it.

-That's not true," he said, his voice hoarse from so much arguing. Connor, what's wrong with you, I don't understand you? You always hated Max and now you are his most fervent admirer.

-I'm not, but when I told you to find your life, your passion, I didn't mean you should do it with a man like that. Honey I know you, you're a sweet woman with good intentions and that's the model of men who tear people like you apart -. Connor began to feel sorry for her friend and relaxed the tone of the discussion. Why is he with you? Has he already asked you for money?

-No!" I shout offended, "Do you really think I can't conquer a man if I don't have any money in front of me?

-Honey, that bricklayer is not the kind of man who falls in love with people. Believe me, I know them well. I'm sure he's been hanging out with others besides you.

The doctor felt her blood begin to boil. Doubts about her age may have assailed her more than once but having her best friend highlight them over and over again made her explode with rage.

-I may not be that young and I may not have tits the size of two melons, but that doesn't stop me from being able to win a man. I have many physical and non-physical virtues.

-And he's not the type to value them. You'll throw away a marriage for someone who's not worth it. Fuck, have you thought about what you'll do with him when you have one of those fancy meetings you usually have? Will you wear a T-shirt to highlight his tattoos so they don't notice his shortcomings?

-That's enough! Let me make my own decisions.

-Not when they're so wrong. You're infatuated with a good fuck. That's all it is. When the novelty wears off, you'll feel empty.

Connor grabbed her shoulder to try to hold her in place so he could convince her when a deep, heavily accented voice spoke coldly from the doorway.

-Either you let her go or I don't answer.

-See what I'm talking about? He murmured in her ear before turning to face the six-foot-nine man who was talking angrily to him. Are you going to hit me?

-No, I'm going to kill you if you don't let her go right now.

Connor released her smiling at her apparent victory. She was demonstrating to her friend the blackened temperament of her beloved lover.

-That won't be necessary, I'm leaving.

The Scotsman walked out the door in triumph. If Brenda knew Brenda at all she knew perfectly well that this caveman demonstration had not pleased her in the least. She could say what she wanted but that brute was not for her. Of course she wanted her to be happy and feel free from her bonds but exchanging Max for that deadbeat was not a good choice. He would take advantage of her, use her, get who knows what and then discard her like a used clenex and he wouldn't allow it.

He walked determinedly towards the street, he needed to breathe some fresh air. He couldn't remember ever arguing with his friend the way he had and that made him hate that cheap bricklayer that much more. Because of him his friend, his sister, was more distant than ever. He cursed him again and again when in the distance he visualized a car most familiar to him.

"Fuck no...Fuck..." he thought as he broke into a run. He had gotten over a hundred yards away from the building but if he ran with all his might he might be able to stop an impending tragedy.

Truths and lies

-Are you all right?

Brenda's tension was all too evident. She tried to calm down but the argument with Connor still kept her upset. When she remembered everything he had said to her her blood began to boil again.

-I'm fine, but I don't want you to do it again. Brenda spoke with an unfamiliar authority.

Akim approaching at his side stopped in place with his body frozen in surprise.

-Are you talking to me?

-Yes, you. I don't like it when you go around threatening to beat and kill my friends.

-I was holding you by force. He answered between his teeth.

-He wasn't going to hurt me. You can't go around threatening me. I don't like it. She said annoyed.

-So he insults me, he offends you, and I'm the one who gets beaten up?

Brenda closed her eyes trying to focus. Akim was right. She was taking all her discomfort out on him. She was sure Connor had provoked him.

-I'm... I'm sorry... I think Connor tried to prove... -She preferred to keep quiet about the thousand reasons why Connor thought they should separate and that she was sure he tried to show. I'm not being fair with you but I can't do it anymore.... -She said, tired emotionally. The weight of the breakup of a marriage was tearing her up inside, if she added to that the incomprehension of her friend that was already the debacle. Akim might have made her feel like never before, she might even have smiled at his side like a complete, desired and passionate woman, but was it really worth so much suffering?

Because she was sure that this way of the cross had only just begun. When she talked to Max there, the world war would reach its peak.

The young man reached out tenderly and stroked her face with a finger until he reached her chin and lifted her up to look at him.

-He will understand, it won't be easy but he will understand. I will take care of showing him how wrong he is.

-Do you really think so? -she asked suspiciously.

-Do you still doubt it? I would do anything for you.

-Why Akim, why are we here?

Akim saw the doubt in her eyes and would have hanged the devilish Scotsman there and then, but decided that she needed all his sincerity. She stretched the length and breadth of her body and with sweaty hands spoke with complete sincerity.

-Because I love you. Because my life makes sense when you wake up next to me and it's lost when you leave.

Brenda felt a warm drop begin to run down her cheek. Strong arms comforted her with a passionate kiss. She closed her eyes and let herself be enveloped by forbidden and sinful sensations that she was sure the world would never understand. She had fallen in love like a teenager with her favorite song, like a bee with the sweetest flower, like a woman with her true love....

Max walked into the office totally happy. He had been away from home for almost a month and was sure Brenda would be delighted with the surprise. Recent times had proved to be very hard. George's death, the constant traveling had taken him too far away from his wife and he was ready to make up for lost time. She was his soul mate.

He entered the building delighted with the changes, the work seemed to be going from strength to strength. Surely she would be happy. He turned down the hallway toward his office when the image he saw hit him squarely. Wide, tattooed arms wrapped around his wife possessively as he kissed her like there was no tomorrow. At first he shook his head trying to clear his head. What he was seeing had to be a mistake, it had to be. He thought over and over again of a thousand reasons to justify it but he could not. His blood was boiling hot in his veins. Her breath began to shorten when she could finally articulate and curse out loud. That young man was not only kissing her once, he was grabbing her around the waist to hold her close to his body, surely burning for her. Max threw the small suitcase on the floor ready to enter and hang the wretch when he was held by a steel body that stood in front of him to stop him.

-Let me through!

-I can't. You're too upset and you'll do something stupid.

-I'm going to kill him! -He spat angrily as he glared at Connor with the greatest of his hatred. You...you knew and you allowed it. You bastard bastard." He shouted as he struggled to try to free himself but the Scotsman stood in his way.

-I will not deny you my qualities but now you must think before you act or you will lose her forever," he said flatly.

-That damn bricklayer is going to let my wife go.

Max faced Connor stretching his long body to show him that he was willing to fight him and anyone who got in his way.

-Wait! Damn you Max. He replied as he held him by the shoulders. You don't understand. He's going to ask for a divorce.

Max stopped in place without moving. Connor's words had never crossed his mind. That idiot was with the wrong woman, he'd break her face, maybe they'd argue and the situation with Brenda would be tense for a while, but divorce? For that whippersnapper? His head was spinning in confusion. He was unable to think clearly. Max's insides began to churn inside. Was there more to this than what he was seeing? The man growled angrily and dodged around

Connor to run to the office door and swing it open on its hinges. The artist cursed loudly and ran after him knowing the inevitable was ahead and he hadn't been able to avoid it.

Prisoner of your decisions

Akim was caressing the sweetest mouth of his dreams when in the next instant he was dragged backwards by the shoulders as a closed fist collided with his jaw causing him to lose his balance and fall to the ground. His hand went to his lip to verify that it was bleeding.

-But what horns... -She raised her face and saw him. He was about to respond to the attacker when he felt Brenda's small hands pleading on his torso.

The young man who initially believed the attack came from the Scottish idiot, gave up instantly upon verifying the identity of his attacker. "He already knows." He thought contentedly. That may not have been the way she wanted him to find out but this was better than having to keep sharing it. Maybe the situation wasn't so terrible after all." He said stroking his bruised chin.

-You son of a bitch. You son of a bitch." Are you afraid of me? -Akim smiled sideways, bringing up his lowly suburban years and wanting to answer. He hated him too. Jealousy towards that man clouded him from day one. That blissful architect represented the greatest of his fears and he was delighted to have a good fight until he left him passed out on the floor.

-Whenever you want. He answered with a withering glance and pulling Brenda's hand away with the utmost delicacy.

-No! Please... Akim... Max... Don't!

They both seemed to stop at the plea of their beloved because they stopped instantly but not without looking at each other like caged wolves.

Brenda approached Max and grabbed his arm to try to pull him away but he wouldn't move. He kept looking at him looking to be attacked and Akim wished with all his might that he could. Watching her approach him and try to calm him down with gentle caresses on his arms was making him desperate with jealousy. He felt like ripping her away from him, holding her tightly and screaming at the top of his lungs that she was no longer his. "She belongs to me! She's mine!" he thought furiously.

-Please Max... we need to talk.

The man turned around vehemently to plunge his reproachful gaze deep into her heart.

-Talk? What exactly do you want to tell me? I didn't feel like I was forcing you?

-Max, please, let's go somewhere else.

-What for! Are you going to explain to me why you were in the arms of a common bricklayer? An ignorant bully who can't even speak? Is that it, Brenda? Do you want to tell me why you're acting like a whore with a brainless guy like this?

Akim was about to throw himself on the architect when Connor intervened holding him tightly from behind. Akim pushed him with all his strength and managed to get free, holding Max by the collar of his shirt, lifting him into the air.

-You can insult me as many times as you want, but don't ever call her that again.

-Or what? You think I'm afraid of you?

Max opened his arms high and let go of his grip and then jumped on his neck and began to hit him with all his might. Akim didn't give it a second thought and responded to his attack with a right straight to his eye that left him prostrate on the ground. The architect trained twice a week at the gym and was quite strong but it was no comparison to the street classes Akim had received. His muscles formed in village fights and senseless wars were incomparable.

The young man was breathing heavily waiting for his opponent to get up so he could hit him again when Brenda threw herself to the ground next to the unmentionable one.

-That's enough! Akim, please leave..." she pleaded feebly, "Max and I need to talk.

-No!" he shouted angrily as he couldn't tell her out loud that he hated to see her on the floor looking after him. Damn it. That man had provoked him. He was to blame for her reaction.

Brenda quickly reached into a box of Clenex for a piece of paper and wetting it with some water from a bottle on her desk, she held it up to her husband's eye, which was beginning to swell.

-Brin... -His voice was barely audible. He also had a bloody lip. He was in pain too, he needed her too....

-Leave us alone...please. She answered without looking at him.

Akim gasped for breath as rage surged through his body, churning his insides. He knew he should leave but it was too difficult. He walked towards the exit and slammed the door with all his might. That damn fool made it clear with his fists, he didn't want to lose her and would do anything to keep her. That made him shudder with fear and doubt. He walked down the hallway a few steps until he came to a halt against a wall, which he angrily punched.

-You look like you've lost your job. Connor's voice behind him made him tense up even more.

-Will you never leave me alone?

-I can help you.

-You? -He answered without a hint of amusement. Are you going to tie a noose around my neck? -Connor grinned, and Akim wanted to practice boxing with his head as a sack.

-You can't imagine how delighted I would be, but no, I'm going to make you another offer. I have an art office in Barcelona. I may not like you but that doesn't mean I don't recognize that you have an innate gift. You made that clear at my exhibition. Your work was brilliant.

-Barcelona... -he murmured amused. A bit far, don't you think?

-Maybe, but you've just lost your job and you clearly need it.

-I will find another solution. He said feeling trapped. That damned Scotsman was right, work was essential for a man of his class.

-You know that if she separates she won't have as much money. Yes, well, she's a professional and a very good one, but the greatest wealth comes from Max. Without him the accounts will plummet.

Akim knew he had reached the maximum quota of offenses. With a reaction that the artist did not foresee, the young man grabbed him by the neck and dragged him against the wall where he left him embedded as an advertising poster.

-Hey, uh... What's going on? -Nikola rushed over, trying to intervene and separate them.

-Your friend just lost his job and the girl. Connor said smiling without a hint of fear.

Akim held him even tighter by the scruff of the neck. Confusion seized him instantly. What was that fool talking about? Losing the girl?

Connor noticed his cloudy look and stirred until he managed to get loose. He stretched his clothes slowly as he enjoyed the mason's desperation.

-With Max here your hopes are zero? -Haven't you seen him? Five minutes at her side and she has chosen him. He's by her side and not with you, that means something, don't you think?

Akim clenched his fists in a furious rage. He had to get out of there or he would commit a series of chain murders and that meddlesome Scotsman would be at the top of the list. He walked angrily toward the lockers. He would pick up his helmet and get away from this madness as soon as possible.

-Accept my proposal and leave! Don't be an idiot. You've had her for as long as it took him to arrive. Connor shouted loudly but Akim could no longer listen. He jumped on the bike at full speed.

Thoughts swarmed through him like hundreds of woodpeckers mercilessly drilling into his brain. "Five minutes... you've lost her... he took her away from you in five minutes..." The idiot's screams made him unhinged. That was not true. She would talk to him. Tonight she would be by his side and they would start a future together. This could not be a fantasy. The love he felt for her was too deep a reality to forget.

The argument with Max continued at his house. They screamed, cussed and cried together until the early morning enveloped them in the thickest of darkness. Brenda was no longer sure of anything. At first she felt she was right. With Max the passion was gone. The woman he wished her to be was a role she no longer wished to play. It seemed shameful to admit it but that was the reality. In his marriage he had acted as he should or as expected but never as he wished. Over the years she had transformed into that woman that both her father and her partner desired. She needed to find her own light and think of herself before others.

-I'm sorry, none of this was planned," she said for the hundredth time, but the slamming of the front door told her that Max could no longer hear her.

She leaned back in the seat of her car exhausted by so much tension and crying her heart out. She did not want to make him suffer. It was never her intention, but what should she do? She couldn't go on living a farce, much less continue to deceive him. Max didn't deserve it. She wiped her face and looked out the window of her convertible. The pain tore at her soul, but a part of her breathed free. A new stage was beginning where her desires would become reality, her thoughts would no longer be silent and her character, good or bad, would be hers and hers alone.

Akim opened the door to her house and approached the car without speaking. He looked as exhausted as she did. He had probably been up all night just like her. He would have liked to tell her that he was happy to be on her doorstep, that he hoped something good would come of it all but tears flooded his face and throat again. The words stuck silently. The pain of almost twenty years down the drain was too overwhelming and he couldn't hide it. He got into the car, closed the door and hugged her. There were no reproaches, no complaints, only understanding. He would never know how important that attitude would be for her. The young man gently kissed her neck and after many, many minutes in silence he whispered tenderly to her.

-Let's go in, I need to have you. He caressed her face gently and nodded his head. She needed him too.

-Whatever you want to talk about, I'll give you as long as it takes me to drink this beer.

Connor sat down next to Max, surprised to find him in such a state. When he called him to meet him in that pub he was sure he would find a man in pain but the image of the architect was much more than that. The man was a total wreck. He never believed that the snooty king of kings could be in such a pitiful state.

-You can't let yourself be defeated... -He said as if reading her thoughts.

-Oh no? -Max took a huge sip of what would be his fifth beer of that early morning. What are you here for? Did you come to enjoy yourself?

The Scotsman raised his finger to the waitress to serve him another one just like his colleague as he sat down next to her.

-He told you." It was not a question.

Max didn't answer, he just drank without looking up from the thick wooden table.

-Connor, why don't you go away and leave me alone. You've done it. She asked me for a divorce, isn't that what you wanted?

-No," he said, choking on what seemed to him to be a lie. For many years he thought Max was the castrator of his friend's courage and illusion, but now he wasn't so sure. Max smiled half-heartedly to himself and took another sip of the longest.

-It may have been that way in the past," he said, trying to justify himself, "but the situation has changed.

-Yes, it seems so. He replied bitterly.

-You can't leave home. You have to stay there.

Max looked up but his neck remained bent towards the table. The glow of pain and drunkenness glimmered behind his pupils and the artist felt truly sorry for the man. It could not be said that they were friends, in fact they always got along like cats and dogs, but they had known each other for almost twenty years, they had shared many birthdays together and more than one Christmas and the memory caused him deep sorrow.

-You know, despite all your accusations, I always loved her. He stated with a sorrow that tore at Connor's heart. You may not understand me but I was only looking out for what was best for both of us.

-I don't think this is the time for statements. Connor shifted nervously in his seat in the face of the accusations of a husband racked with grief.

-Listen to me, we both made mistakes and I'm willing to overcome them if you do.

Max snorted over the beer foam as he answered her dizzy from alcohol and grief.

-Why are you here? I'm no longer part of his life. You should be happy. You're free of me. Now you'll be her little friend forever. You'll be able to take her on the paths you've always wanted. Now she'll be free... free from me... -The architect closed his eyes and finished his big glass in one gulp. He was about to get up when Connor held him by the arm.

-He is going to destroy her. The husband stood on the spot with a confused expression.

-What are you talking about?

Connor was happy to get her attention. With a polite gesture he asked her to sit back down while he ordered her another pitcher of beer. If he was right, and he was, Akim would take advantage of Brenda, tear her apart emotionally and financially and then dump her for a cheap disco gogo girl. He was her friend and would fight for her welfare even against herself. Max may not have been the accomplice she had hoped for, but he was the best she could count on. The architect was emasculating, uptight and very, very prissy but she had no doubt how much he loved her. If that low-life bricklayer bully hurt Brenda the two of them would put him in his place. Max sat extremely interested in her story. He had no doubt that the artist's words gave him hope that until just five minutes ago he had not had and he wanted to hold on to them tooth and nail.

Stones in paradise

-You must leave. Akim shouted in obfuscation for the umpteenth time as Brenda paced nervously through her office. She was tired of arguing in her workplace.

-He asked me for time to reposition himself. I can't throw him out. It's his home too.

-To hell with the house. You move in. Bring your things to mine today. Lucien and my father would be delighted to have you. He said hopefully.

-That's not possible and you know it. I have my life and my routine, I can't be the little friend you bring into the house and have to put up with.

-You're not a friend. Fuck, Brenda, you've been separated for more than a month and he's still under your roof," he replied, biting his tongue to keep from insulting her out loud.

-Please don't be a child. Your home is also your father's and your son's home and I have not yet....

-He said nervously as he dragged his hair tightly behind his fingers. -he said nervously as he dragged his hair tightly behind his fingers.

-I'm not ready to live with someone, let alone a whole family. Please try to understand me.

She was tense and he hated himself for being the reason for her distrust. He wanted to confess to her that his life began and ended with her. That if he was acting strange the last few weeks it was because of fatigue and that new night job but that it had nothing to do with the strength of his love.

He knew he should come clean but she would no longer see it the same way once she knew the truth. Brenda talked about understanding and twenty thousand reasons that justified her decision not to leave or to keep Max under her roof but he found them impossible to comprehend. The unmentionable one was planning something and he knew it. One night he had stormed out and hated her guts, only to arrive the next day submissive and eager to have what he called an amicable breakup? Hell no! he thought, dead jealous, the unmentionable one was planning something and Brenda couldn't see it. God, the fear of losing her made his skin crawl.

Akim approached her, trying to calm his fears, those that always dominated him when he thought about his future, and hugged her tightly from behind. His arms held her, preventing her from moving. If words were as easy as writing or painting he would explain to her that the air was no longer breathable oxygen if she was not by his side, he would explain to her the hundreds of reasons why he could not forget her or show her the thousand and one nights they still had to discover together.

-Brin... -His mouth searched for her like a thirsty man in the desert. He needed the warmth of her body to be enough to say everything that his choked words could not.

Brenda began to give in. The burning began to set them on fire as it always did when they brushed against each other. Akim grabbed her head by the nape of her neck and with his calloused hand held her to pull her against his lips. That mouth was the sweetness of a better world. He closed his eyes to fly into his wife's arms when the insistence of his phone made him curse loudly. Brenda amusedly broke away and pulled him close to her. They both looked at each other and were gawking at each other when Akim saw the total change in her face. The lines around her eyes accentuated and the chocolate glow in her eyes disappeared the instant she held the phone out to him.

-Lola... -She said as she read the name on the screen and walked away instantly.

His hand tried to stop her by the wrist as she answered but was too late.

-*Tell me... Yes... yes... well...*

Lola was sweet-talking, supposedly to inform him about a schedule change in the night shift, but he was barely able to hear her. His gaze searched for a Brenda who was deliberately dodging him. She fidgeted nervously through folders of reports and hurriedly put them in her briefcase. Akim didn't know how to hang up faster. She knew the doubts that used to assail her about her excessive maturity, and the call from an explosive Lola didn't help in the least. -She said in increasingly terse monosyllables, trying to cut off as soon as possible. She was walking towards the door. She was thinking of leaving -Yes...*I said yes!* -He shouted angrily before cutting off and trying to stop his doctor who was running out the door.

-Wait.

Rachel poked her head out of the door at the same instant Akim was trying to hold her by the elbow.

-I'm parked wrong. Shall we go now? -The friend asked, surprised to see their faces.

-Yes.

-Are you leaving? It's late. He said, watching the clock strike almost seven in the evening.

-Yes, we have an appointment.

-Well... -He answered choking, trying to find out where? with whom?

Brenda was about to walk out the door when she turned to speak to him with something in her eyes that looked like sadness.

-If you want, can you wait for me and have dinner together? I won't be long." She commented hopefully.

The young man said inwardly all the curses he knew in his language and in all the ones he knew. That night he was working and had to be in the room before ten o'clock or at least that was what he understood from Lola.

-I'm meeting some friends... -He lied trying to justify himself. Brenda looked down and said goodbye without even looking at him. Shit! -But tomorrow is Saturday," he said hurriedly, "if you want first thing in the morning we can.... -He didn't have a chance to propose his plans.

-We'll talk. She said leaving without looking at him.

The young man clenched his fists so tightly that his fingernails left marks on his palms. If he could, he would run after her, grab her around the waist and calm all her doubts. He would explain to her that Lola's youth and beauty were water under the bridge compared to the brilliance of her experience or the warmth of her kisses. He would ask her forgiveness a thousand times while with his caresses he would erase one by one the half-truths he never dared to explain. He would assure her that he was no longer the ill-tempered bully he used to be and that all this was the sole responsibility of his love for her.

Romantic songs sprang up by the thousands in his heart and thoughts describing his feelings gushed out of him, but she was gone. She had left and he had missed a golden opportunity to come clean.

Brenda walked to the car next to Rachel trying to fill the emptiness she felt in the pit of her stomach. It was Friday and he was out with friends, like most nights in the last few weeks, she thought ruefully.

-All right?

Rachel asked interestedly and Brenda tried her best to forget about Akim and focus on her friend. The poor woman's eyes were dark with grief. Since George's death it was the first time she had managed to get her out of the house. She looked at her sadly. Rachel wore no makeup, she was no longer smiling. She felt guilty about her husband's death and that had to stop. As a psychologist she knew perfectly well that mourning for a loved one was obligatory and necessary, but not guilt. Rachel had to let George go and move on with her life, no matter how difficult it might be.

-Everything is perfect.

-Where are we going? -he said, starting the engine.

-To the Las Amazonas meeting center.

-No, I don't want to. I'm not interested. He replied remembering his last fight with Carol. Those women don't interest me anymore.

-I know and I wouldn't force you if it wasn't necessary, but Esperanza needs us. Brenda tried to appeal to her feminine solidarity and seemed hopeful when she saw the look of doubt on her friend's face.

-Esperanza? What happened? -she asked interested.

Well, I had got their attention. That was enough for the moment.

-Start while I tell you about it.

Rachel reluctantly agreed and Brenda celebrated her triumph. She had to bring her friend back to life and if her plan worked, this would be her last night of guilt.

An end, a beginning

The women's screams were getting louder and louder. Carol charged with suing them and a thousand other stories as Brenda knew the end was near. If I managed to upset her with so little, maybe if I pushed a little harder....

-Liar! You're both lying bitches. You sold us out!

-I didn't do it! And if there's a bitch here, it's you, the one who abandoned her daughter, who hid her and now comes to give us moral lessons". Rachel shouted heatedly in Carol's office.

-Do you like to give lessons? -said Brenda, provoking her even more.

-But who do you think you are? You're not even part of the brotherhood. You have no right to have an opinion," he shouted, making the walls shake.

-Don't talk to my friend like that! -Rachel shouted on the verge of exploding.

-No, let her speak. Why don't I have rights? Isn't this a feminist group? Well, I happen to be a woman, hard-working, independent and a firm believer in our equal rights, why shouldn't I have a say?

-I don't want them in my group! Go away once and for all. Go back to where you came from.

-I want to collaborate. Brenda commented completely serene. It seemed that with each calm answer she offered, her interlocutor lost more and more of her nerves.

-Do you want to collaborate? You want to give us a handout. Carol laughed rudely. People like you only know how to offer charity. They are incapable of putting themselves in our place.

Brenda looked at her curiously. So that was her weak point? She felt underappreciated? She was already close, very close to getting it.

-I work with many charities. She said, poking at the wound. The woman transformed. Her eyes reddened with fury and Brenda knew that here was the true leader of the Amazons. The fake she would soon bring to light.

-Beneficent? Sure, the rich always think they sign up for a march of good intentions and get heaven. I'm sick of them coming here with their donations but leaving without showing their faces. They say they believe in equality but when the meetings are over they go home with their hubbies stuffed with money. Ha, I laugh at their feminism and the mother who bore them. I'm sick of it. The rich broads playing equality and the poor little Amazon idiots raising the little flag but when they get home, they make up to see which one of them is the sluttiest and steals the other one's husband. I don't give a shit if they kill each other, I'm here for what I'm here for.

Rachel's eyes widened in disbelief, but Brenda was very happy with the confession, now she needed the final blow.

-That's why you sold them, you talked to journalists to give them the scoop, didn't you, how many advertising contracts did you sign in exchange for agreements with influential businessmen? -You wanted the movement to fall and no longer put pressure on the political forces, didn't you Carol?

-Only you can have money? -she said, showing her teeth in rage.

-No, but I earn it with my work, not by tearing down the rights of hundreds of struggling women. Brenda tried to press, she needed a full confession.

-I am only concerned about my own.

-What about your daughter? You never thought about her?

-If it were up to me, I would have drowned her in a bucket of water when she was born. I'll collect what I promised, disappear, and let those whores kill each other. They're all selfish pigs who will never amount to anything. They'll grow old fighting over stupid things while I enjoy my retirement in the Caribbean.

-Those politicians bribed you well, I see. Brenda said, waiting for his affirmation.

-I'm not complaining, now if I may? -He said smiling to leave.

-I don't think you're going anywhere. The doctor stood between her and the door.

-Do you think you can stop me, doctor? Do you think anyone will believe anything you say? I will deny everything and those stupid girls will believe me, because I am their leader. She said with a raging bitch smile.

-Are you sure? Hope please... -She said aloud before the door opened.

The young woman entered with a laptop showing with cameras the meeting in the adjoining room full of Amazons. They all looked up at the loud speakers and could not believe what they had just heard.

-You!

The woman tried to pounce on the young girl but Rachel jumped in to defend her. The two fought on the floor until Brenda, Esperanza and other members of the group came to the office to stop them. The leader's face was unhinged as she was dragged towards the exit.

-He has fooled us all.

-He has used us.

-He laughed at us.

-What are we going to do now?

They all spoke in disappointment. The disappointed women looked at each other feeling used and helpless when Brenda decided to climb up on a chair to get the attention of the hundreds of women who murmured in grief.

-Please, girls, one minute. One minute of your attention!

The women did not seem to hear her. They were overwhelmed by heaviness and disappointment. Esperanza decided to bang on the microphone. It made such a deafening metallic sound that the women fell silent as they covered their ears with their hands.

-Girls, we are all hurt and disappointed. I more than anyone but the doctor is here to help us. Thanks to her and her contacts we were able to learn of my mother's criminal plans. Let's listen to her. What have we got to lose? The women looked at each other as they quieted down to listen. Brenda thanked Esperanza for her intervention with a smile and began to speak like a queen to her entourage.

-Dear Amazons, you have been deceived as fighters and as women. You may be lost, angry and disillusioned at this moment but we can't let scum like this get in our way. Great women before us fought for our rights and we cannot let ourselves be defeated now that we are so close to achieving them. No matter how much they beat us or how much they try to step on us, we will always stand up because we are women, we are fighters. We are...

-Amazons! - They shouted with their hands held high with their fingers in v's.

-But how are we going to organize ourselves? We had goals, ideas, dreams... and now we've lost everything....

-No, not at all. We must go forward. One false leader has deceived you, but another will lead us to victory," the doctor shouted.

-They all looked at each other in intrigue as Brenda came down from her chair to hold Rachel's hand and look up at her admiringly.

-No, you're crazy.

-Not at all. I don't know a more honest and hard-working woman than you. You managed to get ahead and make a place for yourself in the world. You love unconditionally, you believe in our rights, you fight for injustice and you are the funniest woman I know. There would be no better candidate than you.

-I can't... George...

-George would be proud to see the woman you have become and that he always knew you were.

Rachel began to cry and Brenda hugged her while the women as if possessed by the new winds shouted out loud the name of their congregation.

-Amazon! -Amazon!

-Rachel, our leader! - Esperanza shouted and the others followed her.

-Yes, because we are strong, we are women, we are Amazons!

Brenda let go of her friend and made way for hundreds of women to come forward to embrace and support her.

-Thank you, without you I would never have been able to unmask my mother or accept that she didn't love me. Esperanza said gratefully.

-You are stronger than you think. From now on you will live your life without dark pasts and learn to accept the affection of people who really love you. He said, looking out the door at a young man as thin as a broomstick waiting in the distance. Go to him and be happy. You deserve it. Esperanza ran to Peter who waited for her with open arms.

The women talked non-stop and Brenda knew she had to leave. This was Rachel's night. She and her Amazons had a lot of work ahead of them but hers was done. She hailed a cab happy with life. If it wasn't so late she would call Akim to tell him. She got in the car, gave the driver the address and smiled as she realized how important this man was starting to become in her life. In just a few months he had made her feel what in years she had never achieved. Lovers, friends and partners all rolled into one. Maybe Carol was right and the world was not entirely fair and that tomorrow would bring difficult problems, but today was hopeful. With Akim she felt alive, a woman, an Amazon, she thought amused, and she didn't want to lose him.

If life offered her oranges, she would make orangeade and let the lemons go to hell, she said to herself, happy with life.

She was in love with a younger man and he was in love with her. Society and social norms be damned. Have I thought that? Yes, I've thought it and I'm glad I don't have to shut him up, she thought as she felt how unfair she had been to him over a simple, stupid phone call. I'll talk to him tomorrow, she told herself excitedly.

A picture, a thousand words

If he were a dog he would surely be in a better mood, Akim thought as he walked through the crowded room. Young girls in skimpy clothes and muscular men were showing off like cattle waiting to be bought. They were smiling cheekily as they, glass in hand, scanned each other for the quickest and most delectable prey on which to satiate their appetites. He smiled unwillingly at the thought that this world was something far away that he no longer wanted to be part of. If it weren't for the money, he would be lying down with the woman he desired and not necessarily conversing.

-A drink?

-I'm working," he replied sparingly, trying to discourage her, although Lola didn't seem to mind.

-What nonsense. Everyone drinks here. Come on, honey, don't reject me. He said with a sonorous double meaning.

-I already did. He replied, moving his lips in a mock smile.

-Why are you so mean to me? -Lola spoke like a little girl as she brought her rounded breasts closer to his torso.

The woman was a perfect connoisseur of her charms and did not skimp on using them. The skimpy mini-skirt left her long and perfect legs in full view. A strapless tank top and a tight-fitting top highlighted a figure that any mortal could consider a knockout.

-Lola, please, I am working. You know perfectly well that nothing will ever exist between us again.

-You say that now, but you won't resist for long. You know that I can give you exactly what you are looking for. She commented, pressing her body against his and stretching out the tips of her toes to bring her face close to his.

Akim cleared his throat as he held her by the shoulders to stop her advances.

-If what you're talking about is a good fuck, I appreciate it, but I'm not interested.

-For the time being, for the time being...

The man shook his head. That woman was not insistent, she was a kamikaze. How could he tell her without being rude that he was no longer interested in her heart-stopping tits, or her magic powder, or if she disappeared from his life forever?

-Lola, please... -He was about to explain to her that he should aim his lethal weapons against another target when she, without warning, grabbed him by the neck to kiss him with unbridled passion. Akim could not get over his astonishment when they were already separated.

-Don't do it again," he mumbled.

-Daddy, you're being very mean to your baby, but you know I'm crazy about you and I forgive you everything.

The woman left satisfied and Akim shook his head. He wanted to return home, lie down to sleep and get some rest before rushing off to Brenda's house. He glanced at the clock contentedly and headed for the machine to clock out. Thinking about her was even changing his mood, he thought amused.

-Do you have them? -Lola asked the man who was smiling and looking at his cell phone screen.

-Yes, and they are perfect. And since when did you say you are together?

-Two years.

-Two years... -The man whispered between delighted and disgusted - Son of a bitch...

Lola kept the hundred pounds in her cleavage while she smilingly commented, fluttering her eyelashes like a naughty girl.

-I hope this makes her friend realize that Akim is not for her.

Max put away the cell phone with his ten photos and left without answering. That woman, that place and the presence of that filthy bricklayer in the room disgusted him. That bastard was probably taking advantage of his wife to get money out of her. He made her believe he was in love with her when in truth he was fucking that two-bit whore. Max wanted to smash his face in right there, but he couldn't let his rage get the better of him. He would continue as planned. In a few days, that damn bricklayer would be a bad memory and when he disappeared, his marriage would have to be patched up a little, but nothing insurmountable.

Akim arrived home exhausted from exhaustion. That night he had intervened in a fight between two drunks, a heated argument of a jealous couple and he had also had to stop the continuous advances of an insatiable Lola, he was dead. He threw his clothes on the bed without even the strength to take off his clothes. It was after four in the morning and if he hurried he would have a little more than four hours before getting up to wake Brenda with breakfast in bed. Remembering her made him smile hopefully before falling into a deep sleep. In the morning he would go to her house, hug her and bring her to his bed to spend the entire Saturday together under the covers.

Ultimatum

Akim was especially optimistic that morning. Seeing his doctor in just a few minutes cheered him up even more, he thought drying his hair with a towel and then tossing it into the laundry bin. He dressed at full speed. He wouldn't eat breakfast, if he hurried he might still find her inside the bed. The phone rang and he cursed under his breath when he saw who it was. His sunny day was beginning to cloud over.

-Yes *Philips I know...I understand it is not the full amount, but soon you will have a second income...yes soon...yes I know...I do not need you to threaten me...I will pay...I am not afraid of you and it is not necessary....*

He angrily cut the cell phone and threw it on the table ranting loudly when he discovered the look on his father's face. "Shit, I didn't see him come in," he said to himself cursing his bad luck. He knew all too well those crossed arms and those eyes throwing poisoned darts.

-I've got it all under control," he said, knowing that it would do him no good to lie. The man knew him too well.

-What a mess you're in.

-I said I have it under control.

-And that's why you work as a pack mule? -His father sounded angrier than he meant to, and Akim noticed it in the slump of his shoulders. Who is this Philips?

-A moneylender. He said as he felt cornered.

Her father opened and closed his eyes a couple of times to sit down the next minute in the chair in the small living room.

-How much?

-You don't have to worry. With the new job I'll get it paid off soon.

-His father raised his voice and Akim became defensive. They both had equally rotten tempers.

-Stay out of my life.

-Damn it, how much!

-Ten thousand. He replied with his temper somewhat lowered as he recognized his father's authority.

-And how much have you paid?

The young man was about to tell him to go to hell. He didn't like to feel like a little boy who was scolded for stealing candy, but the truth was that he had eaten candy without permission and quite expensive ones.

-Two thousand...

-Fuck...fuck...fuck...fuck! You have any idea what those guys are going through! -What the hell were you thinking?

-To tell you the truth, I wasn't thinking much," he said mockingly.

-Why? I have a job, Lucien is well, we don't lack anything. His father got up from his chair and began to walk nervously.

Akim listened to the downpour for what he considered too long and felt that his father was not one to judge.

-Are you sure, Dad? Have you seen the house we live in? Tell me, how old is the newest piece of furniture? When did you last rest? When did Lucien buy a toy without first asking if we could?

-This has nothing to do with us... don't try to fool me. He said apologetically.

-No, damn it. It's with me! I'm tired of being the poor guy who could have been a lot but came to nothing. The one who had possibilities but had to lose them. I'm tired of watching people from below. I don't want to be a spectator.

-Did you do it for her? -. He commented with sorrow in his voice.

-No! It was for me. I wanted to prove to her that I was worthy. That I could live in her world without embarrassing her. I wanted her to know me, to give me...

-His father finished the sentence for him with barely a whisper.

Akim slumped back in his chair as he clenched his hands around his hundred. He knew he had made a terrible mistake, he wasn't stupid enough not to recognize the danger in people like Philips but if he had to do it again he would do it a thousand times over to get what he now had with her. Brenda had met another man besides the dirty, poor bricklayer. Those days they dined, danced and shared an intimacy she had never experienced with anyone. If Philips tried anything with him, she didn't care, it was worth the price.

-Don't worry about me, I'll be fine. He said trying to calm his fears.

-I don't care about you. She looked at him with a frown on her face, and her father bluntly clarified.

-You have been unconscious but you are an adult and responsible for the foolish things you do, my fears are for your son.

-Lucien had nothing to do with this." His father looked at him cheekily and Akim cursed at the realization. They wouldn't hurt him." He said more as a wish than a reality.

Their silence was interrupted by a bell ringing loudly.

-Are you expecting someone? -Akim asked, knowing that if it was Philips he would hang him rather than let him near his son. Cautiously he opened the door and swore loudly when he recognized the visitor.

-What are you doing here?

-I've come to make a deal." Max spoke confidently as he walked in with a folio-sized envelope in his hand.

Akim could not look at that man and stop comparing himself. That guy exuded an elegance that made him hate him more and more. If the circumstances were different, if he had been born here, if he were not a damned outcast, he thought, angry with his life and his damned circumstances.

-I have nothing to discuss with you, you can go.

-I think this will interest you," Max stepped through the door and tossed the envelope on the living room table. Both he and his father looked at each other quizzically.

-And what is that supposed to be? -. He asked, pointing to the brown envelope.

-I want you to disappear from his life. I give you one day to say goodbye.

Akim opened his eyes and the next moment he pushed his head back and laughed as hard as he could. He thought that this day was slowly going bad, but Max brought joy back to his face.

-What makes you think I'll do it? -He replied amused, thinking that the man had suddenly gone mad.

His father did not ask permission and opened the envelope. His face was drawn like a poem and Akim frowned trying to figure out the reason.

-What's wrong?

-You'd better take a look.

The father held out his hand with a handful of photos. All dated the night before. He looked at them again and again without getting out of his astonishment. How could he have this material in his hands? That was not possible, he said to himself nervously.

-This is not...

-What it looks like? -Max asked, knowing that now he was the funny one. Well, it looks like it to me. In fact, I took the pictures myself.

-You... You! You were spying on me... -he mumbled.

-Yes, and I would do it again to expose you. You have deceived her. You told her a lot of lies to get what you wanted.

-That's not true. These pictures are crap and mean nothing. He said tearing into hundreds of pieces the one of the kiss with Lola.

-You can break them all, I have many more on my computer. He replied victoriously.

Akim approached with clear intentions of smashing his face in when his young son appeared in the living room, causing him to stop. He may have been a wild bully but not in front of the little boy.

The boy, who was heading for his father's legs, was stopped by his grandfather's strong arms.

-She will never believe a lie like this. Akim spoke with confidence.

-He will do it because it is the truth. I saw you myself.

-You wretch, you haven't seen anything because there was nothing. There is nothing between me and that woman. He replied angrily.

-I don't give a damn what you say. I want you back in the pit you should never have come out of. I want you out of our lives.

-Ours? Asshole, she left you.

-That's my problem. Take your money and go.

-What money! -He said, clenching his fists and thinking seriously about knocking him out right there.

-In that envelope you have a cashier's check. I hope it's enough. If not, tell me what your number is. I'll pay you whatever it takes to make you disappear.

-Do you think your money's going to convince me to give it up?

-If you have any dignity, you'll accept it and leave without me having to show her proof of your deception. I don't want you to break his heart.

-You son of a bitch! -Akim was about to hit him when his father let go of the little boy and stepped between the two men who were foaming at the mouth.

-Sir, I think you'd better leave my house.

Max glanced behind his shoulder at Akim who was stretching over his father to meet him with his gaze.

-You have today to say goodbye. Not a day more or I will tell you the whole truth.

Max left and Akim's father picked up the envelope with the photos and the check to take them away from his grandson. The boy was not old enough to understand the messes of the heart. Akim hit the wall so hard that his knuckles bled and some of the cement was instantly uncorked.

I don't see you

Brenda was looking forward to seeing Akim that morning when Max walked in the door. He looked exhausted and she felt sorry for him. After all she was to blame for all his woes.

-I need to have lunch together," Max said angrily as he saw her all dressed up and imagined where she was planning to go.

-Today, now Why?

Max had studied every word. His actions were not spontaneous at all. Everything was as well designed as the blueprints of his most precious construction.

-We need to see my lawyer. There are details we can't leave to chance. As you know, we have a lot of things to finalize before.... -He was unable to pronounce the word divorce out loud.

Brenda shook her head and accepted their proposals. Max was right, they should spend some time on that hard task. She would explain with Akim later.

What should have been a few hours turned out to be the whole day. Max seemed content with everything that was proposed and Brenda felt hopeful that he was a little more relaxed. Maybe the last month had helped her to accept that their relationship, though over, was actually a new beginning for both of them and so when he proposed a drink at a nearby place she gladly accepted. Max would always be an important person in her life and she wished it would always be that way.

The two entered the place and Brenda was surprised with the choice of the place. Very crowded and with an atmosphere that she was sure Max didn't like, she didn't understand the reason for his choice but she preferred to keep quiet. Girls showing off their bodies and men demonstrating their qualities was not the kind of pubs Max was used to, but if these were his new tastes, she would not be the one to judge him.

-Are you sure here? -He said as he watched him sit down on a soft sofa in a booth in the living room.

-Yes. He said without further ado.

Brenda agreed and sat down, not wanting to argue. She was sure she wouldn't go back to a place like that after that night. That place with so many mini-skirts and semi-naked breasts was not for her. They ordered a couple of drinks and Brenda was about to comment some nonsense about the place when the image from two steps away left her speechless.

Lola and Akim were there. She was approaching him as if with all rights and he was smiling with his arms crossed. The air began to go out of him and the blood stopped rushing through his body. The cold settled on his skin and he felt the world begin to crumble before his eyes. Max checked to see where his gaze was lost and reached inside his jacket to take some pictures. He spread them on the small table in front of them and Brenda felt gagging begin to rise in her windpipe.

-What is this? -She said trying not to cry and knowing that her question was quite stupid. The evidence was more than obvious.

-I'm sorry, but I couldn't let him keep cheating on you," Max replied, moving closer to her to the point where his shoulder was pressed against hers as he fiddled with the photos. They've been together for two years.

Brenda looked at him with her eyes watering with tears. The pain in her heart was so strong that she thought she could not bear it. She felt cheated, stupid, humiliated.

-No, it can't be, there must be some explanation. This is not true." He tried to get up, but Max wouldn't let him.

-This morning I went to his house. I offered him money to forget about you... and he deposited the check.

Max seemed so sincere that he surrendered to the evidence. Money? Had she been used for money? Had she fallen into a stupid trap of two con men? Had she believed their words of love when they were really only after money?

-How much? -he asked with barely a voice. He needed to know how much his pain and stupidity was worth.

-Twenty thousand pounds.

Max spoke confidently and Brenda felt her world fall apart. How could she have been so stupid? How was she capable of believing that such a young man could...of her...of her...? She stood up and almost fell if it wasn't for Max's strong arm holding her in place.

-I... I... I... have to go... -She said as if she were a drug addict. She had to go outside. She needed to get some air.

-I will accompany you.

-No! No... -She said the second time without shouting. I need to be alone.

-You're in no condition, don't be silly, I'll take you home. We'll get through this together. I'll be by your side." Brenda looked at him, trying to focus on his image, although it was very difficult.

-I said I want to be alone and that's what I'm going to do. Respect my opinion, if only because I don't even have the strength to breathe.... -She said choking and Max looked down ashamed.

He spoke so confidently that Max made a face of disgust but she cared little for his feelings. Her chest was open, her heart broken and her pride trampled. She had to get home any way she could and lock the door so that no one would enter. She walked hesitantly, bumping into as many people as she could. The young girls with high tits snorted at her stomping and seeing them so pretty and young all her fears crushed her like a cold slab. Idiot, how could I be such an idiot? Lies, they were all lies.... They all had a price, a price.... She raised her hand as best she could and a cab stopped instantly to take her away from there as soon as possible.

Akim was walking around the room checking the order when he saw Max paying the waiter. That idiot this time would not get away with it. He came up behind him and spoke with restrained fury.

-I'll wait for you outside. He said threateningly and predicting a good fight.

-I don't care if you rot, I'm not even interested in punching you. For me you no longer exist.

Akim looked at him intrigued and instantly noticed the photos scattered on the bedside table. No, it couldn't be what he was thinking.

-You son of a bitch, you're waiting for her! -he growled angrily.

-You starving bastard, don't act with me. I know you cashed the check. You don't need to keep playing the role of a young man in love.

-What horns are you talking about?

-Max smiled victoriously as he looked toward the door.

Akim told himself that it could not be too late. He insulted the whole world before running like a soul carried by the devil himself. He dashed across the room with all the speed he was capable of but there was no one at the door. She had left. He tried to go for his bike but Lola appeared behind him.

-If you leave without permission you will lose your job.

Akim cursed out loud. Fuck them all, he was losing her, he should run after her and explain himself. He was about to tell her that he didn't care about the money when someone hit him hard, he tried to answer back but two others rushed in to hold him by the shoulders tightly and pin him down while another one punched him in the center of the stomach.

-Philips...

Other Contemporary Romance books with a heavy dose of romance, passion, action and adventure by Diana Scott.

<u>Infidelity Saga</u>
Book 1: After You (Susana, Oscar and Nico)
Book 2: It's for You (Susana and Nico)
Book 3: The Custody of Your Heart (Mathias and Blue)
Book 4: Game of Passions (Lucas and Carmen)
Book 5: Sorry. I Fell in Love (Carlos and Barby)
Book 6: Tied to a feeling (Blue and Matías)

<u>Stonebridge Series</u>
Book I: Hidden Treasure
Book II: The Days We Miss
Book III: Until You Came Along.

All rights reserved
Copyright
© 2020 Diana Scott
@dianascottromance